WHERE SHE WENT

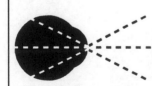

This Large Print Book carries the
Seal of Approval of N.A.V.H.

WHERE SHE WENT

KELLY SIMMONS

THORNDIKE PRESS
A part of Gale, a Cengage Company

GALE
A Cengage Company

Copyright © 2019 by Kelly Simmons.
Thorndike Press, a part of Gale, a Cengage Company.

ALL RIGHTS RESERVED

Thorndike Press® Large Print Core.
The text of this Large Print edition is unabridged.
Other aspects of the book may vary from the original edition.
Set in 16 pt. Plantin.

LIBRARY OF CONGRESS CIP DATA ON FILE.
CATALOGUING IN PUBLICATION FOR THIS BOOK
IS AVAILABLE FROM THE LIBRARY OF CONGRESS

ISBN-13: 978-1-4328-7392-9 (hardcover alk. paper)

Published in 2020 by arrangement with Sourcebooks, Inc.

Printed in Mexico
Print Number: 01   Print Year: 2020

For my daughters and all their squads.

For my daughters and all their squads

ONE

MAGGIE

As the woman approached the glass door of Maggie O'Farrell's salon at quarter to six on a humid Saturday night in early November, all Maggie saw was hair. Not her dark clothes, not the rain gloom of her face. No, Maggie saw chestnut curls, so voluminous they appeared to grow sideways out of the woman's head, the kind of hair you needed to buy a separate seat for on the trolley. Hair like that traumatized women. They were celebrated as infants — "look at those curls!" — then mocked in middle school for not knowing how to straighten them, control them.

Sometimes Maggie believed she could understand all women's thoughts and experiences as she massaged shampoo into their scalps. They sat in her chair hour after hour confessing their wrongdoings, spilling their sad histories, but she was seldom surprised.

The overarching story Maggie had almost always guessed.

But on that weekend, her bone-deep exhaustion got in the way. Instead of motive, secret, narrative rising from the stranger, there were coiled, springy strands that would take over an hour to smooth, precisely when she was ready to go home and put her feet up.

Why hadn't she turned off her neon *Bubbles & Blowouts* sign? Maggie had chosen this location on the edge of the Philadelphia suburbs because of its visibility — all glass, set on an extended curve so people could see it, pink and glowing, in every direction. She wanted women to come in off the street and feel welcome. But not ten minutes before closing at the end of the week.

Maggie's assistant, Chloe, was putting the last of the empty mini champagne bottles in the recycling. Her blunt bob had been blond last week but was currently strawberry red, and her large, blue eyes scanned the salon constantly, taking in every little thing that needed to be done. A few pink-striped paper straws were scattered on the whitewashed wood floor, bent at unfortunate angles. Chloe picked those up almost the second Maggie noticed them. They reminded Maggie of her daughter Emma's Barbie dolls, still stored in a box in her crawl space for when she graduated college and had a daughter of her own.

There was no more chilled champagne for this woman approaching the door. Maggie looked back down at the till, counting twenties, planning to announce this as soon as she stepped inside.

The door opened with its wind-chimey jingle, but then Maggie heard something equally familiar. A sound she'd heard late at night, ear tipped toward the door, for years. Holster slapping against hip. Nightstick swinging from a chain, squeaky rubber-soled shoes. Not the *tip tap* of high-heeled girls at all.

Maggie looked up. *Great,* she thought, surveying the dark shirt and shiny badge. Huge-haired cop? She'd probably expect a discount, too. Maggie knew the drill. Before her husband, Frank, was killed, he took every advantage being a lieutenant afforded him. They'd laughed about these things, the small flirtations and badge flashing that had resulted in saving the family money. Now? *Payback,* she thought. *Payback.*

"Mrs. O'Farrell?" the cop said.

Maggie froze. Every hair on her arms stood at attention at the sound of her name. The formality of the *Mrs.* The gentleness of the punctuation. What a question sounded like when you damn well knew the answer.

She closed the till slowly, as if she could make time stop. She knew how this would go. When a cop came to your door and said your name, there were only a few seconds before everything changed. And here it was again — the last precious moment, the unknowing.

Maggie knew the next question was not going to be *How much for a blowout?* but *Are you the mother of Emma O'Farrell?*

She met the woman's eyes, which were large and long-lashed and might be expressive under other circumstances. Circumstances that didn't require you to keep your cool.

"Ma'am?"

"Yes."

"Detective Carla Frazier. Is your daughter's name Emma?"

Behind her, the soft swishing of Chloe's broom stopped. The clock ticked louder. The last shampoo bubbles popped in the sinks. And Maggie's heart beat against the cage of her chest like a small, desperate bird.

"Yes," she choked out. "Yes."

"We were contacted by an officer in the second district, following up on a wellness check?"

Maggie knew from all the years married to Frank that the second district was the farthest reaches of North Philadelphia. Where Semper University was. Where Emma was, on what the city called a blue scholarship, for the children of officers killed or gravely injured in the line of duty. Not a full ride, because so many officers were killed or hurt nowadays, Maggie supposed they couldn't afford it, but full tuition and half room and board, and that had been enough to make her grateful. Emma had always planned to go there — a state school was all they could even think about, and Maggie couldn't bear her being far away in Pittsburgh — but she was facing work-study and loans or possibly a gap year to work and bank some money. And then, suddenly, it all melted away. Semper meant *always* in Latin. And Emma had pointed out that meant their school slogan — "Once a Semper, always a Semper" — made no sense. Her smart girl. Her witty girl. A child who was wholly deserving of a scholarship.

The day the mayor announced Emma's scholarship, on a podium in front of half the police force of Philadelphia, Maggie sat in the front row and wondered if the reporters there would ever print the real story, the reason for this generosity. That Frank had been gunned down in front of his mistress, who was also his newly assigned police partner. So two of Maggie's deepest fears had come true at once.

She had found out about his affair not by going through his pockets or finding texts on his phone but by being ambushed in an interrogation room. Could Maggie tell Captain Moriarty about her own whereabouts that day? Had she known where her husband was and what he was doing with a female detective in that car parked in an alley? Had that bullet missed its intended target, the woman next to him?

She'd had to admit, with tears streaming down her cheeks, that she hadn't known Frank was having an affair. That she'd had no idea. She had to confess not to being a murderer but to being a goddamned fool. And then the look on Moriarty's face. That he'd spilled a secret about another cop. That he'd broken the goddamned code. Did he think she wouldn't notice his guilt?

That woman, her husband's partner, would never be called by her actual name in their house. Maggie referred to her as Salt. As in salt in wound.

"Is she dead?"

The officer looked around the salon.

"Is there somewhere we can sit?"

12

"Is she dead?"

"No, but —"

"Is this your first time?"

"My first time?"

"Delivering bad news?"

"I never said it was bad news."

"You asked me to sit down."

The woman took a pen and notebook out of her pocket, scribbled something. Maggie wanted to hit her over the head. Taking notes, like that was important right now. How would she feel if Maggie started *sweeping*?

"Look, my husband was on the force, so just spit it out. Now."

"Your daughter's friend Sarah — you know her?"

"Yes, Sarah Franco."

Sarah was the only person from Lower Merion High School who also went to Semper University. The girls were good friends but thought it might be a bad idea to room together — after all, college was about meeting other people, expanding your horizons. But that decision had cost them — their dorms were far apart, anchoring the ends of the sprawling campus. Sarah in Graystone, Emma in Hoden House. How they'd groaned when they had gotten their housing assignments. A big campus was always so exciting until you were hungry, late for class, or in need of a friend. But the girls had vowed to meet midquad in their pajamas if they had to, to keep in touch. Emma's dorm was near Bairstow Stadium, and given the school's fanaticism over the football team, the Semper Sabres, Sarah said she'd be over there all the time anyway. Maggie had been happy, thinking of the two girls dancing with the sabre-toothed tiger mascot, faces painted yellow. In Maggie's mind, they looked like something lifted from the college brochure. Still, Maggie was a pragmatist, and yes, a worrier; the sheer number of students, the ring of frat houses, the jogging paths obscured by trees — were there enough blue emergency lights in the world to make up for all that? She had loaded Sarah's number into her phone, just in case. If she couldn't reach her daughter; if she didn't respond to repeated texts or calls, she could call Sarah, and she could run and check on her. Wouldn't Sarah's mother want the same safety net? She still remembered the set of Emma's lips when she'd asked Sarah for her contact info. She was embarrassing her daughter. She was being ridiculous.

But now this.

"This afternoon, Sarah contacted Emma's

RA, said she hadn't answered her texts last night, hadn't shown up for any of her classes, and her phone went to voicemail all day. She said this was completely out of character."

"She had perfect attendance in high school," Maggie said dumbly. But she was thinking why the hell hadn't Sarah Franco called *her,* in addition to the RA?

"So the RA opened the room and called 911."

"What . . . was in the room?" Maggie said slowly.

"Ma'am, I really think we should sit down."

"What. Was. In. The. Room?"

The detective's mouth hung open, like she needed an infusion of air, more breath, to form the words.

Maggie ripped her apron off, told Chloe to lock up, and ran to the door.

"Where are you going?"

"I'm going to Semper, and you're driving me there."

"Ma'am, this isn't my jurisdiction. I'm simply —"

"Don't 'ma'am' me. The first hours are critical, and we're now a whole day behind."

In the car, Maggie clicked on her seat belt. The detective radioed ahead to the second district, asking for campus escort, then pulled out of the parking space and headed east on Montgomery Avenue.

"Put on your lights. It'll be faster," Maggie said, and after a few seconds, the detective reached down and flicked the flashing light bar switch.

The streets were still wet from the morning's rain, and the traffic lights and neon signs looked like blurred watercolors as they picked up speed. That, or maybe Maggie's head was about to explode, and this was what the world looked like right before. A colorful, swirling send-off.

"I guess you've picked up a lot being a cop's wife," the detective said as she crossed City Line Avenue, touching the far edge of Philadelphia.

"No," Maggie replied, rubbing her temples. "I picked up a lot watching *Dateline* while my husband slept with his partner."

Two

EMMA

Years before Frank O'Farrell was killed, someone had already taken him away. Even Emma could see her father had been performing a slow vanishing, a marital sleight of hand for years. Once when they'd all gone to the Jersey shore for the day — a rare Saturday that Frank didn't have paperwork to do or a case to work — Emma and Maggie had sat on a dune, watching Frank walk up and down the beach, and her mother had told her that she thought of marriage as driftwood: constantly reshaped by time, water, wind. But Emma knew driftwood didn't stay put. It ended up in the bottom of your backpack with a pile of sand. It floated away for someone else to pick up the pieces.

The morning after her high school graduation party, Emma couldn't sleep, woke early. In the kitchen, small gifts and envelopes still sat on the island, and balloons waved their bouncy congratulations in the corner. Half of a yellow-and-gray sheet cake — her college colors, but was there anything grosser than gray frosting? — waited on the counter, her name sliced in two. *Ma,* it said.

She stopped, surprised to see her father bent over, crouching, rooting in the dishwasher for the silver cake server. Cake and coffee for breakfast, his favorite. But why was he home? He stood up from his crouch, then stared out the window, oblivious to her or even to the coffee maker, singing its last gasp of steam. His eyes were fixed on something — a pattern in the lawn her mother had neatly mowed for the party, a bird settling into the weeping cherry tree. Beauty out there, past the patio with the last of the Solo cups and dewy crepe paper, all the stuff she'd have to clean up, something bright that held his attention. She'd always thought her father's job kept him separate. A lie to help her believe it wasn't her fault he stayed away. But that day, two weeks before his death, she saw that it was something else. Even when he was home, his mind and heart were elsewhere.

And then, just like that, he was actually gone. Her mom started watching crime shows while pretending it wasn't because she missed him and wanted to stay close to his world. But there was no way for Emma to do the same. What was she going to do — play cops and robbers? Sign up for a criminal justice class?

She didn't like thinking about the way he'd died. Didn't like picturing the crime scene photos or imagining how the witness looked — the female detective with a blood-spattered blue shirt half torn off her body by something that wasn't a bullet. Blood, sex, guts, drama, blended together with teddy bears and rocking chairs, and all of it, the total, made her father loom larger than ever, like those monuments in Philadelphia parks that were twice life-size. She'd looked at them as a kid, those Yankee soldiers on horseback, and wondered where there were stallions that big, huge as dinosaurs.

The day before he died, Emma had fallen ill with stomach cramps and vomiting and was taken by ambulance to the hospital. Maggie called Frank three times, five, ten, from behind the thin curtain of the ER. No answer. Finally, she begged Emma to call him from her phone.

"Maybe he's not picking up because it's me," she'd said. "Maybe he'll pick up for you?"

But he hadn't. As they prepped her for an

emergency appendectomy, Maggie assured her that her father loved her, that there was an explanation. Covering for him still.

And her mother's secret prayer, that Emma had heard her whisper just before the morphine drip sent her into sleep: that if something had to go wrong, *please, dear God, let it be her husband and not her daughter.*

Emma woke up; Frank didn't. She'd come out of surgery, woozy and feverish, and knew just from looking at her mother's face that her father was dead. She was missing a part of her body and a part of her family, but she felt heavier, a weight on her chest. It was all on her now.

After that, she saw her family as driftwood, too. Three whittled down to two, and two wasn't enough. Two was a broken triangle; two was a roof without walls. Two was barely holding on.

From that day forward, Em had promised to always let her mother know where she was. She'd seen what it could do to someone, the untethering, the *where are they.* Even when she went to college, that first few weeks she'd texted her mother every night before bed their shorthand — *NILY.* Short for *Night, I Love You.* She'd say it to

Maggie, and Maggie would say it back. Even when Emma was shit-faced. Even when she was totally exhausted. Even when someone looked over her shoulder and said, "Oh my God, you are *not* texting your mom again."

Their phones autocorrected to *NILY* the moment they typed in the *N.* Maggie had even knit Emma a pillow that spelled out *NILY* in pink and white for her narrow dorm bed.

Emma cried a little when Maggie gave it to her and said, "Mom, if I ever get a tattoo, it's gonna be *NILY*."

And Maggie replied, "Em, if you ever get a tattoo, I'm gonna kill you."

Later in the fall, when Maggie had stopped by her dorm with two dozen oatmeal chocolate chip cookies she'd probably spent half the night baking and cooling, then drizzling with yellow icing, Emma opened the box and thanked her, then gently told Maggie that a lot of the other girls' mothers didn't text them three times a day. That the other local moms didn't "drop by" on a Sunday because they were in the neighborhood. (No one was ever in Semper University's neighborhood unless they were lost or buying drugs or heading north to another city.) Also, she added, "No one here really eats cookies."

Everyone in her dorm knew about the freshman fifteen, which could just as easily turn into thirty if you weren't careful. Already, there were girls selling their too-small jeans on Poshmark. Some of them drunk ate, but no one ate sugar when they were sober. Emma had seen how boys liked girls who were lean but muscular, how their gazes held when a certain body type walked by. The thought of them looking at her that way, the possibility, tasted sweeter than frosting.

"Maybe girls don't eat them, but cute boy athletes do," her mother had said. "Don't a lot of the football players live next door? In Riordan?"

Her roommates were bent over their phones, but she knew they heard her mother's chirping. And yes, she'd seen the boys moving in next door, boys so tall and wide, they looked like another species, lifting carefully packed boxes of books effortlessly, palming pillows in one large hand. But Maggie's gaze had lingered on them a little too long. *Cougarish,* she'd thought. Emma didn't say anything, but her mother was being totally embarrassing. Boys. Cookies. Jesus, was she twelve?

So even though they were separated by

only a dozen or so miles, Emma's "here" and Maggie's "here" had to slide away from each other. Emma still missed her mother but forced herself to let go. She'd seen her roommates let their mothers' phone calls go straight to their vacant voicemail boxes. They didn't even seem to miss their moms when they were puking and needed ginger ale.

Emma pictured the divide between her and Maggie vividly sometimes, when she had trouble falling asleep, when she worried about a paper she didn't understand or a party she wasn't invited to, but didn't want to rely on her mother's voice to rock away her problems.

In her mind, where the dangerous edges of campus gave way to the beauty of the city and City Line Avenue held the suburbs from spilling in, she imagined that long boulevard as a kind of border wall, with her happy but clueless childhood pinned to it like a memorial. Turquoise Beanie Babies and red plastic barrettes, pink tutus, Poké- mon cards, and Justin Bieber posters. The demarcation of before and after.

Maggie got the message. Emma didn't have to spell it out, didn't have to break her heart completely. And she'd just begun to back off. At Halloween, no decorations and frosted pumpkin cookies arrived at Emma's door. Two days passed, sometimes three, before a heart emoji popped up in her text alerts. Emma had suggested a Sunday afternoon phone call, trying to anchor things, instead of FaceTiming every time they each saw something that reminded them of the other — a funny episode of *Friends,* a macaron decorated like a flower, a dog wearing goggles on the back of a motorcycle. Her mother had to learn to enjoy those things on her own for a while.

And Emma was seeing other things, new things. More differences between her and these party girls than just how often they spoke to their mothers. They drank like boys and danced like strippers. Shotgunning and twerking, skills Emma hadn't mastered during her time on the high school yearbook staff. And some boys wanted more than cookies after parties, a lot more. There was shit going down in the dark stairways and cramped bathrooms she not only wouldn't share with her mother but couldn't.

Because Emma wanted to figure it all out on her own. Because after what had happened to her father, Emma would have to be a complete bitch to make her mother worry about the small crimes of college. The in-between offenses, the misdemeanors of he wanted, she didn't; of he filmed and they laughed and she cried.

No, she couldn't worry her mother.

But wow, yeah. Look how well that had worked out.

THREE

MAGGIE

Maggie hadn't gone to college, but she had a picture of it in her head, and the day she'd moved Emma in, everything she had imagined in her mind, she saw on campus. Yellow Frisbees sailed in the air; boys in long shorts ran across clipped green lawns. Clusters of girls sat in the shade of trees, their nervous giggles absorbed by the low, weeping branches that brushed the shoulders and collarbones peeking out from their carefully chosen shirts. Burgers grilling, balloons waving. And table after table of older kids offering instant friendship in exchange for signing up for something. It was like a street carnival filled with clean-cut teenagers performing the roles of clean-cut teenagers. And the dorm rooms! Brightly decorated with photo boards and fuzzy throw pillows and colorful desk lamps blinking on and off, a friendly coded hello.

How could anything but fun happen in a place like this?

On her subsequent visits, fueled by episodes of crime shows on Investigation Discovery, she was slightly more aware of the fringe-y neighborhoods she drove past before she reached the waving banners that trumpeted Semper's accomplishments. The yellow-and-gray flags flapped their welcome in the wind, like the United Nations, like an Olympic village. She supposed they were designed to assuage the realization that you'd driven through the most economically depressed, drug-torn part of Philadelphia to get there.

The campus itself was a mix of new, towering buildings named after generous alumni (*once a Semper, always a Semper,* at least if you had money) and old stone structures meant to signify tradition. There were unusual sculptures like the fifteen-foot-tall light bulb outside the liberal arts building and modern pulsing fountains scattered throughout, to remind you of the prestigious college of art. Decades ago, Maggie remembered they had dyed the water in the fountains yellow to celebrate a football victory, and they'd been widely mocked, with kids posing for photos, pretending to pee into them.

27

Many of those yellow canvas banners used photos and quotes from famous alumni. Emma hadn't known who half the people were, but Maggie did, and that, she supposed, was the point. To impress parents, who paid the bills, and not kids, who wanted to know whether the food was good and the other kids were attractive.

But college looked amazing to someone who had never been, whether that someone was eighteen or forty-six. Some of Maggie's friends and Maggie's own sister, Kate, had mocked higher education as a rip-off, thought it unnecessary. *Go to a trade school!* But Maggie had always wondered what it would have been like to be young and free but still safe. Half in, half out of adulthood, instead of being thrust into the work world at eighteen.

The fact that Maggie had wanted to be part of it, to share it with her daughter, wasn't all that surprising. But what surprised her more deeply was how she'd glossed over all of it with optimism, how much she'd bought into the brochures, the videos, the campus tour led by a perky brunette. How a smart, savvy working mother could be blinded by a campus tour guide who could walk backward and answer questions at the same time.

It wasn't till the day in November when she arrived with an entourage that Maggie saw things differently, through another lens. Walking with Carla and Kaplan, a policeman from the district, the RA — Tim somebody or other — and a burly campus security guard whose name badge simply read *J* was like cutting a swath with the grim reaper. The way the crowds parted and kids ducked away guiltily. For that was college too, she realized. *What rule or law or mother's promise should I break today? What can I get away with and try to hide?*

Maggie's heart pounded as the security guard swiped his badge and held the door, letting them in to the first floor of Hoden House. Four stories high, a simple brick building that had always been a dorm, unlike some of the others that had been retrofitted over the years as Semper grew. Horowitz Hall, which used to be the English department, had a soaring room on the third floor the kids called the Ballroom and a parapet on top that was only available for study by reservation. Hoden House was nothing like that, no-nonsense, each floor precisely the same, stacked like pancakes, smelling like beer.

They went in single file, past the check-in desk where a security guard who couldn't

29

be older than college age himself nodded at them. As they waited for the elevator, kids made a quick detour for the stairs; no one wanted to be trapped in a small space with the official-looking entourage. Three badges, two passkeys, and a mom? No thank you. Not with tequila breath or red eyes or stolen bananas from the salad bar.

"Did, like, something happen?" a passing girl asked the RA.

"No," he said. "Just a precaution, Robin. Don't you worry."

The girl's face lit up at the sound of her name. He remembered her!

"Is Robin on Emma's floor?" Maggie asked, and he shrugged. "You don't know?"

"I have three floors. It's hard to keep everyone straight."

Upstairs, the north corner. A passkey swipe and they were inside Emma's suite. Two double rooms and a single, plus a bathroom, small kitchen, and living room. Empty. Quiet. All three bedroom doors shut. So different from the bustle of that first week of class. Maggie had met all these girls at move-in, memorized everything she could about them. She repeated their names to herself: Annie and Morgan, first door to right. Taylor, the end of the hall. And straight ahead, the minute you walked in

30

the entry, Emma and Fiona, the roommate her daughter didn't know, the lottery she'd chosen to play. How happy Maggie had been, hearing the Irish name and seeing the tiny cross around the girl's neck; how relieved Emma had seemed when she'd seen how clean Fiona's side of the room was and how pretty her clothes. Fiona was taller, but they were the same size. They could borrow. They could share. What had they shared now?

The door of Emma's room had paper still taped to its door — a colorful Magic Marker rendering of the girls' names, drawn by the orientation team on the first day of school. A childlike contrast to the way the girls — who'd all moved in before Emma — had decorated their small living room. Two fuzzy white throw pillows. A blue butterfly chair by the window. An end table shoved up against the wall that held nothing but a blender and ten shot glasses, each from a different college. Painted wooden plaques from T.J.Maxx mounted above it, announcing *It's wine o'clock* and *#TequilaTuesday*. And although Maggie had been shocked by the alcohol shrine, she'd been calmed by the art on the door, a kindergarten teacher's kind of welcome.

As the RA unlocked the door with his key,

Maggie noticed the paper curled at the edges, and the ink had run down the *F* in Fiona, bubbling the fibers, blurring the word.

"No crime tape?" Maggie's voice was as authoritative as she could make it.

"No crime," Kaplan said, and the word *yet* hung in the air.

"Where are her roommates?" Maggie asked, their memorized names a chorus waiting in her throat.

"Still trying to locate," he replied.

"All of them?" she said, eyes widening.

"Yes. Along with her boyfriend."

"Boyfriend?" Maggie spat it out like a stone in fruit. "Emma doesn't have a boy-friend."

The glance exchanged by the four others made Maggie feel sick inside.

"Using the term loosely, from the looks of things, Mrs. O'Farrell, I think she does."

The door swung open, heavy, banging against the wall. It hurt Maggie, that bang-ing. It felt like a bruise.

On the left side of the room, messy, tangled sheets, an odd woodsy smell in the air. A pair of handcuffs on the pillow, unlocked, beckoning. A condom wrapper on the floor, opened, spent. The bright blue of the package calling to Maggie, signaling her own naivete, her own stupidity. It was the same brand as the five-pack she'd tucked into her daughter's suitcase with a note: *Semper means always . . . be safe!* A smiley face below. A heart. Astroglide on the nightstand, squeezed in the middle grotesquely, violently, like someone in a huge hurry.

But all of that, added together, multiplied, divided, and symbolically rendered in any way imaginable, wasn't the part that would stay with Maggie.

What haunted her was the right side of the room. The side of the room that was completely empty.

FOUR

EMMA

Emma didn't know what she wanted to be when she grew up. She just wanted to grow up.

She'd always been the youngest in her class — born in September but not held back a year in kindergarten like so many others. Perennially a little smaller, more naive. Coming up short, always running after a piece of knowledge the others had first. Not school, but other things. Personal things. She'd pretended to have her period for a whole year before she'd gotten it, carrying tampons in her backpack, complaining about cramps and PMS based on symptoms she'd Googled, without any real understanding of how bad, how devastating it could be. When she'd finally gotten it, on a Thursday afternoon that was stained into memory, she'd wept like a child in her mother's arms, in disbelief that it could be

34

this gruesome, this painful, and last for forty years! Like a prison sentence! *How do you stand it, Mom? Every month?* she'd cried. She couldn't believe every woman in the world she'd ever met, seen, or known had endured this, had carried this secret. Her friends, their teachers and neighbors, strangers on the bus, her mother, her aunt Kate, her freaking *grandmother* who still had it, all walking around like the cool girls at school, as if it was nothing. And it wasn't nothing.

That was the first lesson she'd learned, that you had to push those feelings down. Her mother stood on her feet for nine hours a day, every day, no matter what, just to keep things together. Her mother's mother had worked every day except Sunday in her grandfather's Irish Isle store — correction, *their* store, she'd told Emma once, declaratively — for the same reasons. Grandma, who worked so hard that she'd had a little breakdown that no one ever talked about, who had gone off someplace to rest for a week. They'd never thrown this in Emma's face, but Emma knew. Women worked. They worked hard, harder than men. But men like Frank got the gold stars, the Purple Hearts, the mayor's commendations, the sobriety chips, the whatevers. No one would give her mother a medal for washing hair and paying her bills while enduring cramps. No freaking way. Women had to do more.

As she grew older and the age-related differences between her and her classmates grew smaller, she was convinced these striations would all be gone by the time she went to college. Everyone had a driver's license, had tried pot and drank beer. Everyone had some level of sexual experience and survived the singular trauma known as high school. Every time she liked a boy who didn't like her back, every time a teacher redlined a paper for using the wrong word, every time she saw another girl's outfit in a store and gasped at the price tag — she'd think, *College. This will all be erased at college.*

After her mom left on the first day, she looked around her suite at the four other girls. Annie and Morgan, who met each other in summer camp but laughingly said they hated each other then, were both in the CGP, College of General Prep, which encompassed most of the education-oriented majors but was widely known as the school with the lowest standards. CGP: crayon, glue, pencils.

Taylor, who was enrolled in the business school but planned to minor in theater, wore vintage glasses and had a sideways smile. Fiona, like Emma, was in the College of Arts and Sciences with an undeclared major. She was pretty and polite and organized, quick to loan out her scissors, lint roller, thumbtacks. *We're all freshmen,* Emma thought. *We're all equals.* Those first few nights, laughing and passing around a bottle of cheap pinot grigio, she actually thought she'd found some BFFs.

The cracks began to show a few days later, when girls in other dorms invited some of them to pregames but not all of them. Fiona claimed she'd tried to include them but that it was a "whole different squad." That made sense. The rooms were so freaking small — you couldn't squeeze everyone in. Even at the big frat houses, you had to have your name on a list to get in.

Annie and Morgan had met other girls from their camp and hung out separately with them, doing nothing but singing campfire songs and drinking s'mores shots (or so it appeared on Instagram). Fiona spent a lot of time doing laundry; she had Shout wipes and a steamer and a lamb's-wool buffer she kept next to her shoes. Emma had heard her coming in late at night, heard the light clang of the hanger as she put away her dress and the soft swoosh of wool going over her shoes. She'd started looking at her own shoes differently, seeing the road dust, the edges of mud, errant blades of grass. Did Fiona pay such close attention to everything or just her own things? Emma had known girls like that in high school, who asked things like *Who does your eyebrows?* As if they didn't already know: *No one. God does my eyebrows.* But so far, Fiona hadn't said anything like that. But then again, Fiona didn't say much.

Taylor left campus often with her drama friends. They went into Center City Philly to see small, up-and-coming shows. They went to New York some Saturdays to go to Broadway. It was as if they had better things to do than hang out in dorm rooms.

Emma didn't really have a group outside her roommates, but she figured that would come with time. She had one friend from high school — Sarah Franco — who lived on the opposite side of campus and had a work-study job that took up a ton of time. They saw each other maybe once a week. And Emma had signed up on move-in day to write for the school newspaper's blog and tried to strike up conversations with others at the journalism table. But many of the kids there seemed quieter than she was. Or, they were just awkward or busy, and she was too eager and desperate and blathering.

No one in her suite seemed concerned about this almost instantaneous splintering of the roommates, because they were too busy. They bonded over that at least, the being busy and the being lost. God, how they'd gotten lost. Even kids who went to huge high schools — Taylor had eight hundred kids in her graduating class — even those kids found the campus large and bewildering. They'd all had stories about getting lost and being late and getting yelled at and honked at by professors, security guards, RAs. There was a kind of freshman look; like tourists, they stared at everything with a weird combination of amazement and confusion. And when they relied on Google Maps to get to buildings, turning in circles, looking at their phones? That was a solid giveaway. A few nights in the beginning, they'd taken selfies and tagged them #freshmanface. But they didn't share them with anyone, not even other freshmen, and their group chat soon dwindled to nothing.

But the truth was, even though she was overwhelmed in some ways, Emma wasn't as busy as everyone else. She'd gone to a rigorous high school, and compared to it, her classes seemed almost easy. Yes, she had to keep up with the reading and pay attention, but something about the way the subjects were outlined and served up in class reminded her, vaguely, of eighth grade. It was as if her professors were trying to be serious but still bite-sizing everything for the lowest common denominator.

Another difference that became clear right away was that she didn't have as much money as everyone else. She ate at the dining hall when others went out or ordered in or paid Ubers to deliver. She suggested cooking together to her roommates, pitching in to make chili or Irish stew. They repeated the words *Irish stew,* as if she had just suggested they eat dog shit. And fucking Fiona, who was one million percent Irish, had not even stood up for her.

The night of the first big football game, against the Ohio Burrs, they'd all had shots of vanilla vodka in their room as they painted their faces. Then the others had dispersed, bouncing off to separate parties. Emma had waved to them and pretended she had somewhere else to go, too. She fake-walked all the way across campus, after white-lying to their faces, saying that she was meeting Sarah even though Sarah had not texted her back and that she'd see them all later at the game. *Go Sabres!*

As she wove through the throngs of kids coming to the stadium in the opposite direction, she held on to the hope that she'd run into someone from one of her classes, someone she'd met at her dorm orientation, when they'd played those get-to-know-you games. Emma would remember those fun facts! She'd know who had a pet iguana and who loved opera and who thought unicorns were real until she was eleven. She'd recognize those girls in a crowd and shriek "Unicorn girl!" and they'd bond and share whatever horrible alcoholic concoction was available. She'd swallow it gratefully as the price of admission.

But she saw no one she recognized. She wandered around for a while before going into the enormous, pulsing stadium. She knew what her mother would say — *Make friends with the people sitting near you! Other people are alone, too!* But that was advice that worked in third grade, not now. Drunk friendships didn't hold. Emma had danced and laughed with a girl at a party the first week, and when she'd seen her the next day and waved, the girl looked at her like she was a stalker. Still. There were thirty thousand people here. Emma had been alone her whole damned life, and she was not giving up.

A few days after the game, Emma received an email asking her to make an appoint-

ment with the editor of the *Semper Sun.*
She'd been inside every building on campus
— it was a goal she'd set the first week, a
freshman bucket list — and Emma saw
quickly the disparities between structures.
The journalism building was on the far
northeast edge of the liberal arts school and
dated back to the early 1900s. It was charming on the outside — always featured on the
school's videos — but cold and leaky on the
inside. Its computers were old, its desks
pockmarked with pencil wounds and burns.
In contrast, the new business school campus, with its glass and steel towers, had a
juice bar and a sushi restaurant.

Emma had been early for her appointment
by ten minutes. She'd shaken the hand of
the editor, Jason Cunningham, briskly. She
had showed him a link to samples from her
high school paper, her column about study
habits that kids had ignored but teachers
and parents had loved. Jason had glanced at
it for two seconds, nodded, then asked if
she had ever written anything humorous.
Um, no.

Did she have any hobbies that might make
good behind-the-scenes pieces, like fencing?
Fencing? Funny? Emma had been stunned
by these questions — did she look like she
did stand-up or jousted? It was only later

that night, when she walked away with her one, singular assignment — *to find something interesting to write about and then write up a pitch and pitch it to him* — that she saw their conversation framed in a different way.

Jason hadn't assumed anything about her. He hadn't been sexist or stereotypical or click-bait-y. He hadn't asked her to do a fluff piece on fall fashion or a stupid college YouTube video series on the fastest way to remove makeup after being up all night. He simply had a list of things that he needed, and without making a single snap judgment, he had asked her if she could fulfill them.

That night, she stared at herself in the bathroom mirror as she brushed her teeth. In the hallway outside came the short taps of high heels, the lower thumps of booties, the sounds of a herd of girls going out for the night. There, in the harshest yellow light, with the odd mix of bleachy disinfectant wipes and peachy Dove deodorant always mingled in the air, she tilted her face up, down, and sideways. Squinting and half smiling.

Mysterious? Snarky? Clever? Athletic? All these years, she had looked in the mirror and wondered constantly about pretty or hot and whether she'd stay stranded at cute forever. What a waste. What a stupid, utterly futile waste. Maybe she *was* funny.

Maybe she *could* handle a sword and a shield.

Maybe she should stop limiting herself, start looking at other possibilities, exactly the way he had.

Jason, Jason the editor, had edited her.

FIVE

MAGGIE

"She's not here," Maggie said dumbly, then caught a glance between the policeman and the security guard that stopped short of an eye roll.

"Yes," Carla said slowly, carefully. "That's why we —"

"No," Maggie said and shook her head. "I mean this," she said, sweeping her hand above the bed, "is her roommate's side of the room. Fiona. Emma was on the right side. Those might be Emma's sheets, but all her pillows —" Her heart seized, thinking of the *NILY* pillow she'd knitted. "I mean, all her stuff is gone."

Carla nodded, raised her eyebrows. "Maybe they switched sides? Maybe the roommate is gone, too?"

"Can I look in the closet?"

The policeman put on a pair of gloves and opened the door. "You can look, but don't

45

touch anything."

Maggie frowned. Dresses. High heels. Someone else's clothes. Shoved to the back, jeans that might be Emma's. But the rest?

"Could they be sharing a closet?" she said.

"And what, a bed, too?" the policeman said.

"Let's not jump to any conclusions," Carla said.

"Well, this *is* college," the RA said and sighed.

Maggie should have been offended, but she wasn't really listening. Nothing in this room made sense. It didn't look anything like the cheerful room she'd helped set up. No photos mounted on foam core, no class schedule tacked to a bulletin board; just bits of tape and yellow crepe paper and crumbling holes where those things used to be. As if someone had ripped it all out in a hurry, so no one else could see.

Maggie rubbed her eyes. "Could she have moved rooms and I didn't know?"

"Well," the RA said, "they're not supposed to, not without telling me and filling out request forms. And they have to have a good reason, not just, 'Oh, she was mean to me.' "

"Was she?" Maggie asked. "Mean to her?"

"No idea."

She scanned his face for a piece of information, but he looked away and put his hands in his pockets the way boys did, as if he didn't know what to do with his own appendages.

"She's not staying here," Maggie declared. "There's no makeup, no caddy of shower supplies." She gestured around the room. "No robe, no towels, no books."

"Maybe she uses e-books."

"No computer, no backpack, no —"

"Okay, okay," the policeman said. "Thanks for the inventory. We get your point."

"No," she said, "I don't think you do. Emma is not living in this dorm room. It would be impossible for a girl to live without all those things."

"Well, it's certainly being used," the policeman said, nodding toward the bed.

"You don't know that," Maggie said. "It . . . could be a prank."

Carla's eyes reflected empathy. That Maggie could be that clueless, that deluded.

"When you texted her in the car and I told you to act normally, what did you say?" Carla asked.

"I said, 'Hey, honey, just checking in.' "

"Anything else?"

"Just a bee emoji. For, um . . . honey?"

Maggie's knees started to shake a bit. She could not believe she was standing where she was standing, justifying her texting techniques, explaining habits that should be plain as day to an investigator. How could they only see what was here, not what was missing?

"Is there anything you could text that might feel important but not panic her?"

Maggie nodded. She took out her phone, chose a moon emoji, then added *NILY.* She took a deep breath and hit send.

When they heard the pinging text alert in the room, Maggie's heart nearly stopped.

Now everyone knew what Maggie knew. Because what teenaged girl goes anywhere, even down the hall to the bathroom, without her phone? Before anyone could speak or locate the phone, another chime came from the doorway.

"Located the boyfriend," the cop said.

"She doesn't have a boyfriend," Maggie said.

Six

EMMA

Emma had entered college thinking everything about it was going to be interesting. She envisioned worldly people from different backgrounds, states, countries. But it seemed almost everyone in her dorm was white and their idea of a hobby was spinning class. Outside Hoden House, there was more diversity, so she chatted up people in class, at the cafeteria. She got a lot of one-word answers and apologies for having to go. It turned out it wasn't that easy to ask people if they had any unusual hobbies. It was like asking them if they were freaks and wanted to confess their serial killer traits.

So after a solid month of searching and praying to God to send her a fellow student who did taxidermy in the common room or made moonshine in her bathroom, she wondered if she had simply been deluded about college.

Emma had been friendly-ish in high school with Lizzie Burton, a girl whose mother travelled constantly on business, who threw parties on weeknights and ditched school to go see foreign films and bought her essays on the internet and was always dating someone in a band. College was just full-on Lizzie Burton.

The best she could come up with were a few Adderall addictions and girls doing boys' laundry for money. She pictured Jason's face closing like a bud when she said the word *laundry*. No. That was too small, she thought. Finally, she found a group of Irish dancers who practiced in the corner of the gym every Tuesday, but when she'd pitched it to Jason, he'd said someone wrote about them last year.

It took her a while to realize that her interest wasn't just rooted in journalism but rooted in Jason. She wanted to be the person he saw in her. There was something about his quiet calm, the way he tilted his tortoiseshell glasses up onto his nose delicately, with one slim finger. The way he spoke with just the right number of words, no adjectives, nothing extraneous. The smart boys she'd known before seemed to flaunt their brains like chess pieces. Not Jason.

Since Emma wasn't coming up with any original ideas, Jason had asked her to edit other people's stories. This meant being on call before deadline, being a good speller, and having a fast, decisive touch. She liked the responsibility, enjoyed the chime of the alerts. She'd say to anyone nearby, "Gotta go. Jason needs me."

But after a few weeks, Jason asked her to come into the office to talk. She'd dressed carefully for that meeting, trying to look pretty without looking like she was trying to look pretty. A plaid shirt in shades of green and brown that matched her eyes. Boots that made her look taller, since he was tall. She had to be careful about being too intentional. For he was observant, too; she didn't want him to notice her ministrations.

When she arrived, he was typing quickly but lightly, his fingers almost dancing across the keyboard. Most guys she knew pounded the keys with the wide pads of their fat fingers.

"Just a sec," he said without looking up. "Okay," he said at last, flipping his laptop screen down. "Sorry about that."

"No worries," she said.

He sighed. "I hate that phrase."

"Oh. Well, I'd never use it in my writing. Still, you don't think it's useful?"

"No. Not with 'that's okay' or 'fine by me' still in the vernacular. We don't need to take anything from Australian surfer culture to supplement."

She blinked.

"You did know that, right? That the phrase migrated from Australia?"

"Well," she replied, " 'cheers' is British, and everyone says that. So I don't think we're at any risk of becoming less American. Besides, people hate Americans, so why not dilute?"

"You're awfully cynical for a freshman."

She shrugged. She didn't know if cynical was good or bad.

"Well, Emma," he said and paused, and she realized it was the first time she'd heard him say her name. He said it softer than others did, not emphasizing the *e,* sliding the *m*'s.

"I know you signed up for the blog. But you're a good editor. And we need someone next semester, because Robb is going abroad."

She opened her mouth, but he held up his hand.

"Just hear me out, please," he said as he put his hand down, and the *please* made her forgive him a little for that hand. A little. Her mom, she knew, would never let a man hold up his hand to silence her. "It's harder to find editors. Everyone can write a hashtag, but they can't form paragraphs. And no one can spell. It's a lost art, like good handwriting."

Emma wondered if she confessed at that very moment to having good handwriting — because she did, in fact, have beautiful, loopy, Instagram-worthy handwriting — if he'd demote her further to addressing invitations to their holiday parties.

"I appreciate your confidence in me," she said. "However, I don't want to give up on the idea of blogging."

"The idea of blogging," he repeated softly.

"Okay, on blogging."

"Well, you're not blogging, so you were right the first time."

She felt her cheeks turning red, which she hated about herself. It was such an Irish thing, and his family was probably totally bougie and English, and her family had probably been their maid and butler a few centuries ago, and she felt all those things at that moment and wanted to die.

"I'm sorry," he said. "That sounded cruel, but —"

"No, you're right," she said. "I haven't come up with something to write, and writers write, right? But I will."

"Okay," he said.

"You don't believe me."

"The world frequently surprises me. But a little advice? Stop looking so hard. There's probably a story close by."

She nodded perfunctorily, promised to be in touch, left quickly, and fumed all the way home. He had given her the most basic, vanilla advice. Write what you know? Jesus! How stupid did he think she was?

And she was so angry, she didn't know whether to prove him wrong or prove him right, but one thing was for sure. She wouldn't need anyone to edit her story. Whatever subject she chose, she'd do the work of two, and he'd appreciate her twice as much.

SEVEN

MAGGIE

The policeman didn't look much older than
the RA, and perhaps because of that, Maggie kept speaking to Carla. She knew the
officer had zero jurisdiction, but she was
there, and she seemed to be an actual human, and who knows, maybe she had a kid
herself. She'd already broken protocol by
bringing Maggie to the campus, and maybe
Maggie could convince her to help. Maybe
the roommates would have a lead they could
follow up on together while this baby boy
cop who probably wasn't married and
definitely didn't have a daughter himself
and likely hadn't ever handled a real investigation was busy learning how to tie his
shoelaces. He had a full head of hair but
shaved his head — a look that Maggie had
always found suspicious, like they were trying to hide something essential about themselves.

But when the cop — Kaplan was his name; the RA was Trenton, Tim Trenton — said they had the boyfriend and he turned to go interview him, she asked Kaplan how far it was, if she should walk or drive in the car.

"Neither," he said. "We don't interview witnesses with other people around."

"Other people? I'm her mother," she said firmly.

"All the more reason," he said.

"And wouldn't you say he's a suspect, not a witness?"

"And see, this is exactly why we don't. There's procedure to follow, as I'm sure you're aware more than anyone. So I advise you to go home, get some rest, and we'll call you if —"

"Go home?" she said incredulously. "I'm not going home when my daughter has been . . . been . . . kidnapped, or taken, or —"

"There's nothing that indicates that, ma'am. There's no need to panic."

"Are you kidding me? You need to collect fingerprints. You need to spray this room and hallway with luminol. You need —"

"Mrs. O'Farrell, please. You said so yourself — her things aren't here. Her backpack is gone —"

"All students leave their rooms with their backpacks!"

"Ma'am, kidnappers don't pack up people's stuff when they take them, okay? Your daughter has almost certainly moved residence and neglected to tell you or follow the dorm procedures."

"But her phone is here!"

"All due respect, that doesn't mean anything. Another possibility is that she gave away her possessions. Was she exhibiting any signs of being depressed, any family history or anyth—"

"I can't believe this," she said. "If Frank were alive, he'd have your head."

Kaplan shot Carla a look that spoke volumes.

"I'm staying right here," Maggie said. "Until her roommates come back."

"You can't do that," the RA said.

"I beg your pardon?"

"We can't just randomly let people hang out in a shared suite. It's not fair to the roommates. They have stuff here, valuables."

"What about my daughter? She's not valuable?"

"I didn't say that."

"You don't even know who is living in this room! Maybe I should tell the dean of students what a great job you're doing keeping track of the kids in the dorm!"

He sighed. "Have you ever tried to control hundreds of eighteen-year-olds?"

"As a matter of fact, yes, I have. I hosted post-prom," she said hotly.

"You can wait in the common room by the elevators for a couple hours."

"I can't believe this," Maggie said.

"Just drive her back, if you wouldn't mind," Kaplan said to Carla.

"I'm not going anywhere!"

"I'll stay," Carla said.

"Let me know if you get eyes on the roommate. And in the meantime, Mrs. O'Farrell, try to relax? Because I bet you five dollars I'm going to find her over at the boyfriend's apartment, with a backpack full of . . . stuff."

Maggie took a deep, audible breath. "She doesn't have a boyfriend."

Maggie rubbed her eyes. She'd seen cops interviewed on television, shedding tears over missing kids who were the same age as their own children, claiming the cases had gotten to them. But those cops were rare. Even when her husband had been shot in the line of duty, even when one of their own went down, it had been nearly impossible for her to get information. The detectives solved it quickly enough — leaned on every young drug dealer in the neighborhood till they found one who'd talk — but they hadn't told her what they were doing at any juncture along the way.

In the common room, she scanned the dozens of posters affixed to the refrigerator, wondering if Emma had been drawn to one. A play that night? A concert? She didn't see anything. There were, however, greasy cookie sheets stacked in the sink. So much for no one eating cookies.

Suddenly, she turned to Carla. "The phone," she said.

"I'm sure Kaplan will get it and pull the records if he needs to. And her bank account, too. Usually takes a while, though. Might not know anything for weeks."

"No," she said. "That's not what I'm saying. I pay that bill. I own that phone."

"Okay," the officer said slowly.

"And I want it back. Now."

EIGHT

EMMA

Emma left Jason's office and decided she'd been doing it wrong, all wrong. She needed inspiration, not observation. She bought *New York Times* and the *Washington Post,* digital subscriptions to the money she couldn't afford, and spent every free hour not reading her assignments but reading the papers. Corruption, collusion, unions. Were the university cafeteria workers unhappy with their conditions? she wondered. Were the tenured professors overpaid, and the adjuncts ready to revolt?

On Monday nights, she allowed herself a break to watch *The Bachelorette* and let her brain turn to mush like the rest of the dorm. She had been sitting with Taylor, eating terrible gluten-free pretzels and rosé wine when Fiona came in.

Fiona glanced at the screen, then asked if they were hungry, dangling a brown bag from a restaurant Emma had never heard of. "Pad thai," she said. "I only ate a few bites."

Taylor said yum and jumped up, grabbed a fork and plate.

"Oh my God, look at all the shrimp."

"I know," Fiona said. "It's an awesome place."

Fiona refilled her water bottle from the Brita, then refilled the Brita from the sink, probably because there were witnesses. (Emma was constantly finding the Brita in the fridge with just a few drops in the bottom, just as she found the toilet paper roll with a single sheet clinging to it like a life vest.) Fiona was beautifully dressed, as she always was. A black crepe dress with sleeves that fluttered just right over her upper arms, a flippy skirt that showcased her long legs. Cherry-red high heels that were probably by some designer Emma didn't know, and lipstick that seemed to match. Emma had never seen Fiona in loose sweatpants or a T-shirt. Even her workout clothes were stylish; she had little sweaters and wraps she only wore to and from the gym.

"I'm going to take a quick shower."

"Okay," Emma said.

Fiona always showered at night, which was fine by Emma, since she liked to wake up with a shower and hated going to bed with wet hair. The thought of it soaking into the pillow made her queasy. But Fiona rarely washed her hair; she had it done at Dry Bar every Friday and tried to make the blowouts last as long as possible.

"This is delicious. Do you want a bite?" Taylor asked.

"No thanks," Emma said, glancing at the huge mound of noodles on her plate. "I guess Fiona is one of those girls who doesn't eat on dates."

Taylor laughed a little. The first week of school, they'd both seen lithe Fiona drunk-eat a microwaved cinnamon bun in bed at 3:00 a.m. They'd all gone to Mabel's Diner one morning after too much sauvignon blanc and watched her order oatmeal, then proceed to eat half of Annie's cheesesteak and poached eggs, taking small, swift bites. They knew what she was capable of in private, if not in public.

"I don't think her date wants her to be too full," Taylor said with her mouth full.

"What do you mean? Is she seeing someone controlling?"

Taylor put down her fork. "Oh my God, you don't know."

"Know what?"

"Look, she's your roommate, so I just assumed."

"Assumed what?"

"That you knew. You knew her from before, right?"

"No."

"Wait, what?"

"Nope. We went through the roommate lottery."

"Oh, right. She didn't want to risk any idiot from her Podunk town. But still. Don't you talk?"

"She never talks about who she goes out with."

"Well, now you know why."

Emma frowned. "I do?"

"Because she goes on daddy dates."

"She eats out with her father?"

"No, you knucklehead, her sugar daddy."

"What?"

"You heard me. She dates older men who pay her."

"Wait, what?"

"Yup."

"Pay her, like, money? How much?"

"A lot. Like, a lot a lot."

"So . . . I mean, does she sleep with them?"

"Well, she has an endless supply of those disposable shower caps from four-star hotels, so you tell me. Maybe they're just

63

watching movies and getting room service. I shouldn't judge."

"Jesus! When did she tell you this?"

"I was complaining about money a while ago after going to New York and spending, like, five hundred dollars, and she suggested that I should stop working at the computer center and try something new and fun instead. I thought maybe she was talking about waitressing on roller skates or something, ha-ha. But she said she'd paid off her student loan and had next year's tuition banked."

"Really?"

"One of the guys gives her investment advice, too."

"That's totally insane. And here I thought she liked showering at night because it was relaxing."

Taylor laughed. "So get this. Then she tells me that I'd be good at it. That I'm a natural."

"Well, you *are* flexible. We've seen you twerk and do the floss at the same time."

"Ha-ha, no, she said it's basically acting. Act like you're interested. Act like you like them. Act like you're grateful when they pay you money out of their children's inheritance."

Taylor paused to eat more of the pad thai

and offered Emma another bite. Emma shook her head. She was having trouble processing all this already without the multitasking of chewing. She wasn't sure if eating Fiona's sugar daddy's food would make it easier or harder to understand.

"Damn," she said. "I knew a girl in high school whose cousin did webcam stuff for money, but that's tame. That's like modeling, and this is like —"

"Prostitution?"

"You said it. I didn't."

"I'm sorry. I just figured you knew."

"Fiona's not a big talker."

"She's probably all talked out, pretending to care about these dudes."

"So there's, what, a call service? Or a . . . pimp or madam or something?"

"There's apps. And I think there are clubs, too."

"Clubs? Like a physical space?"

"I think so."

"Well, this explains why she goes to mass twice a week, not just once."

Taylor laughed with her mouth full. "You're funny, Emma."

"No, I'm just Catholic. We have this terrible habit of telling the truth."

"Well, don't say anything. Let her tell you first."

"Okay."

"Maybe you can find a subtle way of bringing it up."

"So wiping down every surface in our room with Clorox wipes, is that not subtle enough?"

"Again, funny."

Much as she appreciated the compliment and camaraderie with Taylor, who was the most interesting of all the roommates, Emma couldn't recall ever feeling younger or more naive or more suburban. Taylor had been so matter-of-fact about it all.

She picked up the bag from the pad thai place. It had a red logo printed on the front, a bit smudged with oil but still readable. *Paco's Thai Palace.* Underneath, in loopy script, *Thai me up, Paco!*

A website was listed, but no address or phone. She'd never seen it, never heard of it. It must be far off campus, in another corner of Philadelphia. Maybe it was near one of the so-called clubs, or maybe it was the club? Emma had a hard time picturing a fun, pun-loving Thai restaurant as a bordello, but it certainly painted a colorful picture in her mind. Red lanterns, umbrellas in bright drinks, desserts lit on fire with tiki torches, all served to women in short dresses clapping their hands in delight while men stroked their legs beneath the table. Yes, it evoked a lively picture all right.

A picture that might accompany a very, very interesting story about college students and student loans. A story so close to home, it was lying in the extra-long twin bed right next to her, wrapped in soft pale-blue T-shirt sheets, hair coiled in a silk scrunchie, wearing a pink Korean face mask, scrolling through designer handbags on Rue La La, yawning.

NINE

MAGGIE

They were lucky: the door to the suite was still open. Maggie didn't know if it was ineptitude on the security guard's part or if one of the other girls was home and just being very, very quiet, but she didn't care. Down the hall, she'd noticed other girls streaming in and out of another door freely, no keys. Not everyone locked their doors. Why? Why had it been locked before and not now? That question would have to wait.

She was just glad that they didn't have to get anyone else involved to get inside. They'd listened at the door before entering — two heads up against the wall — to the singular sound of an empty apartment. The hum of a refrigerator, the drip of a bathroom sink, the creaking of someone walking on the floor above. The sound of nothing, really, but the kind of sounds that had kept Maggie up for years. The sounds you could

68

never get rid of, no matter where you lived or how well you insulated yourself or how much red wine you allowed yourself. (Two glasses, no more, except on holidays. Except when your daughter went to college and you missed her. Except when it was a Saturday.) Her sister said she'd sleep better if she stopped watching true crime shows at night, but Maggie thought they calmed her. It took her a few months to realize they made her feel closer to Frank, like the old days when he used to tell her everything about every case he worked.

Inside, it was clear from the row of open doors that no one was home yet. But those doors had all been closed earlier. The girls come and gone, clearly, perhaps waiting in another room. How had they missed them? Another party in their hallway? Or had they crept up the stairs at the end of the hall to avoid Maggie seeing them in the common room? Maggie imagined some kind of alert on an app, like Waze — *Cop ahead. Parent on the side of the road. Seek alternate route.*

Maggie thought back to move-in day, when she'd asked Taylor (who seemed the friendliest, the most reasonable of all the girls, not stiff and formal like Fiona, not ditzy like Annie) if she could have their phone numbers, in case of emergency.

Emma had intervened, a look of horror on her face. "Mom," she'd cautioned. A stop sign, a red light, in one word.

"It's okay," Taylor had answered, and Emma had said *No, no, it wasn't* and stopped the transaction. Emma had turned to Taylor and said, "only child," and Maggie had wanted to add, "only parent." But embarrassing her daughter had not been part of the plan. She'd wanted her to be happy, to fit in. Not be the weird girl with the overprotective mother and dead father. And now, part of her regretted that decision, but she also knew that none of those girls would answer her call anyway. But would they answer Emma? She wasn't sure.

In Emma and Fiona's room, she heard a sudden peal of laughter from three floors below, on the sidewalk, and when Maggie glanced instinctively toward the window, she noticed it was open an inch.

"This wasn't open before," Maggie said.

"Huh. I think you're right."

"I know I am." Maggie was, first and foremost, a mother. She'd come late to the role of wage earner and left early the role of wife — for even she would admit, long before her husband had died, she'd stopped being a wife, just dropped it off her resume, allowing it to fall from the to-do list forever.

Mother was what she was and what she'd been good at. She could live forever on four hours' sleep, hush a crying baby with a few swings of her arms, whip up cupcakes on short notice from just a few things in her pantry. She was smart enough to edit a term paper, calm enough to teach parallel parking, and she'd always known when she came home from a night out if someone had thrown a party in her absence. She'd notice the smallest thing wrong — the fireplace poker turned sideways, the bottle opener tossed into the wrong drawer, all the Crystal Light packets used up — and just know. Compared to those things, an open window was a big thing. A big thing a mother would notice.

She went to the window, looked down. She stood there watching the kids on the sidewalk, two boys and a girl, which was always trouble. The worst combination imaginable. If there was a third boy, there would be a chance of overruling each other. If there was a second girl, there would be a chance of getting away. Maggie stared at them as if she could will their motives to be pure. They laughed hysterically at something and swayed in that way that said *drinking but not drunk.* She didn't recognize them; it was clear they were just out for a walk, just passing by, just stopping because one of them said something so funny, the other two almost wet their pants. They weren't important, but suddenly, everything was important. The window was open, the sky was inky, people were laughing outside, and her daughter was missing. How did all these things fit together? Suddenly, there would always be an addendum, a phrase at the end of every thought, action, and piece of news. Da dum da dum da dum and my daughter is missing.

"Too high to jump," Carla said.

The words didn't calm Maggie; they put more ideas in her head. *Jumping?*

"I guess the roommate waited for us to leave, came home for a minute, and cracked the window."

"To blow-dry her hair," Maggie said. "To keep her cool."

"Or to vape, more likely."

"Girls blow-dry their hair a lot," she said defensively.

"College kids vape a lot," Carla said. "Take a look." She pointed to a couple down on the sidewalk, passing something between them.

"Damn, I feel old," Maggie said, and Carla smiled.

"The phone sounded like it was in the

bureau," Carla said. "Why don't you look, so I can keep my job."

Maggie opened the top drawer. Inside was a pile of bright lace thongs and bras that weren't her daughter's, couldn't be her daughter's — and underneath them was Emma's white iPhone. She put it in her pocket and nodded her thanks to Carla.

She would take it somewhere private and put in Emma's password, which she knew, she was sure, was *KOALA,* which was Frank's nickname for her. He had always called her things that ended in an *a* like her name — Arugula, Calendula, Mozzarella, but Koala had started it all. It was one of those sweet things he did every so often that forced Maggie to think highly of him again. He seemed to know exactly when to employ that sweetness, and once Maggie finally noticed that, the manipulation, the ebb and flow of it, it made her angry all over again. It was Frank's job to manipulate people, but Maggie had been so young when they'd met — just seventeen to his twenty — that she was sure he'd gotten all his practice cajoling her.

Still, the phone was a victory. She could at least start to put together a picture of what was happening — who might have summoned Emma, what they had said, when she last spoke to someone. All texts, group chats, always. The police would be yet another step behind, talking to a not-boyfriend, waiting for roommates who were likely not coming home anytime soon. On a night like this, you could wait for a group of girls, Maggie knew, for a long time. Past the party, the after-party, the drunken hookup, the fourth meal, the walk of shame. They could be here all night, waiting for girls who would be too drunk to even speak to them. And then what would they do? Was it even legal to read the Miranda rights to girls so drunk they couldn't speak? Was waiting for the drunks a methodology, a technique? She tried to remember an episode of *Dateline* or a case with the steely Paula Zahn, who dug deep but with hair so soft and eyes so kind that the parents of dead children didn't even feel the wound, that featured testimony from teenagers who were drunk or high. She couldn't remember. But that was what was about to happen, and she was pretty sure Kaplan would use it as another excuse to delay.

Go get some sleep, grab some coffee, crack jokes with your coworkers, fill in your lieutenant who says something innocuous like "try again," try again, fail again, rinse and repeat. Regular citizens wondered why police investigations took so much time, but Maggie knew exactly why. Cops moved on cop time, as if they were saving themselves, storing up their energy, for quick bursts of adrenaline, the pursuits, the chases, the takedowns. In between, you needed to conserve, or you'd burn out.

But Maggie was in a hurry. She didn't need to save anything up for later; she would happily burn herself out over and over again. As they walked back to the common room, she noticed Carla glance at her watch.

"You don't have to stay," Maggie said.

Carla nodded. "I thought I'd maybe wait with you till Kaplan gets back."

"There's no need, really."

"Will you be . . . okay?"

"I'll be fine. I'll just stay here, keep my eye out for the roommates."

"You're going to try calling from your daughter's phone? That's why you wanted it, right? To see if the roommates would answer her call instead of the RA's?"

"It's worth a try. I don't think it'll work, but still."

Carla frowned a little, then nodded. Maggie could tell she didn't know about teenage girls. How they didn't listen to voicemail. How they didn't answer their calls or texts unless someone exciting or important was guaranteed to be on the line. And she had a feeling, a terrible gut feeling, the roommates didn't want to hear from Emma. That that was why her phone was in another girl's bureau drawer, and everything else she owned was gone.

"You have Kaplan's number, right?"

Maggie nodded.

"Well, here's mine. Call me anytime if you want to talk. The police station in Ardmore is close to your house. And call Kaplan if the roommates show up, okay?"

"Okay," Maggie said, but in her head, she was thinking, *Maybe, maybe not.*

She thanked her and waved goodbye and watched through the doorway as Carla pressed the button for the elevator, then got in. She counted to sixty, eighty, a hundred. Long enough for Carla to leave the building. Long enough for her to reach her squad car.

Then Maggie left the sticky, empty common room to wander the other hallways. Quiet now, no laughter or water running. She considered knocking on doors but knew the wrong move could get her thrown out. She also knew the girls she wanted to talk to weren't the quiet ones. Still, something stuck in her mind. Why would bright girls

76

leave the door unlocked? Unless they were going somewhere very, very close by?

She went out to the elevator, typed in Emma's password. Koala17, just as she'd assumed. But she stared at the short list of contacts and the handful of apps. No Facebook, no Instagram, no email. What had happened to her daughter's phone? There was only Uber, Lyft, Snapchat. She opened Uber. Emma's last ride had been almost a week ago, to Center City. She opened Snapchat and was both relieved and disappointed to see a longer list of contacts, but all of them had coded names and bitmojis, and it was hard to imagine who was who. Still, she remembered another parent telling her about the Snap Map, that you could see the last place a person had chatted from, so she clicked on TayBae, which she guessed was Taylor. Her last location appeared to be on the same block as Hoden House or the one right next to it — Riordan — sent thirty minutes before.

Unlocked door. Roommate gone somewhere close. It added up to a party very, very nearby. But where? Which building? What floor? How many chances would she have to find it before someone realized someone's mom was raiding all the parties? It was hard to tell. And in thirty minutes, any of the girls could have moved on to the next one.

She walked out into the lobby and flagged down the first scantily clad girl she saw.

"Hey, where's the best party tonight?" She lowered her voice to a whisper. "I'll buy the vodka."

TEN

EMMA

Three days after Taylor's revelation, a Thursday, after listening to Fiona come home every night in a different pair of designer high heels — for she had a whole closetful, made of different colors and materials, which now made perfect sense — Emma freed up a morning to start researching the story, and she started out with the safest, simplest, do-it-in-your-pajamas way she could, by Googling things. She quickly found a couple of the websites Taylor had alluded to, both of which denied her free access — you had to identify as a "daddy" or a "baby" and log in. The baby path asked her to upload a photo and requested a nominal monthly listing fee — a fee that, she was horrified to learn, was discounted 50 percent if you registered with a college email address. *Targeted,* she thought. And she wondered if there were other ways they recruited.

She quickly exited. She couldn't sign up without an invented persona, and she'd better not try anything further on her computer, from her room. She ran over to Lenape Library, which wasn't the closest library — there was a smaller one in the science building — but it was her favorite, because it was quiet. Even the second floor, with its long rows of desks and green lamps, where students often worked in groups, was filled with nothing above whispers. The computers were on the ground floor, in the back. She'd never used them; only the kids with laptops in the shop or no computers of their own spent time here, so she was surprised that you needed a college email address to log on. Shit. She was trying to cover her tracks, after all, be anonymous. She typed in the only other college user name and password she knew: Sarah Franco's. She'd explain to Sarah later; they'd find a way to laugh about it, she was sure.

Once she was online, she created a fake Gmail account under the name George J. Pigg, then used it for the daddy email path on OurArrangement.com. No photo required, but a monthly fee that was five times higher than the sugar baby's. On the sidebar of the site was a scroll of college logos, as if they were proudly affiliated. Wasn't that illegal? One thing was for sure — if she wanted to go undercover as a daddy or a baby, she would need a bit more money than she currently had. This struck her as a serious barrier to entry — wouldn't anyone desperate enough to want to "baby" to pay off her debts be unable to afford the listing costs plus the clothing that fit the dress code, which was described as "classy" and "perfectly coordinated"? There were YouTube videos full of advice about how to create the perfect profile, how to appeal to just the right daddy by what you wore and how you did your hair. Watching them, even with headphones, even with the screen angled away from the whole world, toward the wall, made Emma gag. Girls helping other girls prostitute themselves with video tutorials? And the founder of OurArrangement.com, with his comb-over hair and pudgy hands wrapped around a champagne glass, was straight-up creepy AF. How the hell was this legal?

She also found a four-year-old *Inquirer* article claiming that hundreds of Philadelphia college students, male and female, were engaged in a variety of activities to pay off their student loans, one of which was "sugar-babying" or "sugaring." The highest percentage of participants, they claimed, came from Semper University. The article didn't mention the websites or a club — maybe this was a newer phenomenon — instead alluding to private networking events by invitation only. The sources were unnamed restaurant workers and a local businessman. The businessman said it wasn't illegal for friends to meet friends of friends at a restaurant and for them to buy each other presents. That was all that was happening here. When asked by the reporter if he'd ever participated, he'd laughed and said, "I said it was legal. I didn't say it was moral."

This struck her as the kind of story that would make a series, but there were no follow-up articles. She looked for the author, Cara Stevens, on the *Inquirer* website, but she apparently didn't work there anymore. When she searched the author's name, a hodgepodge of results came up, so she retyped "Cara Stevens, journalist" and found one, only one, living in Vancouver, working for a tiny magazine. *Probably wasn't her,* Emma thought. Maybe she'd married and changed her name. Maybe, after her breakthrough series was shuttered for shoddy reporting — how on earth had she ascertained that the majority of students came from Semper? — she quit and became a teacher.

She walked to the subway and took the first car into Center City. It was only a few stops, but it always freaked her out to go aboveground and see that the planet wasn't actually covered in yellow banners and completely populated by people all the same age. There were grown businessmen and women, grandparents, moms with babies, kids on field trips. It was jarring, going into the real world, but also a relief. You weren't surrounded by people looking at you, trying to figure out if they wanted to date you, fuck you, borrow your clothes, use your biology notes, or make fun of you later for something stupid you said. No one cared if you had every flavor of vodka under your bed, had a Free People leather jacket, had pot brownies or cigarettes or any form of currency they needed. College was a lot like prison, Emma decided. It made it a lot harder to adjust to the outside world.

She headed east to Paco's Thai Palace, passing bright storefronts, smelling the odd mix of wet sidewalk and musty awning and fried onions she'd always associated with the city, with her childhood. Part ruined, part delicious. So different from the manicured spaces on campus.

She walked in, sat at a tiny table in the

back, and ordered the lunch special. It was $11.99, which was a lot of money to her but not a lot of money for food in Philadelphia, she'd come to learn. When the other girls ordered from Grubhub or Uber Eats, she always looked at the receipts they'd thrown away, still stapled to the greasy brown or white bags, and tried to calculate how much they were spending, wasting, throwing away, as if she could measure the difference between their lives and hers.

The restaurant was a few blocks off Rittenhouse Square, clearly designed to appeal to millennials, with pink and blue cocktails, chairs that swung from the ceiling, a roof deck. But it had gotten great Yelp reviews for the food, too, despite its goofy name, and from the comfort of her padded booth, Emma watched a parade of young office workers line up for takeout. No one in the restaurant looked remotely like a sugar daddy or a daddy of any kind. Babies, yes; daddies, no. A hunting ground, maybe, but not during the day. She'd have to come back at night to judge it properly. The shrimp pad thai special was delicious, and despite its huge proportions, Emma ate most of it. She didn't want to be seen bringing it home and didn't want to waste it. She vowed to skip dinner, paid the bill, and went outside.

She looked up and down the block, considering her original hypothesis — that the restaurant wasn't the club itself but near the club. She headed west, passing a shoe store and a high-end baby clothing store, which she found ironic. A nice detail that might fit into the story. An office supply and repair store had a filmy, yellowing window and locked door, and she wondered if it was a front for something. *I mean come on,* she thought. *Who needs typewriter repair?*

The rest of the block was more upscale, a mix of dentists and lawyers with residences above. When Emma looked up, she saw a guy watering a fiddle fern on a balcony and a woman talking on her phone and drinking coffee from an oversized cup. People home in the middle of the day, rich people with trust funds, people who didn't have to pay off student loans. Had they seen anything from those windows?

She shielded her eyes against the sun and looked across the street — a cheese shop, a gift shop, a CVS. She crossed the street, kept walking. An upscale men's store, Beck's, took up most of the next block, a store so bougie, it had valet parking. On the corner, a bar/restaurant with a coat of arms on the door and a one-word name: London. She tugged on the door, but it was locked.

Open for dinner only, she assumed, until she saw the small type etched below: a private supper club. *Holy shit,* she thought. Maybe her hypothesis was correct. You drew in the men from the store and the girls from the bars. Who needed advertising? Who needed a website or an app or listing? Still, the club didn't look very big. She stared up at the windows above street level. Offices? Residences? Massage rooms? That seemed sleazy, and everything she'd heard about this phenomenon had led her to believe that it was high-end, classy. And God knows there were plenty of hotels around to serve that need. She walked over the men's store and smiled at the valet, who smiled back. She was glad she'd worn a dress, washed her hair.

"Hey there," she said. "Can I ask you a question?"

"Sure," he said.

She felt confident now, practiced from all her introductions and questions aimed at strangers at school.

"Is Beck's open at night?"

"Wednesdays it is."

"You ever work Wednesdays?"

"I alternate, yeah."

"So, I was wondering if there's also valet for the supper club?"

86

"Oh, no," he said suddenly, his face falling. "You're going there?" The disappointment dragging down the corners of his mouth, the slight blush across his lightly freckled cheeks, said everything to her.

"No, no," she said, and he brightened. "I . . . my boss asked me to check it out. For a, uh, client visiting. For dinner."

His face brightened. "Well, we usually handle valet for them."

"You do?"

"Sure. Same owner."

"Same owner," she repeated. She wanted to ask who that was but was certain that wasn't necessary. She could find that out easily. She hesitated, wasn't sure the right question to ask next.

"So . . . how long you work for your boss? How well you know him?" He was asking her questions now, too.

She had to be careful. She was not as good at lying as she was at asking.

"I . . . just started."

"Ah, well. I hope he's good to you. And he doesn't get any ideas."

"What do you mean?"

"Like sending you to that club or something."

She frowned. "So . . . you don't like that club?"

"That's an understatement."

"Is it a young crowd, then?"

He laughed. "Half of it is."

"What do you mean?"

"Well, when they drop off their car here with me, it's not. But when they pick it up, it is. If you catch my drift."

Of course, Emma the journalist caught the drift just fine. But undercover Emma running errands for the boss, would she catch it?

She frowned, screwed up her face in a way she knew looked childish, and that was the point. "Half old, half young? In the car?"

"Yup."

"Oh!" she said, feigning surprise.

"Yeah. Gorgeous girls, too. Kinda makes you sick."

"So the cars must be nice? For you, at least. To drive."

"Most of them, but not all. You'd be surprised."

I bet I would, Emma thought. Since the world was starting to seem incredibly surprising.

"Wow. Well, thanks for the info."

"You're welcome. I'm Michael, by the way."

"Mary," she said, extending her hand, the fake name rolling off her tongue quickly, easily, more easily than she thought possible.

"You be careful with that boss of yours," he added.

"I will."

"Maybe I'll see you again," he added. "But not on a Wednesday."

"Thanks, Michael."

He'd given her a lot to think about, and she was confident he would remember her if she needed him again. Her first source, after her roommates!

She walked to the corner and opened Snapchat, just to see where her roommates were. She wasn't sure how often Fiona checked the app, but it could prove helpful. She could follow Fiona and test her hypothesis. She stared at the map, squinting. Annie, Morgan, and Fiona were all at the same location, and it wasn't the dorm. Wasn't even on campus. When did Annie and Morgan ever do anything with Fiona, who kept to herself? She scrolled in and saw that they were at a boutique clothing store on Walnut Street. Shopping? For what?

She stood there a few minutes, trying to decide if this was meaningful. Or if she should go there, since it was eight blocks away. Then it struck her, with horror. *If I know where they are, they know where I am.*

Here, next to the private club that might be a freaking whorehouse.

She turned off her phone, then headed back to the subway along Chestnut Street. She went into the first electronic store she saw and bought a new burner phone.

ELEVEN

MAGGIE

Maggie shouldn't have been surprised that there were three liquor stores so close to campus, but she was. They'd lived in the city, in South Philly, for years, but in that neighborhood, on the exact opposite end of town, the stores were few and far between. Frank had always joked that this was by design, to try to keep their Irish relatives sober, but Maggie knew there had to be strict ordinances about how many licenses were issued, where, and when. In Pennsylvania, liquor stores were technically controlled by the state, but in the last few years, the rules were starting to relax a little, carving out ways for "state stores" to be connected to other stores, so consumers didn't have to make as many stops. But kids? Catering to college kids with money and a party to go to? That did not seem in line with the goals of the state. This small outpost had a bodega inside it with a few aisles of snacks and magazines as well as an aisle of alcohol and wine.

Maggie stood in line with a handle of vanilla vodka, waiting for the young man behind the counter to ring up the lottery tickets and 5-hour Energy drinks and Doritos of the people in front of her, all of whom looked young enough to be students but weren't. They wore uniforms — colorful scrubs, a mechanic's shirt. People who worked in the neighborhood, not people who studied. Still. Three liquor stores on this block. The things you don't notice on campus visiting day. The things you don't care about on move-in day. The things that aren't clear to you until someone calls you from campus and tells you something you never wanted to hear about your child. Drunk. Hurt. In handcuffs. Missing. Or, God forbid, all of the above.

The girl waited for her outside, on the corner. Before she'd agreed to their transaction, she'd asked Maggie who she was looking for. Maggie had hesitated for only a second, then decided she saw enough youthful empathy in her to tell her the truth. She was skinny, tiny as a child, with a puff of blond, curly hair that didn't quite reach her shoulders. Fine hair that suited her, but she probably hated it, wanted thick straight hair. She wanted the hair of an older girl, not a fairy child. Not what she had. *She could never be served,* Maggie thought. Never. This girl would be showing her driver's license and rolling her eyes at servers until she was forty-five. Maybe she was young on the inside, too. Not so tough. It had been pretty easy to convince her.

"My daughter is missing," Maggie had said. "And it's imperative that I find her roommate."

"Oh my God," the girl said, one hand going up to her mouth. "That's so scary."

"Yes, it is."

"So, the roommate might be missing, too," she said, her eyes widening.

Maggie hesitated only a second before deciding to agree, to roll with it. "Yes. Their room looked very suspicious."

"There could be, like, a serial killer on campus."

Maggie swallowed. "Yes. Do you know a girl named Fiona?"

She shook her head. No. She didn't live in Hoden House; she lived in Riordan, the dorm next door, with lots of athletes. But they all went to the same parties, texting each other, looking for the ones that had the most alcohol, the most boys. And sometimes, late at night, maybe the most food. Food was probably the most elusive quantity of all, but Maggie knew girls didn't like to eat in public, in front of boys. That was for later, in the safety and anonymity of their dorm.

On the buckling sidewalk, the girl looked unsteady in her high-heeled wedges, as if they were small blocks of cement that couldn't quite hold her up.

They crossed the street, and when they were back on campus, under the flapping yellow flags, she held her hand out toward Maggie's plastic bag and said thanks.

"Oh no," Maggie said.

"What? I told you where the party was."

"You're taking me there."

"But you have the address! It's right over there!" she said, pointing. Her voice was whiny like a child's, too.

"I have to go in."

"I can't take you with! You can't just go in! I thought you were going to, like, stake it out. You know, watch who comes and goes."

"My daughter is missing. I have to go in."

Maggie took an elastic from her wrist and pulled her long hair up, into a high ponytail. She smoothed the sides and top by feel. She took a red lipstick out of her purse and put it on, again by feel. No mirror. The girl watched her incredulously.

"Okay, you look a little better, but still —"

Maggie unbuttoned her cotton shirt, letting a tiny bit of her black lace bra show. Right after Frank died, Maggie had gone out in a fit of grief and jealous rage and bought all new underwear. Bras and panties that fit, that matched. No holes. No sensible, Catholic-girl cotton. That made her feel, somehow, whole and desired again. No one to see her that way, but that hardly mattered. She put on her underwear and drank a little wine and watched TV without apology, like the grown woman she was, not the repressed Catholic girl with the alcoholic relatives she used to be.

Maggie pulled the tail ends of her shirt around her waist and tied them.

The girl looked at her sideways, in a way that reminded Maggie of a puppy. "Okay, maybe if it's dark?"

Since it was, in fact, dark, Maggie sighed. She didn't have time to explain the world to this girl. That age was on a sliding scale and that if they both lived in a world where a girl who looked eleven could be an adult who needed to drink, then a woman in her forties with the right clothing and Ariana

Grande hairdo could look twenty-five. Had she never heard of J.Lo?

"Give me your shoes," Maggie said suddenly.

"What?"

"We're trading shoes."

She looked at Maggie in horror. "Ew, no!"

"I'll throw in twenty bucks."

The girl looked down at Maggie's feet.

"Wait, are those . . . Allbirds?"

"Yes, and they cost four times as much as what you paid at Target."

The girl unbuckled her wedges, and Maggie untied her wool sneakers. They were one of the few brands of shoes comfortable enough to work in all day, and she loved them. But she loved her daughter more.

A man passed them on the sidewalk and didn't even glance down, as if this was a common transaction, women trading shoes. No wonder men made terrible policemen.

"But I'm not going in with you, okay? I can't."

"Fine," Maggie said and handed her the vodka.

"Okay, well, good luck with everything," she said. "With your daughter and all. She's probably . . . just with some guy, you know? Have you thought of that?"

Maggie smiled at her. "Do me one more favor?"

"Um, okay."

"Call your mother tomorrow. Call your mother and tell her you love her." Maggie's voice broke when she said it, and even here, in the noise of the world, the girl could hear it.

Their eyes met, and the girl's looked even paler blue, liquid with sudden tears, like the sea. Maggie could see the toddler in her, the little girl holding a melting ice cream cone, a scrape on her knee. Suddenly, she felt a wave of nausea. She was a baby. A baby with vanilla vodka. Maggie bit her lip and said a prayer. That God would understand the bargain she had just made. And that this girl, this young girl from a small town or farm somewhere in the middle of Pennsylvania, who hadn't grown up in the city, who had no older sister to guide her, who didn't belong on a campus of thirty thousand students, who desperately needed vodka as currency to fit in, would be safe. That she would trade the vodka more than drink it. No matter where Emma was or would be, let this girl be safe and not drink too much tonight.

"I will," she said earnestly, nodding her head like a third grader and wiping carefully under her eyes. "I promise."

"And don't drink more than three shots!" Maggie called after her. "Three! You don't weigh enough to drink any more!"

"Okay," she called back over her shoulder.

Maggie watched her walk inside the row home, heard the shrieks from inside as she brandished the bottle toward a friend. Just in time for shots. Just in time for a wake-up cocktail mixed with a little Diet Coke. Just in time to pour a bit into the jungle juice, to add its sweetness to the darker swirling mess inside.

The party was just a few blocks from Emma's dorm, but it was darker here and louder. Not a frat house; there was no flag outside. But this was an elevated kind of housing, something Maggie hadn't noticed on her tour. Maybe it was reserved for seniors. *Great,* she thought. Boys who looked thirty. Girls who looked twelve.

The whole block pulsed with rap music and laughter. Rap had always confused Maggie. All those words. All those rat-a-tat rhymes. It was like listening to a podcast at double speed, trying to catch up, trying to make sense of it all before the next tangled stanza appeared. But she also knew the messages weren't meant for her; she wasn't supposed to understand it. The puzzle of it all, the speedy glory of figuring it out, belonged to another generation, like the crossword did to hers.

Now, the songs in different houses, different parties, competed with one another, overlapping, like jumbled code. Were these all students in these rentals? And if there were faculty, staff, someone else here, how could they stand this level of noise?

She waited a few minutes, then walked in. A crush of bodies dancing in the small, dark living room. Arms in the air, beer dripping from cups, foam running down their arms. Sticky, like toddlers. Maggie wanted to put them into a bathtub and scrub them down.

In the back, the kitchen, and beyond, a courtyard deck. She moved through the room, trying to avoid being spilled on, and stepped into the kitchen. Coolers on the floor, plastic bags of ice in the sink. Her feet stuck with every step, which made her wince. It was dark enough that no one noticed her but light enough that she could see — and she didn't recognize anyone. She said a small prayer that the girls would be outside and not upstairs. She really didn't want to know what was going on in the bedrooms.

She smelled pot, tobacco, and something sweet she couldn't put her finger on. Perfume, she guessed. Some awful, sugary, celebrity perfume. If it was a hair product, she'd recognize it — they all had such distinct, annoying scents, especially dry shampoo. Girls would come into the salon, and she'd know exactly what they used on their hair. If it was anyone else's house, it could have been honeysuckle or herbs, something growing, but she didn't think the occupants of this house owned flower pots. From the looks of things, they didn't even own furniture. No sofa in the living room, no table in the kitchen, no folding chairs in the courtyard. But there were twinkling lights hanging above. Row after row, carefully strung. For what they paid for them, Maggie knew, they probably could have bought four chairs. But for what?

Maggie had only seen all of Emma's roommates together once, but she had a picture on her phone of the girls outside the dorm room on move-in day. They'd laughed and posed in front of the Hoden House sign, and Taylor had called out "Hottie House!" She didn't need to open her camera app again, in the dark, to look at it. How many times had she stared at it after leaving her daughter, memorizing it? What a girl looked like the exact day she grew up. Maggie had gone home and studied that photo at night, as if wondering if the wings, the parachute, the launch pad would be visible. Could Emma handle it? Was she ready? Of course she was. Emma had a good head on her shoulders, was organized, smart, studious. But what about the others? Had they been ready, able, tough enough? Or were they like the girl Maggie had just met?

The photo in her memory contained the practiced poses of girls raised on social media. The tilted heads, the bent arms, the knowledge of their best angles. One dimension. Even in video, they didn't quite seem whole or real. But how did these girls look in the actual world? When someone wasn't watching, when they weren't posing, when vodka and pot and who knows what else — cocaine? molly? — softened it all and exposed the parts they didn't want seen? The double chins, the flyaway hairs, the big ears hidden by flat-ironed hair. When it all became obvious that they were human, mortal, what would they look like? If they became real again, suddenly, standing right in front of her, would Maggie even recognize them? *Yes,* she thought as she moved toward a young woman standing near the fence, close to the keg, she would. Unlike the police, unlike another parent, unlike a girl who'd seen them sometimes at a party.

Because Maggie O'Farrell would recognize their hair. First and foremost, yes. And there it was. Dark-brown hair. Long and swinging, with a tiny amount of copper in the undertones, not gold. And not colored, not altered in any way. Virgin hair, the rarest thing. Proof that there were still plenty of girls left in the world who didn't try to become blonds, who didn't spray their ends with lemon juice in the summer or try to layer on something neon, fake, and bright like they'd stolen it off of My Little Pony. Shiny brown hair, Anglican. Touched far more often by spotlight than by sunlight. The hair of the girl in the middle of the picture. Taylor.

TWELVE

EMMA

Emma decided not to follow her roommates for three very simple reasons. One: her feet hurt. It was too close to Uber and too far to walk in her Converse, and the number two reason occurred to her as she headed toward the train station — there was nowhere to hide. If they'd been closer to campus, it could have been an accident, running into them, but how would it look now? Still, as she wove through the terminal at Suburban Station, joining a small parade of students and business people, all of them ignoring the homeless men sitting near the walls, lumpy and smelly and dark as bags of trash, a third smaller, stupid, completely annoying reason roared through her, inflaming her cheeks with embarrassment and anger. Her hair had always had a tiny hint of red in it, mixed with the mostly gold highlights that came out every summer, and when she

103

blushed, as she was too prone to do, it just made everything about her look red. Red as a slap, red as a scab.

She flushed not from effort or fear or flirtation — all of these caused it, too — but from hurt. They were all together without her. Shopping. Having fun. Eating lunch. Talking shit about her. They were hanging out without her, and it didn't matter if one of them was a slut or they were all basically sluts, if Fiona had recruited every single one of them. It stung. How stupid she'd been to think they just all had their own busy lives! What a freaking idiot to think they were just busier than she was! She felt like an absolute fool, the youngest always, still behind in the ways of the world.

Riding the train, the truth of it all sunk in hard, filling her chest with a tight kind of dread. What else were they hiding from her?

When she got home, she deleted everything on her iPhone that wasn't essential, disabled the GPS, and put it in the top drawer of her bureau, underneath her pajamas. She'd only open Snapchat from the dorm from now on, to find information, not to give any away. They would never know when she left or where she was going or what she was doing. They could be secretive? Well, she could be, too.

On her laptop, she disabled iCloud, turned off location services. She taped over her camera, disabled the microphone, cleared her cache and her search history, and emptied the trash permanently.

She'd never had a long-term boyfriend to hide something from. Not a parent. No one. Her mom never snooped; she didn't believe in it. Maggie wasn't a pushover, she wasn't a fool, but as Emma had overheard her telling her aunt Kate before carpooling kids to a concert on the Parkway, she wasn't going to look through her daughter's stuff like it was evidence. Kids needed some privacy, too.

Emma was unpracticed at something most teens were good at, but she was about to get very, very good at covering her tracks. She would use the library computer and her burner phone. No one would know what she was really up to. This was an investigation now, and it was important that no one around her had any idea what she was doing until she knew what shape it was taking. Especially because, despite Taylor's gossipy half-drunk confession, which, when she recalled her exact words, "she's your roommate, so I just assumed that you knew," she realized could simply be a way of her lording it over her. *I'm closer to her than you are.*

You sleep next to her, close enough to hear her prayers, yet don't know what's in her fucking heart. They clearly were sticking together. Four against one was crappy odds.

Then, as she started to Google the owner of Beck's and look up the Facebook profiles of everyone named Cara Stevens, another sickening thought crept in. That none of her roommates cared what she was or wasn't doing. She wasn't a threat or a problem. No one would ever think to search her computer or phone. If they were worried about what Emma thought, would Fiona even have the guts to dress how she dressed and come and go as she did? If Taylor cared, would she have told her what she'd told her? Well. She'd show them, wouldn't she, she thought as she messaged the Cara Stevens in Vancouver first.

As she was reading all about Brian Beck, the owner of Beck's, and his mission to make Philadelphia the best-dressed city in America — a goal Emma thought, based on her childhood in South Philly, where the men tended toward bowling shirts, and her adolescence on the Main Line, where the fathers wore wool sweaters with patched elbows, was an impossible dream — she got a message back from one of her Cara Stevenses. Yes, she was the author of that article, and yes, she'd be happy to talk. Bingo. But she had to call Emma back from a pay phone.

A pay phone? Emma thought with horror. Did they still have those? Well, maybe in Vancouver they did. Vancouver seemed about as far away and foreign a place as Croatia or Tasmania.

She gave Cara the number of her new burner phone, packed up her laptop, and headed all the way across campus to the one place she knew Fiona and all her roommates would have absolutely no interest in going after their little shopping or lunch date. The synagogue, B'nai Sholom. She sat on a low wall outside, alone. The only time she'd seen it busy was on a Saturday or during a Jewish holiday, and even then, it was quieter than anywhere else.

She gathered her thoughts, made a few coded notes in a doc that she named "Lunar Eclipse," and buried it in a folder called "Science Labs." Then she copied it onto Dropbox for later use at the library.

Five minutes later, Emma's phone rang.

"Cara," she said breathlessly.

"Yep," she replied. Her voice was deep and scratchy, as if she'd just woken up. Emma realized there was a time difference; she had to think of that kind of thing.

"Sorry for the subterfuge, but we don't know each other."

"Right. I could be . . . the police, or —"

"If you were the police, I'd be thrilled. Shocked but thrilled. I was more worried that you're a professor. Or a horny man out for revenge."

"I am neither."

"Doesn't sound like it."

"But full disclosure: I'm a female student."

"I know."

"You do?"

"Saw you on Instagram. Cute sunglasses, by the way."

Of course. Crap! She'd have to change her privacy settings on social media, maybe delete her accounts. She'd have to think about that carefully, though; her mother would freak out and worry that something was wrong.

"So, what, you're helping out with sexual assault research, interning at *Rolling Stone* or *Teen Vogue* or something? Somewhere that still gives a tiny shit about investigative journalism?"

"No."

"Well, what story are you working on then?"

"I'm working for the student newspaper."

There was a brief pause, and Emma heard

a sharp exhale of breath. It occurred to her that she'd rarely heard anything so clearly and wondered if pay phones had better microphones than cell phones. If technology was actually going backward. Whoa, that would be a cool story, too.

"You have got to be kidding me."

Crap, she was about to lose her! She had to defend herself and Jason. If not her, Jason.

"I know our paper is, like, nothing to a real reporter like you, but I feel the evidence I've found —"

"No, that's not it."

She paused. "What is it then?"

"Well, is Leandros still in charge at Semper?"

"Yes."

"Ha, yeah. Well, more on him later. Or you can just Google it and find out how in bed he is with all of Philadelphia. So who knows about your story and your research? Just your editor?"

"Yes," she lied.

"So the story hasn't been killed yet?"

"Well, no, that's why I'm calling you. I'm just starting really."

"So you're a freshman and don't know shit about the history of this, right? Your editor a junior or a senior? I can find out.

You'll just save me some time."

"He's a senior."

"Well, neither of you was on campus when my story broke, but he might have been aware of it if he was on the newspaper staff his first year. Okay, never mind. So. What do you want to know? Where do we start?"

"I guess my biggest question is, why wasn't this a series? It felt like a five-parter, or three. I kept waiting for . . . I don't know, other shoes to drop." She winced as she said this — it was one of her mother's favorite phrases. After her father was killed and she found out about his mistress, that's what she'd said. That the other shoe had dropped.

"Yeah, well, it was supposed to be. Till the second installment was killed."

"Killed by who? I mean whom?"

"Technically, by a pansy-ass editor. But officially, by the owner of the *Inquirer,* who threatened to fire him. He had three kids in college, so I understand to some degree, but he's still a pussy."

"Did he give you a reason at least?"

"Oh sure. Said I used too many unnamed sources that they couldn't substantiate. But the real reason was I was about to name some of the clients and one of the restaurant owners and dared to call out Semper University for not protecting its students. I had

110

one of the girls on record. Someone who was about to graduate. But that wasn't enough."

"Did that restaurant owner happen to be Brian Beck?"

"Close. His brother, Sam."

"Brothers?"

"Yeah, imagine how proud their mommy must be. Two pimps in one family. What a gene pool. So how'd you find out about Brian?"

"A bit of intuition, a bit of luck, and a lot of proximity."

"What do you mean?"

"Well, Beck's store is next to this private club. They use the same valet parking service. And the valet parking guys have big mouths."

"Wait, I don't follow. The Beck brothers opened a club on Chestnut Street?"

"Yes. Why? Is it new? I haven't checked it out thoroughly yet."

"Must be new in the last few years. When I was working on this, Sam Beck had just renovated a big restaurant on Broad Street, near the old *Philadelphia Inquirer* building, if you can believe that. Like he was just daring one of us to figure it out. Anyway, the second floor was a private space, and he ran the operation out of there. All by invitation.

Only one bartender and one server allowed to even set foot up there. The rumor was it was his brother's idea, and he had something on him, but still."

"Must have been small if there were only two people working."

"No, it was huge. Half a city block. But they only served champagne, vodka, scotch, and these miniature desserts. Macarons, petit fours."

Was this to keep the girls from eating too much? Was that why Fiona stopped for Thai food afterward? Because she was starving? Emma felt her lack of experience acutely. Maybe sex felt best on an empty stomach. Or, ew, this might have to do with oral sex. She felt suddenly nauseated.

"So it was really just a meeting place, and the arrangement went from there?"

"Funny you should say that. That's what they called it internally. Privately. The arrangement. And that formed their excuse, too: 'The arrangement between two people is up to them. We just introduce friends to friends of friends.' "

"Ugh, I know. I've seen the websites and the apps. So what was the name of that restaurant?"

"Sparks."

"Ugh again."

"So I guess the new location is better for girls from Drexel and Penn. As well as the guys from the store."

"Wait, what?"

"Oh, you didn't think Semper had the market sewn up, did you?"

"No, but it's a state school, and it's bigger and . . . well, you know all that, but it's also —"

"Trashier? Sluttier?"

"Uh, I didn't say that."

"Sorry, I have to work on my political correctness. Too much time in newsrooms."

"Well, I was going to say, maybe less moneyed."

"There are girls on scholarship juggling student loans everywhere. And believe it or not, some girls do it for other reasons."

"For the sex?"

"Well, that's what they've convinced themselves. 'I like sex. I like to experiment.' But it's really the thrill, the danger, the wrongness."

"I noticed you didn't say illegal."

"See, this is the problem. It skirts the law. Talk to a lawyer. Talk to a psychologist."

"Oh, I will. I'm planning to," Emma said, although she was taking notes so furiously about all the people she'd have to call next, her head was spinning.

"And keep meticulous records and notes. Try to get people to go on record. That way if your story gets killed, you can take it somewhere else, somewhere young women's perspectives are valued, like the *Cut,* or *Lenny.* You'd know better than me. Your editor must have balls of steel to let you pursue this."

"He does," she said firmly. And hadn't she felt that about Jason? His calmness, his cool head? That was a kind of strength and certainty. She was sure of it.

"I assume you have a girl on the inside? Is that how this started?"

"Yes," she said. A half lie. She wondered if Cara Stevens had been sitting in front of her, a tough and seasoned professional, if she could tell how much bullshit was propping up her side of the conversation.

"Because that's the most important thing. The girls are being manipulated and harmed, whether they see it that way or not. Especially if they're freshmen. The younger, the better, in my view."

Good, Emma thought. Now if she could just get Fiona to share what was going on with her, she'd have a story. Especially since Fiona was trying to recruit Taylor. Collusion!

"Yes, my, um, source is a freshman."

114

"Good."

"Well, this has been great, wow. Thank you, Cara. You've given me a lot to think about."

"You're welcome. Let me know if you need anything else. And promise you'll be careful."

"I will."

"And one more thing?"

"Yes?"

"When you have a second, DM me a list of your professors."

"My professors?"

"Yeah, just in case."

"In case what?"

"Well, I always suspected that students weren't self-selecting. Someone was recruiting."

Emma's stomach dropped to the floor. No wonder Cara told her to be careful. No wonder she'd been working on a series. She was beginning to understand why Cara had called her from a pay phone. And maybe, just maybe, why she'd left town.

THIRTEEN

MAGGIE

There was not an ounce of recognition on Taylor's face as Maggie approached her. This, Maggie knew, was from a combination of things. One, she was drunk. Two, Maggie looked young in a ponytail. Three, no one cared or remembered anything about anyone's parents. Oh, they'd pretend to all right. The charade started in high school when they accepted your rides to games, when they came to your house at all hours and ate your food, when they were getting ready for a party together in your daughter's bedroom and one of them needed a black eyeliner. Then, yes, they would register your existence. Maybe on those nights, when you'd looked them in the eye and given them something they needed, maybe then they could describe you or pick you out of a lineup. Sometimes they'd eye something on you they wanted

116

— a nail polish color, a tasseled necklace — and you'd feel their gaze linger, registering, filing away.

But most of the time? Mothers were just a blur, part of the background, or occasionally, when you asked too many questions or worried too much, an easily kicked-over barricade in their way.

The converse of the equation, though, which aided Maggie now, was how much the opposite was true. How mothers saw their children and their friends in stark, detailed relief. All the negative things floated up first. Chipped polish. Bitten-down nails. The too-orange edges of a spray tan. The bend in the back of their heads where they'd missed with the flat iron. Mothers saw these things first. They'd been trained to be on the lookout, and they were, whether they liked it or not. So Maggie had no doubt she'd recognize those roommates and no doubt whatsoever that the girl laughing as she dropped a shot of Jack into her Solo cup of beer was Taylor.

Maggie took a cup from a teetering stack and pulled herself a beer, pretending to drink.

Taylor wiped the foam from her mouth with her sleeve. "Cheers!" she said to Maggie.

Maggie lifted her cup toward her. "So what are we celebrating, Taylor?"

Taylor stopped drinking, blinked. The fairy lights above them swayed in the wind, creating shadows across the planes of her face.

"What?"

"Are you celebrating the fact that one of your roommates is gone? Instead of, I don't know, being out looking for her? Instead of talking to the police and organizing a search and putting up flyers like her other friends will be tomorrow?"

She squinted. "Oh my God. It's, it's —"

"Yeah, OMG. It's Emma's mommy. So let's go out front and talk about that."

"No, I —"

"No? Well, would you like me to call your mom and explain instead?"

It was early by campus standards — ten thirty — but late for Maggie. She was exhausted, and Taylor was tipsy, and that's why Maggie suggested coffee, pointing to a place around the corner.

"No," Taylor said, "I'm meeting people here."

"Fine," Maggie said. She opened the gate, motioned outside, and Taylor followed her. They stood on the sidewalk, one woman upright, one wobbly.

"So where's my daughter? And why didn't you and her other roommates report her missing?"

"She's been gone a while."

"I know that, Taylor. Why didn't someone contact me?"

"Because she's not, like, missing. She's just, you know. Elsewhere." Something about the way she spoke gave Maggie the impression that she was pretending to be drunk, not actually drunk.

"Elsewhere?"

"She's staying somewhere else."

"Where?"

"That I do not know."

"Do you know she hasn't been to class? Her teachers haven't seen her or her friend Sarah. So you know her, Sarah Franco?"

"Sort of. And no, I didn't know."

"Don't you have any classes together?"

"One, but it's, like, a lecture. There's hundreds of kids in it."

"So when did she leave?"

"I don't know. Maybe a week?"

"Why did she leave? And why are you ignoring your voicemails, when the police are trying to reach you?"

"I don't listen to voicemail," Taylor said. "I don't pick up for random numbers."

Of course, Maggie thought. No one bothered. Too much time. Life moved too fast for voicemail or messages.

"You do realize they're going to find you? And you're going to have to answer someone a lot tougher than me. So why don't you just tell me where she is and save yourself some time and heartache."

"I told you, I don't know."

"Well, if you don't know when or where, maybe you can tell me why."

"Why what?"

"Why she's quote-unquote staying elsewhere."

"You know, not everyone is cut out for dorm life."

The wind picked up and blew a strand of hair across Taylor's lips. She lifted it away and turned her head so the wind blew her hair back. She stood away from Maggie now, ignoring her, swaying just a little, like a drunk person would. A drunk person in a bad play.

"Is that right?"

"Yeah. It's like camp or having a big family. Emma couldn't deal."

"Couldn't deal?"

"Right."

"So she's staying with another friend?"

"I guess."

"You guess? And what about your other

roommates?"

"What about them?"

"Where are they?"

"Tonight, you mean?"

"Yes, tonight, Taylor. Now. Because I find it astonishing that none of you were reachable on exactly the same evening. All night long."

She said nothing, looked at her feet. This confident, spark plug of a girl, a theater kid, the life of the party, good with people, suddenly couldn't perform. And couldn't look her audience in the eye.

"I don't know. We're not joined at the hip."

"Any Instagram stories or Snapchats from them tonight?"

"I don't know."

"Don't give me that, Taylor. I don't believe you. I can hear your alerts buzzing in your goddamned pocket. You know exactly where they are."

"Look, I don't know what you want from us. We don't know. We don't understand her, okay? The workings of her mind are not, like, normal."

"What do you mean?"

"I mean, she doesn't care about people."

"That's not true."

"No offense," Taylor said, and Maggie steeled herself for what was coming next.

Because when a young person used that phrase, she knew she was about to be offended deeply. "But I don't think you know your daughter."

Ouch. An arrow through the heart. Wasn't that what all mothers feared? That you spent all this time, talking, tending, shaping, and the result would be a complete mystery? Maggie suddenly couldn't breathe. She bent forward a few inches, trying to gather herself, centering her gaze, and in that half second, Taylor turned and ran back inside. Maggie could have followed her, could have embarrassed her, could have stolen her phone from her back pocket. She did none of those things. Instead, she made her first mistake. She called Kaplan and left him a message, told him she'd found Taylor and gave him the address.

Let him get it out of her, she thought. *Let him shut down this loud, underage party and ruin her night for causing it.* Taylor would learn the hard way; she'd learn to be a better actress. Or she'd learn to tell Maggie things first.

FOURTEEN

EMMA

It started to drizzle, a cold rain just steady enough to be annoying, but Emma didn't stop at her dorm for an umbrella. She rushed straight to the journalism building, running up the damp stone steps, sliding a little in her Converse. She was breathless when she arrived and found Jason in a meeting. The conference room, the only large room on the floor, was wrapped in smeary, streaked glass; it looked like dogs had pressed their noses against it. Jason's back was toward her, so she couldn't flag him down, and she realized this was a gift. She *shouldn't* flag him. This wasn't a matter of life and death, after all; it was just a story, and he didn't know anything about it, and it wasn't like anyone was in danger, right? There was no serial killer on campus, no rapist she'd uncovered; she realized, catching her breath and calming herself down, that this was not imperative, time sensitive, or worthy of running, so she was grateful she had the time to gather herself before she spoke. Passion was one thing; impetuousness was another.

She used the time she was waiting to strategize. Would knowing Fiona be helpful or hurtful? Could she count on interviewing her or her introducing her to others? She was suddenly annoyed at herself for not being chattier, more forceful. Even Taylor assumed that she'd known; why hadn't she asked Fiona innocuous questions about her clothes, her going out at night? Why had she just assumed her roommate was simply stylish? And what would Jason think? Would he wonder if there was something wrong with her powers of observation? That she could have slept right next to this girl, who took more time with her clothes and beauty regimens than she ever did with her homework, and not have suspected it was for a reason and not because she was just a prima donna?

Emma took a deep breath. No. That wasn't it. If another girl had behaved that way, Emma might have suspected right away. But not quiet, Catholic girl Fiona. Fiona didn't hide the cross around her neck; she wore no other jewelry, went to mass twice a week, and crossed herself instinctively whenever something good or bad happened. She was from outside Pittsburgh, but she reminded Emma of the girls she'd been confirmed with in South Philly. Good Irish girls. Girls who were raised with stories from their grandmothers and great aunts, of other girls who got into trouble, who strayed from the path. Girls like that don't have indiscriminate sex, and they certainly don't charge for it. Realizing this made Emma feel enormously better. It was the swinging gold cross around Fiona's neck that had hypnotized her, nothing else.

Jason's meeting seemed to go on forever. The real reporters, the seniors and juniors, they were in that room, no one else. She wondered what they were discussing. The lack of equipment? The need for more printers, fonts, photographers? The desire for a generous alumni donor like the business school and the biology lab and even the gym, with its gleaming rows of equipment, had? She wondered what they were working on. If any of them was experiencing the same problems she was.

She watched Jason listening quietly to a guy passionately describing something, gesturing with his arms, swaying his head. Finally, Jason took off his glasses and rubbed one eye. That did not look good to her. That looked like he was tired of listening, that the speech-giver had lost him. She wondered if talking to him after this long meeting, when he'd already grown weary, was bad timing. Maybe she should come back?

At last, they gathered up their laptops and notebooks and stood. A couple of people stretched. Jason opened the door and exchanged a few pleasantries, but the look on his face was clear. He wanted out of that room. She looked at her watch. Maybe he hadn't had lunch?

Outside at last. Still talking to one of the guys. She stood nearby but didn't wave, and he noticed, nodded his head, then finally extricated himself, made his way to her.

She smiled, exhaled.

"Long meeting?"

He shook his head. "It wasn't supposed to be, but what can you do?"

"Yeah," she said, although she had no idea what he was talking about.

"So what's up? You got something?"

She nodded. "I do. But if this isn't a good time —"

"No, this is a very good time, because everybody else in this room," his voice dropped to a whisper, "got a whole lot of nothing." He sighed. "Let's get some air. Can you walk and talk?"

She nodded. It was still spitting rain on and off, but she knew guys didn't care about that. Guys didn't care about their hair, their mascara. Outside, they walked and she talked and he listened. He stopped occasionally to wipe the rain off his glasses, but he let her speak. She tried to be succinct, to emphasize facts, not hunches. But when she was done, he went immediately for the weak parts.

"So you have not spoken to your roommate about her work yet?"

"No."

"And you haven't witnessed her in this establishment or in a car leaving it?"

"No."

"And you haven't been inside the club or found anyone who has?"

"Not yet," she said. "I know there's a lot more work to be done."

"Do you know when the first restaurant was shut down and when the club was built, when they got their liquor license?"

"No, but I will. That's on my to-do list."

"How long have you been working on this?"

"A day."

"A day?"

"Yeah."

"You found all this out in a day?"

"Yeah. Well, I skipped class this afternoon, so . . ."

He took a deep breath in, then rubbed his hand across his mouth. She had a feeling that was a good sign.

"Nice work," he said finally. "But there are more questions than answers, and we need a lot more before we can do anything with it."

"So no one's come to you with this already?"

"No. I know there are girls on every campus in big cities doing this, but I thought it was on the fringes, through the apps, maybe only a couple. There was a story in the *New York Post,* or maybe *New York Magazine,* a while back. But it sounds like your roommate isn't exactly the type you'd expect."

"That's putting it mildly."

"How close are you? I mean, other than seeing her in her retainer or hearing her snore, how well do you know her?"

"Not well. She's quiet and, um, she's gone a lot at night. And now I think I know why."

"Any issues with her, though? Any reason you can't get closer?"

"No."

"My thinking is that if she opened up to your other roommate, she'll open up to you. You need this information firsthand, not second. Otherwise, it's hearsay, gossip. I doubt she'll go on the record, but you at least need her perspective directly. And you need to work that valet. And, best case scenario, get inside the club. Can you waitress? Or bartend? I'm guessing they have attractive servers."

Her breath caught in her throat. Had he just called her attractive?

"I don't know," she said. "I was thinking that I should find out if she's told my other roommates. Or anyone else in her classes. Because maybe —"

"No," he said. "If that gets back to her, she'll be pissed that you're talking behind her back, and you could lose her as a source."

"But she might be recruiting, and that's really the story."

"I think based on . . . what's her name? Your other roommate?"

"Taylor."

"Right. Based on what Taylor's told you, you already know she is. To some degree. So the main focus has to be gaining her trust and getting close to her. Once you have her perspective, you can always widen out."

"Okay."

"And also, don't tell her you're working for the paper. Do they know you are?"

"I don't know that I've ever mentioned it."

"They haven't noticed your Harriet the Spy routine?"

"What?"

"Your notebook, your wandering around looking for a story to bring me."

She blushed and tried to stop it by breathing deeply, which sometimes made things worse.

"I'm teasing you. Don't worry. Anyway, don't tell them. We can always meet somewhere else in case they suspect."

He took out his phone and asked for her number. She explained, breathlessly, that she had two.

"One day and you're already undercover?" He laughed.

"I didn't want them to think I was following them."

"Women and Snapchat," he sighed.

"Guys are worse. They stalk hot girls all the time."

"No they don't."

"They do. Maybe you should be following

that story, too."

He smiled. "Well, first, someone would have to get hurt. It's not a story until someone gets hurt."

"No one's hurt in my story."

He tilted his head and looked at her oddly. "Keep digging," he said. "Maybe talk to a few experts about post-traumatic stress, about sex work and power. Maybe you'll change your mind about that."

They exchanged phone numbers, and as she was walking away, he called out. "One more thing, Emma."

"Yes?" she said, turning back.

"Nice work."

She smiled and walked away, her step just a little lighter, bouncier, than it had been before.

FIFTEEN

MAGGIE

Maggie sat down on the curb outside the house and, while she waited for Kaplan, tried to reach Sarah Franco. She tried not to let her anger come through in her texts; she simply said she was on campus and wanted to talk to her.

Who is this? came the reply, finally, ten minutes later.

Emma's mom, she replied.

I think you may have the wrong number.

After a series of guarded texts, she ascertained that Sarah's old phone number now belonged to a young woman who was not a student. It could have been Sarah, lying to her, Maggie supposed, but she didn't think so. The person on the other end of the phone softened, became suddenly human when Maggie said Emma was missing and apologized for texting a stranger at night.

You know, I had to change numbers because

someone was stalking me. Maybe your daughter is in hiding for a good reason?

Maggie teared up reading that, this advice from a total stranger. A woman who understood.

Thank you. Maybe she is, she texted back.

Sorry I couldn't help you but good luck.

Maggie waited an hour for Kaplan. It was hard to be angry when she knew he was interviewing someone he needed to interview, but really, how long could that take? She pictured him stopping for a burger, taking a break, cracking his knuckles as he called his wife to say he'd be late. The party went on behind her, the thrum of music punctuated by an occasional crash or shriek or peal of laughter. Every once in a while, a chant rose up, the rhythm and call of a drinking game.

She made a list of things she needed to do: gather photos, make posters, find Sarah to help her get volunteers, get Emma's schedule, and talk to her teachers. Her sister Kate could come to town and help, one of her brothers too, she supposed, if she was desperate. Her brothers were immature and disorganized, but family was family. Chloe could take care of the salon without her for a while and would be grateful for the tips. She'd go to the computer center and get help, she thought. There was a whole campus full of resources, and the thought of that buoyed her suddenly, that even lost in an island of strangers and drunk children, there were strengths that could be marshaled on her behalf.

Emma was the daughter of a decorated police veteran who was bravely gunned down in the line of duty. She was a story waiting to happen. Maggie could call a press conference on her own. She could look up the names of the reporters from the TV station and the *Daily News* who'd spoken to her after Frank's death and see if they could help. If Kaplan didn't get the job done, someone else would. People on the force loved Frank. She could find someone, she was sure.

It was past midnight, and the length of her day and the strength of her emotions were starting to catch up with her. So much to do still, and yet a weariness in her bones, a feeling she associated with grief, a feeling she couldn't accept, wasn't ready for. She called Kaplan again, and he was so close that she heard his phone ringing and his shoes scuffing on concrete. She hung up the phone.

"I told you I was on my way," he said. He loomed over her, pants still looking creased, eyes still wide and calm.

"You also told me it was best to go get some sleep," she replied. "So forgive me if I don't believe everything you say."

"Insulting me is probably not your best strategy."

"Well, leaving me in the dark isn't yours."

"You have to let us do our jobs."

Maggie let out a long sigh. How many times had she heard this complaint from Frank? That people wouldn't leave him alone, didn't trust him, couldn't wait for answers. *There's a process,* he used to say. *There's a protocol. Things take time.* But when your child is missing, time is of the essence. Process, protocol, things that sound time consuming? No. Just no.

"What did the boyfriend say?"

"He said he wasn't her boyfriend, for starters."

"Hate to say I told you so."

"No you don't. You love to say that. Anyway, he may be lying. Everyone thinks she was seeing somebody."

"Since you haven't talked to anyone but Sarah Franco and her RA, how do you define everyone?"

He ignored her question and started asking about Taylor. What she looked like, where she was inside the house, if she was with anybody, if Maggie was sure she hadn't left.

"Do you want me to come in with you?"

"No, I —"

"How about you just give me your gun and your badge and I'll go get her? How about that?"

He looked up toward the sky and shook his head. "I'm starting to see why —"

"Why my husband slept with someone else? Is that what you're gonna say?"

"No, I was gonna say why your daughter didn't tell you where she was."

"Yup, just one of those pain-in-the-ass mothers who worries when her daughter goes missing."

"Look, I'm sorry, but the minute I go to that door, kids are gonna skitter like roaches. If I don't make it clear that it's not a raid and I only want her, I'm sunk. So I have to know what she looks like."

"She's out back," Maggie said.

"Good. I'll climb over the fence then."

"Are you kidding?"

"Well, I'll probably use the gate if it's not locked." He took two steps away from her.

"Wait a minute. So this boy, this kid, he told you nothing useful?"

"He's not a kid. He's a twenty-one-year-old straight-A senior who edits the school

136

newspaper and says she was working on a story and probably felt the need to lie low for a while."

"Wait, what? That's ridiculous. Lie low? She doesn't work for the paper!"

"Well, he said she does. And she felt a need to work undercover."

"Undercover? She's not a journalist breaking Watergate, good God —"

"He said he couldn't say more without revealing his sources. I asked if I could look around his apartment, and he said no, not without a warrant."

"Christ, get a warrant!"

"Mrs. O'Farrell, warrants are for crimes. Right now, we have nothing. Nothing but rumor and . . . paranoia. Also, this guy —"

"This guy what?"

"He's solid."

"Are you kidding me? You think because he gets good grades and his professors like him or whatever that he somehow walks on water? Are you kidding me right now? Okay, the mother is the last to know. Everyone says Emma had a boyfriend. He might be lying about being her boyfriend, and we all know, dear God, it's always the fucking boyfriend! And you just what, you let him go?"

"Was I supposed to arrest him for editing

the paper? For liking a girl, even if he wasn't dating her?"

"Did he say that he liked her? How do you —"

"You," he said loudly, "are not being any help to your daughter by being exhausted and hysterical."

Maggie laughed then, a maniacal, tear-splashed laugh that could only come out of the mouth of a mother who wasn't being taken seriously, wasn't being listened to.

"Let me tell you how this is going to go," she said. "You're going to go in there and find Taylor too drunk to speak coherently, or at least pretending she is and fooling you. Then you're gonna tell me to go home and get some sleep and trust in your fucking process, and I'm going to tell you to go fuck yourself, and I'll find the other roommates before you will, okay? I'll wait till tomorrow, when they're no longer drunk, merely hungover, and I'll get it out of them while you're still on your first cup of coffee, filling out paperwork as part of your fucking process."

"I don't need to take this from you." He headed for the door.

"No? Well, prove to me that you can get something done. Steal Taylor's phone, and text her roommates to meet you. Or drag

138

her out here, and I will!"

"If you want me to find your daughter, you need to calm down."

"No, Kaplan, if *you* hope to find her, you need to rev up."

He exhaled in disgust and headed for the back deck.

Maggie sat back on the curb and waited, scrolling through Emma's phone. One voicemail from an unrecognized contact, left over a year before? Could this be important? She pressed play. *Hi, Em, it's Dad . . .*

Tears sprang from her eyes. Of course. This was probably the reason Emma had kept this phone even if she had another, newer one. No nefarious reason. No undercover reason. Sentimental reasons. Fear that she might lose this voicemail in the changeover, in the updating, in the stupid volcanic mystery that was the cloud. *Listen, before we meet you today, can you bring some napkins?* That was so like Frank, so like a police officer, who didn't want to run errands in his uniform. *We have everything else. Thanks, sweetie. See you soon.* His tone of voice, so different when he spoke to their daughter than when he spoke to her.

If Maggie had saved her voicemails from Frank, they wouldn't bring anyone solace. She imagined them all, end to end, a symphony of sharp and flat notes. An aural portrait of the man only Maggie knew. Not the calm tones of the public servant. Not the sweet harmonies of the Catholic choirboy. Not the soothing sound of a devoted dad. No. Her Frank would sound like an animal in a cage, nerves frayed, ready to jump. Maggie wondered, not for the first time, about his lover, the cop named Gina who she'd always simply referred to as Salt. Had she kept his voicemails, too? Did they have the same purring quality as Emma's?

The thought made the tears flow again. She wiped her eyes, shook her head. There was no time for this now. None. She'd gone through her husband's things only a week after his death, thrown out his old socks, donated his shirts and sweaters, given the rest of him away, all the parts that Gina hadn't taken. Emma had looked stunned by the speed and ferocity of her cleanout, but Maggie was done. She'd mourned the person he used to be, but she would be goddamned if she was going to mourn the asshole he'd become. She was done feeling sad over Frank O'Farrell.

Maggie started scrolling through Emma's contacts. *A–E,* all first names. She steeled herself on *D,* thinking that Emma's dad's cell phone number would still be there. But it wasn't. When she got to *F,* she was certain she'd find him. Father. Frank. Sentimental Emma would have kept that, too. But no. Hmm. Maybe *P* for Papa? What was there, in the *F*s instead, was another Philadelphia number, with the rare 215 area code, the one no one had any more. The name? *Future husband.*

SIXTEEN

EMMA

Emma knew the biggest obstacle in trying to be a reporter wasn't being afraid or being new to it or not being smart enough to make connections and figure things out. No. Her biggest obstacle was her tendency to blush. It would be one thing if it only happened when she was embarrassed or attracted to someone; that she could totally handle. But it also sometimes happened when she told a lie. Her mother had scoped this out early and used it against her. She supposed if she was ever in a long-term relationship and tried to cheat on her boyfriend, that he would be onto her, too. Sarah Franco was close enough that she might have noticed, but Sarah was a biology major, logical, left-brained, and tended not to see things other people did. Sarah was the friend who didn't notice when you got your hair cut or had a new outfit on. Sarah had never teased Emma about her blushing. But Taylor? Taylor, addicted to acting and gestures and movements; Taylor, who memorized the walks of strangers on the street in case she'd need them someday in her work, had already teased her about blushing in front of the others, and for that reason, Emma had decided that she needed to talk to Fiona about her job in the dark. As in at night, when they were in bed, or when Emma used one of her mint-green facial masks. That would cover her blush, and that would cover her tracks.

The problem was, Fiona wasn't in a very chatty mood late at night. The first night, she'd answered Emma's questions with single words, like a reticent adolescent: "Where were you tonight?" "Out." "Did you have dinner?" "Yes." "What did you have?" "Chicken." And then, when Emma had asked her who she was with, Fiona had actually fallen asleep. That, or she'd pretended to. Emma knew her tactics had to be wrong. She'd seen Fiona in a group using actual phrases and sentences. She'd seen her drinking, laughing and loose. Maybe when she was tired and ready for bed was the wrong time. Maybe Emma interrogating her reminded her of her mother, her nagging sister, someone she hated. Making asking questions was the wrong thing to do. Maybe Emma should just talk? Or maybe, just maybe, it would be simpler and quicker to follow her. After all, she had to prove she was right first, didn't she? Before she cozied up and got information, didn't she have to prove her hypothesis and make sure Taylor and her love of drama and intrigue and character hadn't just made the whole thing up to see if she could get a rise out of Emma?

She'd spent enough time around drama kids in high school to understand that some of them lived in a parallel universe. They were costumed, not clothed. They performed instead of talked. So it was entirely possible that Taylor viewed the world differently. But how differently? Could she have made this up? Was it part of some performance art for school? When Emma had asked Annie and Morgan if they knew where Fiona was, they both said they thought she had a job modeling clothes. And neither of them had blushed when they answered. They'd looked her straight in the eye, no hesitation.

So first, Emma had to find out if Taylor was lying. That was her justification for tailing Fiona. It was as if she hadn't believed herself, hadn't believed the valet, the ownership and permits at London, hadn't believed everything she'd laid out to Jason. It was as if she was finished before she'd even started, doubting herself completely, half believing that's what it would turn out to be — a Taylor drama. Not a story. Not a story that would change her life.

What had never occurred to her at the beginning, which didn't hit her until later, was that Fiona might not just be exhausted but embarrassed, sad, something. That Fiona might feel old and used and ashamed and not rich and happy did not enter Emma's brain for a while, and she felt badly the moment it did. Before then, she hadn't felt anything but justified.

Most of Fiona's classes were in the afternoon, and when Emma left in the morning for hers, she'd assumed Fiona stayed in bed. Emma was at the Morning Grind picking up a coffee that first Monday when an email came through from Cara Stevens. A link to a book excerpt she might find helpful. A new memoir written by a thirty-year-old who dated an elderly man through one of the apps in New York. Emma had listened to a few podcasts with escorts and sugar babies and read articles written by prostitutes, but this was the first full-blown account she was aware of. The excerpt described how the woman's first relationship had grown and expanded. Starting with drinks, dinner, and sex and then unspooling in the opposite direction. Brunch, shopping, movies. Just like with a girlfriend, there was as much daylight activity as anything else.

This girl had had trouble adjusting to the man's demands, the lack of privacy and space. They started out going to neighborhoods far away from hers; she lived in Queens and the man on the Upper East Side, so that was easily accomplished at first. But New York is a notoriously small place at times, and one day, when he had tickets for a Broadway matinee, their worlds collided. Her hand sliding from his arm the moment she saw her cousin on the sidewalk ahead. He'd patted his own arm, scrabbling, looking for her hand, as if he'd lost money or a piece of jewelry. But it was too late. Her cousin had seen them, and the awkward introductions had been embarrassing, and her cousin, young and sharp and outraged. "Oh, your friend Robert, huh? And where do you two know each other from, huh? You two kids in a book club together?"

Reading this, Emma realized she could be missing out on a crucial part of Fiona's situation by confining her investigation to the evening hours. She finished her coffee and vowed to check the Snap Map every hour, in case Fiona did more than sleep in and eat Starbucks sous vide eggs in the morning. After her Intro to Art History class, her instincts paid off. Fiona was not in her dorm and not in Starbucks or the gym. Fiona was down near city hall.

The next day, Emma skipped class, donned a dark hoodie and a baseball cap, rented a blue bike from the campus station, and waited in Semper Circle, near the fountain at the south campus entrance. She figured the bike would give her flexibility in case Fiona took an Uber somewhere. If she took the subway, she was screwed, but somehow, she doubted Fiona was riding public transportation on the regular.

An hour later, Fiona stepped outside Hoden House and walked down the street. Emma watched, not moving at first. She could be going over to Riordan or Digby, where she had friends. She could be going to get coffee. No. A black car idled nearby, and she walked to it, got into the back seat. An Uber? No. This was a Jaguar. Somebody's driver was picking her up. Emma flipped up her kickstand, pulled her sunglasses down, and prayed that whoever was in the car drove slowly.

The car headed south down Broad Street,

predictably enough. She stuck to the wide sidewalk, where she had less chance of being seen. She knew it was illegal to ride a bike anywhere but the street, but the cops in North Philly had bigger concerns. This close to campus, the concrete was pocked with broken brown and green glass, crushed cans, and discarded Juul pods. Emma tried to swerve around them, worried about the tires on her rented bike. She drove past the Top Hat, the dive bar kids went to for its cheap Natty Light and soft pretzel nuggets with cheese dip. Emma considered it, just a block and a half off campus, as far south as she would ever walk off campus alone, even during the day. She felt slightly safer on a bike but not much. This was not a place anyone wanted to be stranded, in this stretch between campus and city hall. But this time of the morning, it was quiet. Ugly and littered but not loud, not jangling with music and shit talk from groups of people gathered on the stoops and the street, drug dealers, gangs, or just bored neighbors who didn't quite fit either description. It was impossible at night to tell who was who. Unless you were a student, foolish enough, broke enough, or drunk enough to be walking back to campus. People were regularly robbed after dark, and everyone knew it.

Even the materials on Semper's website acknowledged the need for caution.

Emma kept well behind the car to make up for the occasional stop at a red light. She kept pace pretty well, and the timing was mostly fine. Occasionally, she had to pedal faster, on the off chance the car would turn before it hit city hall, but Emma didn't think it would. Broad Street wasn't pretty up here, but the surrounding streets tended to be far, far worse.

Then, a turn signal. Left.

Shit, Emma thought. *Be a mistake. Be an accident. Please don't turn. Please don't turn.* She was on the far right, on the sidewalk; turning left was not going to be easy for her, and it would be conspicuous to panic or veer. That, and she really didn't know what it was like over on those side streets; they could be drug houses or urban pioneers for all she knew, but she did know they would be narrower, smaller, and closer than the width and boulevard sweep of Broad Street. It would be harder for her to hide.

The car was well ahead of her when she finally made her way across. She slowed at the corner, watchful. The block wasn't too bad. A few renovated houses mixed among ones that were falling down. An empty lot on one corner, a community garden on another.

The car was going slower now, so Emma got off and walked her bike. If Fiona looked in the rearview mirror or turned around, would she recognize her? Emma doubted it. She sometimes had the feeling that she was invisible to her roommates. The car stopped next to the garden. *Buying vegetables?* she wondered. Did Fiona have to cook for this guy, too, pick up salad fixings, what?

But no. Another young woman appeared, walking from the opposite direction, in booties and a floral dress, her long, dark hair glinting in the sun. The car idled, and she heard the slide of the window going down. The girl stopped. A brief conversation. Then she opened the back door and joined Fiona inside.

What the fuck had just happened here? Was this a three-way? Or some kind of transport? Emma would never know, would never be certain. As she followed them all the way to Center City, the car pulled up in front of a fancy woman's store, one where you had to be buzzed in, and waited as the girls went inside.

Emma wasn't dressed well enough to follow them. She huddled in a coffee shop across the street and watched from the window as the girl she didn't recognize came out an hour later. Fiona did not reappear.

She got up, stretched. Ordered another coffee, a decaf, and waited another hour. The seats were small and made of concrete, to discourage loitering or to appeal to only skinny people who could balance on them. She watched a stream of people only a few years older than she was walk to work, headphones in, ignoring each other. *This was life,* she thought. Walking around, knowing no one. No one going to the same building you were, no one with the same professor. People on a sidewalk who only had the sidewalk in common. She drank the last gritty sip of her coffee and realized the futility of what she was doing. Fiona either worked there or was spending a lot of money, and at this point, even if she walked out with shopping bags, Emma might never know which it was. She could feel her GPA plummeting to the ground as she watched and waited and waited.

The moment she stood up to leave, two other people dove for her table. *Good luck,* she thought. *You'd be more comfortable sitting on the curb.* She walked outside, annoyed with herself, with the situation. She thought, as she often did when she was in the city, of her father. How did her father have patience for stakeouts? The thought of her dad, always in motion, his foot tapping as he sat, fingers drumming on the steering wheel. How could he have sat still to observe or to wait? And paperwork? It was easy to imagine him running after a perpetrator, interrogating a witness — that she could see in sharp, realistic relief. The rest of it? No freaking way.

She stood on the corner, trying to decide if she should get another bike from the docking station or just walk to Broad Street and grab the subway, when she heard a familiar peal of laughter.

Across the street, Taylor, Morgan, Annie, and Fiona, coming out of the store, shopping bags swinging on their arms. Taylor's familiar laugh, the others subtler, smaller. A cluster of dark denimed legs and high boots and long sweaters, better dressed for this morning jaunt than they ever were on campus. They headed toward Rittenhouse Square, sliding in and out of the molten autumn light, passing through the shadows of buildings high and low, bits of gold sparkling at their ears and wrists, the buckle of a bag, the hardware of a boot. Not toward the subway. Not toward school. Toward the world, another world.

Shit. How had she missed the rest of them

entering the store? When she'd glanced at the menu? When she'd bent down to take a sip of coffee? Had she slurped on that foam too long? She watched them walk up to the next corner, linger at the stoplight. Suddenly, she cared less about where than why.

She ran across the street against the light, hitting the store's buzzer urgently with the flat of her hand. A man in a suit arched one brow at her behind the glass, and she pulled down her hood. Her hair tumbled down around her shoulders, and she saw him soften, open the door.

"Thanks," she said. "I just need a word with the cashier."

The store was landscaped in white wood with very little merchandise in it. The clothes hung a few items to a rack, as if someone didn't want the hangers to touch, clank, mingle.

"Excuse me," she said. "I was supposed to meet friends here after I went to the gym. I think maybe I missed them?"

"Fiona's friends?"

"Yes," she said brightly. On a first name basis?

"They just left," the salesperson said with a tight smile. "Perhaps you can catch them."

"Damn," she said. "Did they all buy new outfits?" She fingered the sleeve of a blue dress hanging nearby. "Because we have this thing tonight, and I was just gonna wear a black dress, but now maybe I have to step it up, y'know?"

"No, Fiona got them matching sweaters. So cute."

"Matching sweaters," she repeated dumbly. This was not what she expected to hear. They were eighteen, not eight.

"For their birthdays," the clerk continued.

"Ah," she said. "Right, because —"

"All their birthdays. So close together in the fall." The girl sighed. "Libra. It's one of the most generous signs."

"Clearly," Emma said, then thanked her and left. It could have been a half-truth, or it could have been a complete lie. Emma didn't know when all of her roommates' birthdays were; it hadn't come up. But she knew Taylor's was in September. Maybe the girls' birthdays were in the same quarter, and that was close enough.

She put up her hood and continued walking toward the square, just in case they were all still nearby. But it didn't matter. Where they were going instead of going to school, who cared? Girls skipped school all the time. She was pretty sure she knew what she needed to know: that Fiona — or maybe even her sugar daddy; who knew who got her that credit card? — was trying to woo them. Or bribe them. That was the conclusion she held on to tightly. Because the other explanation was too painful — that they were all best friends and she wasn't. That Emma simply wasn't invited, even though her birthday was in September, too, and no one had so much as bought her a cupcake.

SEVENTEEN

MAGGIE

Maggie's eyes closed as she waited at the curb. Elbows on knees, head in hands. She didn't know how long she'd been asleep or how long Kaplan had been inside the house when he jostled her shoulder and told her that Taylor was no longer there.

"How is that possible?" she said.

"Well, there's more than one door, a lot of windows, and I'm only one person."

They headed back to the dorm together. Later now, quieter. Inside the hallways, the common rooms, just an occasional girl in flannel pants and a T-shirt, shuffling in Ugg slippers or worn moccasins.

"I'll text the RA one more time," he said.

"The door might be open."

He blinked. "Should I ask you how you know that?"

"Some of them leave their doors open. That's all I'm saying."

The door was still open, but Kaplan knocked, loudly, waiting for an answer, getting none, before going inside. He announced their arrival, turned on his flashlight, but there was no point. No one was home.

"Too early," she said.

"I guess so," he agreed.

He pulled out a business card and taped it to the refrigerator.

They stood in the hallway, and he said he'd follow up the next day.

"It is the next day," she said. Well past midnight.

"You know what I mean. Time to call it," he said, and the words stung. The words of a surgeon when the patient couldn't be revived.

"There's more to do," she said.

"Maybe. And if there is, I'll do it tomorrow."

"You have to collect evidence, get fingerprints. You —"

"We've been over this. There's no crime scene. Her stuff is gone. The witnesses say she's staying somewhere else. I know you don't like it, but you have to accept it. I'll file a report, though, and we'll go fr—"

"Accept it?" She let out a low laugh. "I'm a mother. I don't have to accept anything

157

but what I feel in my gut. And my gut says my girl needs help."

"Well, a gut isn't evidence. We —"

"No, I want more than the report. I want fingerprints, crime tape —"

"I want you to sleep. And if there's still no word from her, after she gets wind of how hard we're looking for her? Then we'll talk."

That he was sounding reasonable and negotiable and almost made sense was the first sign that she knew he was right — she was tired, and she did need sleep.

He pushed the elevator button.

"I have to go to the bathroom," she said. "You go ahead."

"Okay," he said. "There's a ladies' room around the corner."

"I know."

"But you can't stay here. You know that, right?"

"I know that, too."

He left, and she pretended to go to the bathroom in the hallway, then headed straight back to the suite. Kaplan didn't know as much as he thought he knew. She didn't really want to stay there. Didn't want to smell the mix of vomit and hair spray in the hallway. Didn't want to confront a bunch of drunk girls with smeared makeup and slurred words and hope they'd tell her what they wouldn't tell him. No, that was not her idea of a fun evening. And she knew it was probably fruitless. But so, too, was going home. What would going home do but make her feel far away, that the clock was ticking, that she was wasting her time? She needed to be on campus, somewhere, and she needed to reach Sarah Franco. It was late, but she would call her mother's house in Ardmore. She would wake them, scare them, but that was okay. It was all okay when your daughter was at risk.

She realized as she walked once again through the warren of rooms that she didn't feel the presence of her daughter in any of them. No mug, no hair tie, nothing familiar. Not anymore. Was Kaplan right? Had her daughter simply moved and not told anybody?

It wasn't the first time since his death that she missed her husband, missed having a spouse, a partner. But right now, she missed him as cop, not man. What would he glean from this? What would he see or know?

She went to their shared bathroom. In the mirror, she confronted her own worn face, mascara fallen onto her cheeks. She opened a drawer, looking for soap, and there it was. A tiny tub of Lush face wash, Emma's favorite. She lathered the strawberry foam in her hands and slid it across her nose and cheeks. Strawberry, salt, mint. It could have been a drink. She splashed her face, letting it all go down the drain. Watching the pink bubbles pop in the bottom of the sink, she felt the enormity of the sob working up from her diaphragm. A train. An earthquake. A tornado. She gripped the edges of the vanity and let the tears come.

She dried her eyes on the edge of her shirt and walked toward the door. On the way, she had to pass her daughter's room, the crumpled bed, the empty one. She blinked in the low light, stepped in. She was the one who argued it was a crime scene, but no one had listened. She wouldn't touch anything, she told herself, wouldn't turn on a light, open another drawer, wouldn't leave fingerprints, wouldn't obscure whatever evidence was still here.

She sat on the thin mattress and felt the featherbed liner beneath her give way. She lowered her head onto the lone remaining pillow. Emma had come to college with two. Her head sunk in deep. Memory foam. *How ironic,* Maggie thought. How she wished it was true. How she longed for something that retained her daughter's thoughts and fears. But enough of that. Finally, all those thoughts slid away.

Maggie fell into a deep sleep, a practical sleep, the sleep of someone who was paying for this room, who was owed that much, so why the hell not.

EIGHTEEN

EMMA

Emma sat in Rittenhouse Square for only a few minutes before heading back. It was beautiful there: trees dotted with golden colors, a bronze fountain turning glazed green on the edges, restaurants still occupying sidewalks at lunch time, tempting the autumn fates. It would be colder soon, more cars, fewer bikes, fewer walkers. It would be harder to follow people. This thought struck her with great force, that winter would make it all much more difficult. Everyone would be bundled up, disguised, in vehicles. She stood up and headed back to campus, trying to think through her next move. She walked down Walnut again, on the other side of the street from the coffee shop. Ahead, another group of girls approached the same boutique and pressed the buzzer. Emma squinted, doubted what she saw, then half ran to get a better look. As they

162

were ushered in, one of the girls' heads turned, revealing yellow and gray ribbons in her hair. Samantha. Samantha from down the hall, a blond who often wore school spirit ribbons in her hair, a habit held over from cheerleading, she'd told them all in the get-to-know-you days of orientation, when everyone in their dorm shared their weirdest habit and their biggest fear. One of the boys had said his biggest fear was cheerleaders, and they'd all laughed, even Samantha.

She tried to see who the other girls were, if she recognized anyone, but it was too late. They were inside, and the doorman shot Emma a look as she passed. A look that said he was onto her.

Her head was reeling as she headed for the subway. This could not be a coincidence, or could it? Samantha was arguably the prettiest girl on their floor, golden haired and blue-eyed. She was from Wilkes-Barre, chubby by modern standards, curvier than most cheerleaders, and thought anyone who was on a diet was crazy. She had an old-fashioned quality to her and spoke her mind loudly and freely. Everyone knew her, and it was impossible for Emma to believe she was involved in this. She struck Emma as some-one who would be vocal in opposition and who couldn't keep a secret. No, she thought, she had to be wrong. The store probably had a Groupon promotion. Simple as that. Or, she thought with a chill down her spine, the store named simply B, enhanced by Pinterest-worthy graphics inside that encouraged you to "B yourself" and "B beautiful" could be owned by another B — Beck's.

As she waited for the train, she confirmed that it was, in fact, owned by Sam Beck. Discounts, she thought. Discounts for the sugar babies. *B a whore,* she thought instantly, then felt guilty. She was being a little judgy, considering some of these girls had serious money problems. But she'd done some perfunctory psychological research and learned that some escorts didn't need the money. They liked the money. They liked the attention.

She made a note about B and Beck's and the shopping in one of her phone apps, all in code. She'd already deleted everything uncoded relating to the story. She flipped to her list for school and realized she had a paper due in two days, on religion and literature, and hadn't done any of the reading, hadn't cracked open her own Bible, hadn't even thought about God in relationship to words, so she thought about it while she waited, thought about the literature she had to read and more. Her mind kept wandering back to the story. Was there any God in the words she would write for this story? She felt it underneath, holding her up, rooting her to the earth sometimes, this belief that it was all part of a grand plan, that she was here for a reason. She felt something else bubbling up too, something surprising, that she wanted to tamp back down. Judgment. Commandments. Rules of this religious world her family had chosen being broken. She felt her own righteousness and was ashamed. There it was; God was there, driving her, too. But how was God driving Fiona? How had she managed to justify what she was doing, the words she spoke?

Back on campus, she headed straight for Lenape Library, vowing not to do any more work on the story until her paper was done. She'd crank it out, do the reading for her history class, and start fresh tomorrow. But her burner phone rang, interrupting her. Cara Stevens.

"Hey, I just wanted to ask you about your psychology teacher."

"Mr. Grady?"

"Yeah, William Grady."

"What about him?"

"He was on my restaurant list."

"What do you mean?"

"I mean, when I cross-checked the list of credit card customers at Spark's with the list of teachers at your school, he was one of the names."

"Which might mean nothing," Emma said, thinking of Mr. Grady, who was about as ordinary and quiet a dude as she'd ever met. A small man who wore sweater vests and rubber-soled shoes, who didn't even make much noise when he moved around the room, passing back their papers. All this time, when she'd pictured the men, she'd pictured powerful, forceful guys. Maybe even handsome, older, DILF-y men. The idea of having sex with puny Mr. Grady made her sick.

"Correct."

"And might mean something."

"Bingo. Just warning you to keep your eyes open."

"Okay. Anything else?"

"I also had made a note about a kid who used to work at the restaurant who was also a student. I think he'd be a senior now. Timothy something. Last name starts with a T."

"Not — Timothy Trenton?"

"Could be. Depends on how many Timothy T's there are in the senior class."

"I can find that out."

"Yeah, that should be easy. So you know one, huh?"

"Yes," she said, swallowing slowly, a lump building in her throat.

"Any connection to your roommate?"

The thoughts flooded her. How she'd looked around the first day of school and thought, wow, how pretty everyone is at college. How at first she'd chalked it up to everyone being on their best grooming behavior. First day, best shoulder-skimming, leg-baring outfit, still summer-tan, still pale-blue pedicure, smoothest hair, careful makeup that said you weren't trying too hard, you were just born this way. Girls who seemed to work out every day, starting in the morning in their leggings and crop tops, running or heading to the gym. How they'd all heard boys at parties calling her dorm, Hoden House, Hottie House.

"He's my RA," she said quietly.

NINETEEN

MAGGIE

When she felt the hand on her shoulder, Maggie thought it was part of her dream, in which she was in a museum, employed as a docent, shepherding students through exhibits as they kept trying to touch and upend masterpieces. Then, gathering consciousness, she blinked her eyes, sloughing off slumber, trying to wake.

"Emma?" she said, heart pounding, turning in the low light.

"It's Sarah," a soft voice whispered.

She exhaled her disappointment and sat up on one elbow. The room, still empty. The hall, still quiet.

Sarah sat down at the foot of the bed, barely making an impression with her thin frame. The soft waves of her brunette hair, even uncombed, tousled from sleep, shone in the light. She was one of those girls who hadn't peaked yet, who would seem prettier

168

every year.

"You didn't answer your phone. I figured you might be here."

"Yes," Maggie said, sitting all the way up and rubbing her neck, "but if the police had their way, I'd be home. Or in an insane asylum. I can't believe I slept through your call."

"Well, you were exhausted, I'm sure."

"These girls," Maggie sighed, "are avoiding me."

"They're avoiding the police, to be honest. I mean there's probably three illegal things just lying around. And girls are paranoid. At least that's what the RA said when I called him. Asshat."

"You should have called me, Sarah. Not him, me."

Sarah looked down, just as she had when she was in middle school and Maggie had admonished the girls for shrieking in the car or throwing food in the kitchen or one of a hundred small annoyances that didn't matter anymore.

"Yeah, well, I was hoping for a logical explanation first. Like her roommate snored so she'd moved down the hall. Or she had the flu and went to the health center."

"There's a little too much logic floating around for my taste. Too much logic, not enough hunch."

"Hunch equals paranoia, I guess."

"So, Sarah, is there anywhere around here that serves pancakes?"

Sarah smiled. Maggie knew pancakes were Sarah's favorite, knew because she'd always told Maggie she made them better than her own mother, knew it from years of requests, years of making sure there was buttermilk in the fridge, baking powder, real maple syrup. Was there anything a mom wouldn't do to make a kid eat happily, even if she wasn't her own?

"I know a place," Sarah said. "Not as good as yours, though."

"Well, of course not."

It was nearly 6:00 a.m., and the dorm was still empty, as were the hallway and common room. No one home still. The floor felt tacky beneath Maggie's shoes, as if she needed another reason to be uncomfortable in the wedges. As they waited for the elevator, Sarah looked down at her feet, and Maggie shook her head.

"Long story," she said.

"When in Rome?"

"Yes," she sighed. "Something like that."

Mabel's Diner was on the south edge of campus, tucked underneath one of the school's banners, lending it an official air. It proudly stated that it had been there for over fifty years, long before the campus sprang up around it, but it had clearly adapted for the students, serving breakfast all day, for one, and on the weekends, it was open twenty-four hours. And from the looks of it, it was staffed by waitresses who took no shit from drunk college kids but happily took their parents' money and added gratuity to every check automatically. Smart.

The coffee was fresh and hot, and Maggie drank it gratefully. She ordered scrambled eggs and home fries; Sarah ordered a short stack and sausage and promised to give Maggie a bite of pancake. There were plenty of fancier things on the menu — s'mores waffles, pumpkin spice scones, and something truly Philadelphian, highlighted as the house special: scrapple pie.

"A meat pie made of scrapple?"

Sarah made a face. "Only boys are stupid enough to eat that."

Maggie smiled. Anyone watching them — not that anyone was; the diner was empty — might think they were mother and daughter, with their long, dark hair, but if they looked closely, they'd see the awkward silences, the threads of guilt and anger that held them to the spot. Maggie had already admonished her for not calling her first, but

171

Sarah seemed like something else was weighing on her. She took deep breaths between sips of her coffee, like she was gathering strength. It reminded Maggie of the night the girls had confessed they'd had a party when Maggie was out. Maggie had already known, of course, but she had wanted them to come clean, wanted them to suffer through that conversation, because that's what growing up was all about. Difficult conversations. Now, she could see, they might be about to have another one.

"What is it, Sarah? What do you know?"

Sarah shook her head violently, as if she was trying to shake away a memory.

"Nothing specific," she said. "Nothing at all, really."

"What then?"

She shrugged her shoulders, sniffed away a tear. "I just . . . I know she wasn't as happy at school as I was."

"What do you mean?"

"I mean, my roommates are nicer than hers, more fun. More open. She was spending a lot of time alone in her dorm, and I wasn't."

"Well, that's natural, that your experiences wouldn't be identical."

"That's what my mom said, too."

Maggie smiled. She didn't know Sarah's

mother well, but she'd always liked her.

"I thought maybe it was the usual stuff, you know, borrowing clothes without asking, not doing dishes, or getting sexiled —"

"Sexiled?"

"When your roommate brings a guy home and locks you out?"

"Clever."

"Yeah, it happens."

The food arrived, and they each picked up a fork, paused, took bites. The eggs were creamy and the pancakes fluffy. Maggie took the offered bite, dipped it in more syrup, and nodded her approval. She was surprised by the force of her hunger. Some things didn't change, didn't stop, no matter what else was happening.

"But I . . . just feel as if I didn't make enough time for her. Once, at a football game . . ." Her voice trailed off and cracked. "I feel like maybe she needed me, and I wasn't there."

Maggie reached across the table and took her hand. One of them had syrup on her fingers, and they stuck together a bit, which made both of them smile.

"I'm sure that's not true," Maggie said. Another mother would blame the first girl who confessed to contributing to the problem, but Maggie knew, instinctively, that this was not the girl to blame.

"We can't be sure."

"Did you miss a call in the middle of the night? Forget to answer a text last week?"

"No, never."

"Well, honey, Emma knew you well enough to be honest with you. If she needed something or someone to help her, she would have told you."

"Maybe."

"Yes," Maggie said firmly. "I know it."

"Well, I think the same of you. That she would have told you."

Maggie shook her head. "I'm not sure of that at all."

"Then you know how I feel."

They ate a few more bites. Outside, a few more students yawned as they walked down the sidewalk. The city was starting to come alive, inching toward 7:00 a.m. More people awake now, going somewhere. An 8:00 class. A breakfast meeting with a professor.

"So, tell me about this boy she hasn't mentioned to me," Maggie said.

"There's no boy that I know of."

"The police seem to think she has a boyfriend. Based on something someone told them."

"Well, it wasn't me."

"She was working for the newspaper,

though? Did you know that?"

"Yeah, I knew that. She was searching for something to write about, and she called me a while ago, saying she found it. Something juicy."

"What?"

"That's just it, she didn't tell me. We were supposed to get coffee one day, and she cancelled, and I didn't follow up and —" Tears filled her eyes.

"Sarah," Maggie said. "That doesn't sound like something to feel guilty about."

"Yeah, well, sometimes things feel worse than they sound, you know?"

"I suppose."

"During move-in week, we had this, I guess, psychology seminar? Where they explained that high-achieving kids are good at masking their problems. Everyone expects them to have it all together, so they act that way."

"Is that how she was acting? Like everything was perfect?"

That didn't sound like Emma to Maggie. Emma moped when things were wrong, got quiet. And when she was trying to lie or cover something up, she got chatty, nervous, overcompensated. And the blushing! Emma was not adept at hiding what she was feeling; she was actually terrible at it.

"No," Sarah sighed. "I'm grasping at straws, I know."

"How about this," Maggie said. "Let's both stop blaming ourselves. Because we can't do anything about those missed coffee dates or missed signals. We can only go forward, pay more attention now."

Sarah nodded.

"Gosh, I sound like a priest," Maggie said.

Sarah laughed. "I wish more priests sounded like that," she said.

Maggie thought of the church on campus, how she'd pointed it out to Emma on a map, saying that if she ever felt stressed or needed a quiet space in the midst of all these people living together, to remember that she could go there. To sit, reflect. That was Maggie's primary worry, that her only child would not do well surrounded with other people. That she would feel encroached upon, overstimulated. Had she been right? Was that all this was? Was Emma somewhere holed up in an Airbnb just so she could be alone and could get some work done? Did she have a paper due, some reading to finish? Were the police right?

Maggie laid out this theory to Sarah, explained that the police believed Emma was staying somewhere else, on purpose, and just hadn't told anyone.

Sarah shook her head with frustration. "She would have told us."

"That's what I thought, too. But onward. I'll need some help, if you can spare it?"

"We need posters," Sarah said. "We need searchers, we nee—"

"Yes."

"I'll help you," she said. "And there's an organization on campus that will help me get the word out."

"Good."

After breakfast, they went to the computer center and worked on large flyers, printed them out. Maggie bought plastic sleeves, thumbtacks, waterproof tape at the bookstore and gave most of the stack to Sarah. Maggie would cover the dorm area and head to the journalism building. Sarah would hit the rest of campus, focusing on the cafeterias, library, and student union.

They vowed to keep in touch, and as they hugged goodbye, each of them stifled a sob, nearly broke down.

"We have to stay strong," Maggie whispered, and Sarah nodded.

Maggie went first to the journalism building, lingering outside the door until a boy headed for it, slipping in behind him. He glanced at her briefly, sizing her up as teacher or parent, not threatened. Not questioning. She brandished the posters, asked if he knew her daughter, and he said no. She asked if he worked on the paper, and he shook his head.

Inside, the corridors were quiet. The door to one classroom was open, a female teacher gesturing at the front of the room, and Maggie ducked away, out of sight. Kids might not think anything of an unfamiliar parent roaming the halls, but teachers were another problem entirely.

She stopped another student, a short girl whose backpack was stretched beyond the point of ballast, threatening to pull her over backward.

"Do you know where the newspaper offices are?"

"Third floor," she replied.

"Great, thanks."

"But they're closed."

"Closed?"

"Yeah, they distribute Tuesdays, so they always take Wednesday off."

"Do you work for the paper?"

"My roommate does."

Maggie pulled a poster from her stack, asked if she recognized her daughter, and the girl said no, then added wistfully, "She's pretty."

Maggie took a deep breath. Yes, her daughter was pretty. She had to be honest about that salient fact and how much it weighed on her. If you looked carefully, beyond the painted and polished archetypes of young women today, Emma, fresh-faced and healthy, was pretty. Many might see that in her. A certain person might prefer that. And that fact made Maggie both proud and very, very worried.

"Does she have a boyfriend?" the girl asked.

Maggie released a small shrug. "Maybe."

"I bet she does," the girl said.

"What's your roommate's name?"

"Liz Cameron."

"Would you ask her if she knows Emma? Or where she might be?" She handed her the flyer, pointed out the phone number at the bottom.

"Sure," she said. She took a picture of it on her phone, then handed it back.

Maggie headed up to the third floor. It was arranged differently than the other floors, with several classrooms combined in one. She pulled on the locked door, stared through the glass. She taped up a few posters, left.

She spent the rest of the day walking around, asking students if they'd seen Emma, if they knew anyone who worked on the paper or lived in Emma's building. Thousands of kids on this section of campus alone, and she'd only connected with one person whose roommate worked on the paper. One.

At dusk, she went back to the dorm, slid in behind a group of girls, headed to Emma's floor. She was hanging posters in the common room and outside the elevators when she felt a tap on her shoulder. The RA.

"Hi," she said. "Are the roommates back?"

"I'm not sure."

"Have you checked?"

"Look, Mrs. O'Farrell," he said, then hesitated, took a deep breath.

"Yes?"

"You can't be here," he said. "Someone said you spent the night in the dorm. I don't know how you got in but —"

"The door was open," she said hotly. "Do you not counsel the girls in the dorm to lock their doors? Do they realize that someone could be kidnapped and go missing in a heartbeat?"

"We don't know that Emma is actually missing," he said with a sigh. "Please, we can't have this rampant fear. We can't have you whipping these girls into a frenzy. There are all these rumors about a rapist, about a

180

serial killer. It's no—"

"I," she said forcefully, "am trying to find my daughter. And if I scare somebody else's daughter into being careful along the way, well, great."

"Look, you can't be here. Only residents can be here. It's completely against university rules, and the girls are complaining."

"Oh, are they? The girls are unhappy that a mother dares to worry when her daughter is missing for days? Well, tell them to stuff it."

"Look, the police are on top of this —"

"The police," she said through gritted teeth, "are most certainly *not* on top of it."

"I spoke to college administration, and they said —"

"Oh, you did, did you? Well, I think I need to go there next! Straight to President Leandros. Because I have rights, too! And you," she said, poking him in the chest, "you are part of my problem."

"Don't touch me."

She poked him again, sending him back a few inches, and turned to leave. She was aware of him making a call or taking one as she headed for the elevator. She pushed the button, and as she waited, the door to the stairs opened, and a security guard appeared.

"I'm leaving, don't worry," she said, but the man stood next to her, got in the elevator with her.

"I said I'm leaving," she repeated.

She walked out of the building and sat on the bench outside.

"Ma'am, you have to leave campus," he said.

"Fine," she said. She stormed off. She thought about how much a hotel might cost. She thought about how much a disguise might cost and how she could sneak back to campus the next day to go to the journalism building.

She went to a bus shelter on the edge of campus and put up another poster, then sat down and waited for more students to come by. How long could she keep doing this alone? She decided to wait an hour, until it was dark, then sneak back.

Under cover of darkness, she felt more powerful. Long strides, head held high. The power of criminals, the strength of shadows. Anonymous in the invisibility of midnight. Dark sky, dark clothes, it added up to power, and she, with her early nights and her extra half glasses of wine that didn't count, rarely made it past nine. She didn't know this power any more. She only knew the weakness of twilight, the fading of willpower that came the moment she left the salon for home.

She curled up on the bench outside her daughter's dorm and watched the door. The roommates had to come home eventually, if only to get clothes. It was dark. *I'll stay outside,* she thought. *And I'll leave before it's light.*

She wasn't sure when she fell asleep, but once again, a woman's voice woke her. She opened her eyes, blinked. Dark shoes. Dark uniform pants. Dark hair. Olive skin, a mole near her mouth. The streetlight on now, illuminating everything about them both.

"Hello, Maggie, I'm G—"

Maggie held up one hand, stopped her. "I know exactly who you are." She stood up, brushed herself off. "So I guess you're here to help Kaplan get rid of me?"

"Hell no," Gina said. "I'm here to help you get rid of Kaplan."

TWENTY

EMMA

Emma set an alarm on her phone. Ninety minutes. She'd give herself that much time to scan the material and get the paper done before she turned her attention back to her story and following up on what Cara had told her. Writing papers this way was just like journalism, she told herself, writing under deadline. Other students did their papers at the last minute every day.

But she squirmed in her seat, had trouble concentrating. She kept picking up the phone and looking at the time she had left. It reminded her of how her mother acted when they had to get to the airport for an early flight; every cell in her body was on edge, anticipatory. She finally stopped after an hour, when she had a first draft. She'd proofread it and check the footnotes in the morning. Or she'd hand it in and get the B- or the C+ that she deserved for half-assing it. She rubbed her eyes and put her laptop away. She was lucky it was on a religious topic she understood, something any Catholic could outline in her sleep. If it had been on almost any other topic, she'd be sunk. She headed for the communal computers and chose the one farthest from the door. She felt a little guilty suddenly, that unlike the other kids here, she had a scholarship and also a laptop. She hoped none of them had seen her sitting at the other table on the second floor, typing away, packing her things up. But there were plenty of open spaces; she wasn't taking a computer from someone who needed it, and that was all that mattered.

A quick search for Professor Grady brought up cursory, predictable material. Married, lived in the suburbs. A pretty wife whose clothes looked a little artsy and hand-dyed and who taught preschool at a private school. Two teachers in the house? She felt sorry for their kids. A Semper alumni. Attended Radnor High School. In an article about Radnor parks, he was quoted as being part of a lively game of outdoor chess played throughout the summer. He practically had *nerd* stamped on his forehead.

She opened Google Earth, stared at the bird's-eye view of his house outside Wayne.

A green lawn, well-trimmed hedges, target set up in the backyard. Archery? Had to be. A path that looked like it led to the neighbor's house. Or maybe the Radnor Trail, depending on where this street was; she didn't know that part of town well enough to know. She looked him up on social media, expecting little, finding next to nothing. Typical. She remembered her own father's attitude toward Facebook, calling it a burn book, a gossip column. She scrolled over to LinkedIn and found a profile there. Ah. That was actually better. Students connected with their professors on LinkedIn all the time. She asked to connect with him, knowing it would probably take weeks for a response. Then, to cover her tracks, asked to connect with all her other professors as well, then logged off and kept looking elsewhere.

She found an alumni Facebook group for the year he graduated, but it was private, and she had a feeling he didn't belong. There had to be more alumni materials archived at the library — yearbooks, she guessed, maybe student newspapers and programs for the plays? These thoughts skittered through her mind as she dismissed them. They struck her as available but unimportant. She thought of other things that would be accessible — marriage licenses, real estate transactions, the salaries of public officials. She didn't need that info to guess at what he and his wife made; he taught two classes, had tenure. They lived a nice, comfortable life but not a glamorous one, and she was willing to bet their kids went to the private school where his wife taught, and they would go to Semper, too, all at discount. It wasn't a bad strategy for making a teacher's salary stretch.

Still, something bugged her about the house. So neat and trimmed. Too neat? She went back to Google Earth, stared at the skinny, winding path she'd noticed in the backyard. The grass was trimmed at the edges. This was no trampled grass path, no cut-through. It was intentionally made. Was it stepping stones? Brick? Zooming in didn't help; the resolution wasn't crisp enough. But when she zoomed out? It was clearly a designed path that led down to a neighboring property. But wait. No. She plugged in addresses near his house number until she hit the one next door. From there, she could see it clearly. A patio, pool, and hot tub, the aqua tones throbbing in the midst of green, brown. A structure too small to be a house — it was a pool house or shed. Not a separate home. Part of his home, the parcel behind his, another terraced level. An expensive terraced level. How much did a pool and hot tub cost? A lot, she knew. This could mean something or nothing. He could have family money; this was the Main Line after all. But did people with family money usually attend Semper? Only if they were academic fuckups. Not if they were nerds who played chess in the park.

Meanwhile, three of her professors had accepted her LinkedIn requests, but none of them Grady. She switched her privacy mode to anonymous so no one would know she had looked at their profiles, then scrolled through. None of them were linked to Grady, but that could mean nothing. She thrummed her fingers against the keyboard impatiently. Grady only had forty-two connections. Two of them were to Semper professors in his department, one to his secretary. He didn't have a photo posted. He probably didn't have his alerts set up. This was a waste of time, she decided.

She was about to seek out the librarian and ask about historical Semper materials when it occurred to her that someone may have digitized them. Bingo. Of course. A generous alumnus by the name of Stanley Gross had paid for the project. Searchable yearbooks. *How thoughtful of you, Mr. Gross, to make spying on your classmates and friends so easy. Bless you.*

And there he was, Professor Grady, freshman year of college. She was totally shocked, as she often was with older photos of adults, by how hot he'd been. Longish hair, streaks of sun in it. Skin still tanned from a summer backpacking or lifeguarding. Just a dude before he'd chosen a major, before he'd met his wife. Before his life had even begun. There were no clubs or interests listed. Had he joined the chess club? Taken up archery? Did he know what might lie ahead? Did he have a plan? Or was he as clueless and unformed as she was?

She scrolled through the whole class, thousands of them, searching for what, exactly? She wasn't sure. She went through the *G*s to the *Z*s slowly and was about to exit when she realized she'd forgotten *A–F.* And there it was. Sam Fucking Beck. Same class. Similar hair, bigger smile. He looked confident, like he knew more about what awaited him.

She felt an actual tingle along her neck and spine and knew before she even pulled up the search, before the pieces came together, that they would. Precisely. *Same dorm. Same room. College roommates.*

She felt a rush of blood to her head. They

were in it together. She didn't know whose idea it had been. And whether it had been hatched in college, lying shoulder to shoulder in their narrow bunks, surrounded by more beautiful coeds than they'd ever seen, or later, when their paths diverged, and one of them had an idea the other could help with. She imagined their lawyers claiming all this didn't prove anything. Of course a friend would go to an old friend's restaurant! Of course he would! And she knew they would be wrong, without even knowing the particulars. She knew it in her bones and didn't need all the details, not yet. Those things could turn this from story to series, the behind the scenes, the history, the evil plot. She saw it all in her mind, the photos, a timeline, a map, a path. Her path.

In her small notebook, she wrote down the name of every freshman boy who had lived in their dorm that year. Page after page. Just in case. It was somewhere to start, and it seemed as logical a place as any.

Walking back to her dorm, it was crystal clear to her: she'd been following the wrong people. The girls were a given. Whether it was one roommate or all — what did that matter? The part of her that cared about that was the girl in her, not the writer. She felt left out, excluded, jealous in a weird, twisted way. She had to laugh at the absurdity. *Wasn't I good enough to be a ho, too? What about me?*

But the writer in her needed to follow the men, the money, the mechanics of it. The girls could come later. All she needed was one, just one, to talk on the record. *That,* she thought, *would be the easy part.* And she decided that asking Fiona questions was wrong, too. Fiona didn't want to talk. Fiona didn't want to be pursued. When Fiona was home, she needed peace and quiet and space. So there was no reason to trip all over Fiona. No. There were other girls out there, had to be.

She would have to let Fiona come to her, not the other way around. And Emma thought, in her youthful and naive way, that she knew how to do it.

There was a reason Fiona had approached Taylor and not Emma. Taylor acted the part. Taylor looked the part. And that, Emma knew, was fixable. Learnable. Doable.

First stop: CVS.

TWENTY-ONE

MAGGIE

Maggie believed a confrontation with her husband's mistress would have happened at Frank's funeral. She had steeled herself for it, convinced herself it was inevitable, that this woman, this Gina Colletti, a fellow cop who had become his partner, would not be able to stay away. When an officer dies in the line of fire, the whole city grieves. Not just the precinct. Not just the department. The mayor, the citizens, everyone. Gina had been there, after all, during what they officially called a stakeout gone wrong but what Maggie knew had been a stakeout turned into a tryst. When Captain Moriarty had told Maggie it happened outside the Warwick Hotel, she knew immediately. That was Frank's favorite hotel. That was where he and Maggie used to go for a cocktail, back in the days when they did things like that at the end of an evening. That was not a stakeout.

Still, regardless of the reason, it was a Tuesday, and they were newly paired as partners, and they were together and Gina could have been gunned down just as easily as Frank. And even though Maggie's sister Kate believed a fellow Catholic wouldn't dare show her face at a married man's funeral — she'd be in a different church, her own church, praying for her soul, Kate had said — Maggie believed the cop code would take precedence over the God code. She pictured Gina slipping in, sitting in the back corner, dressed in dark tones, sunglasses on, hair tucked in a bun. Or in uniform, perhaps, blending in with the others, as if Maggie didn't know exactly what she looked like.

But it did not happen. And all Maggie's careful preparations — a stylish black crepe dress she'd run out to Macy's for at the last minute, hair blown out just so, a full face of waterproof makeup, and heels, high heels, which she never wore — were wasted. Or maybe they weren't. She caught more than one appreciative glance from the men in attendance, and if even one of them had the thought that Frank was an idiot to give up Maggie for Gina, then it was worth all the money, time, and effort. But no, she had done it all for Gina, and the rest of it, the catering and the kind words and deference to Frank's cousins and coworkers and city officials? That had been for Emma. So Emma would be proud. So Emma would have good memories. But the man she'd known? The man whose sideways smile and dark-blue eyes had turned her head at seventeen? That Frank, Maggie knew, had been gone for a while. She'd been mourning that loss for years, not days.

Maggie stood, brushed off her clothes, and squinted at her. Gina was shorter than she'd pictured. A low ponytail, ragged at the ends. Skin color deepened from late-summer sun, like she went to the Jersey Shore on the weekends. Long eyelashes but dark circles under her eyes.

"You're not as pretty as I thought you would be," Maggie said.

Gina let out a small, tight laugh. "Well, it's been a rough year. But I don't need to tell you about rough years."

"No," Maggie said. "No you don't."

They stood for a few long moments in silence, catching their breath, taking stock of the situation. Maggie was, surprisingly, not angry. It was relief that washed over her, that it had finally happened and she didn't need to worry about it happening, and what feeling was sweeter than relief? Nothing.

"Look," Gina said finally, "Kaplan's an asshole, but he's just following protocol and orders."

"Orders to not find a cop's daughter? I find that fascinating."

"You've got a bunch of things going against you. One, college girls sleep over with boys and friends. Two, teenagers run away for all kinds of reasons. No one files a missing person report right away; they wait. They wait till the kid sleeps it off, till the hitchhiking adventure to see a band is over, till it resolves itself. Three, when shit goes down on a college campus, no one wants the cops involved. They want to handle it themselves."

"Well, they've already fucked it up."

"Nope. They informed you in person. That's a lot more than most people get."

"If you're here to defend the department and what is happening right now, you can just leave. I don't need your public relations bullshit."

"I'm just telling you why, that's all. I don't agree with any of it. I'm just telling you."

"Great. Fine. Thank you. The grieving police widow has been informed of the police handbook. You're off the hook."

Gina took a deep breath, let it out. "I'm

sorry," she said, "but the deck is stacked against you here. I heard Kaplan down at the precinct bitching about you getting in the way, messing everything up."

"What did he say?"

"Something about interfering with evidence and you going to a frat party to confront a witness. Is that true?"

She shrugged. "Technically. Sort of."

"You need some help, and if you keep your mouth shut about it, I'll give it to you."

Maggie wanted to ask her why, why she'd do such a thing, but she knew the answer, and she didn't want to hear it. The idea of Gina Colletti saying her husband's name out loud was suddenly too much. Just way, way too much. But motives aside, she'd be a fool to pass up the offer.

"All right," she said. "Are you going to help me search or with the posters or —"

Gina karate-chopped her hand through the air. "Nah, you can get kids to do that. There's an organization called Take Back the Night that will distribute them for you all over the city, not just the campus. Just get one of your daughter's friends to take them there. Done." Gina picked up one of them and nodded, told her she did a nice job, that the photo was the right size, the phone number, too. "You'd be surprised how many people do a bad job on these, make them almost illegible, make the kid look terrible, at a bad angle."

Maggie imagined creating them all alone, after being up all night, eyes blurry with tears. Of course they did a bad job.

Gina took another breath. "Now, here's what I'm going to try to do. I can get surveillance footage from the camera outside her dorm, the library, the popular entrances, and any of her favorite off-campus restaurants that she frequents. So you find out what those places are. Also, I'll look for cameras outside any recent frat parties or anyplace you think she's been in the past few days. And I can get lists of everyone who is in each of her classes. We can interview them, try to piece this thing together."

"Emma was . . . is . . . a little introverted. I don't think she's made a ton of friends in the first couple months of school."

"They don't need to be friends to know something. Sometimes it's better. It's easier to complain or gossip or whatever about people who are strangers."

"What about enemies?"

"That makes it easiest of all, doesn't it? And then I'll get her phone records and check the cell towers —"

"I have her phone."

"She left her phone behind?"

"Yes."

Gina raised her eyebrows, and Maggie knew what that meant. It was bad, always, for someone that age to go anywhere without their phone. It simply did not happen.

"And Kaplan let you take it?" She screwed up her face.

"Not exactly."

"Okay, well, I'll try to get it unlocked."

"I unlocked it."

"You had her password?"

"She's my kid. I know my kid."

"Okay, well, what was on it? Anything interesting, concerning? Any texts the night she went missing?"

"We don't know when she went missing."

"What?"

"Not sure of the day."

"Okay. Well, still, anything that looked suspicious?"

"Hardly anything. She deleted most of it. Even most of her contacts."

"Then you'll definitely need her records, transcripts, and I can get that. Give me the phone number and the name of your carrier. We can also see where else she'd been before you got the phone."

"So the fact that I have it, that's not gonna

be a problem."

"On the plus side, I'm guessing you own the phone, your name is on the bill. On the minus side, you obstructed an investigation and fucked with a crime scene. Hard to say, but whatever, no one needs to know that right now."

"Do you have kids?" Maggie blurted out.

"What?"

"You heard me."

"No," Gina said quietly, almost apologetically. "Divorced, no kids."

"So you don't know."

"Know what?"

Maggie took a deep breath. How many times could you tell someone who didn't have kids that having kids changed you as immediately as a landslide, a tsunami?

"Know that obstructing an investigation doesn't matter to me. That my husband being a cop and knowing the rules and how things go? None of that matters. Not when it's my kid."

"I'm not judging you. As I said, I'm here to help."

"You don't like Kaplan."

"I don't like a lot of people," Gina said.

Maggie believed her. There was an edge to her, she saw now, the kind of edge you needed to be a cop or a nurse or anyone who had to deal with a lot of people a lot of the time. Maggie had always thought she had that edge, too, from having too many heads in too many bowls of warm water. Sometimes all she wanted, at the end of the day, was to drown them, to take advantage of their trust and erase all those people's heads, faces, beings.

They exchanged phone numbers and information. Gina said she'd be back in touch as soon as she could pull some favors, get what she needed. She warned Maggie that it might take more time than going through traditional channels, but she would do her best.

Maggie listened to her, watched her, couldn't help inventorying her. Her hair needed to be cut, conditioned. Her scalp had spent too many days under a hat, sweaty, unwashed. Her eyes didn't really need makeup; she didn't have a great body; she wasn't tall like Maggie. She looked like she'd wolfed down her share of egg sandwiches and bagels in a hurry. But her skin. Her skin had the warm, buttery quality that you only see in Mediterranean people. Her skin looked like cookie dough, Maggie thought, and it made her sad, suddenly, to think of how her husband might have admired it, touched it. So different from

Maggie's thin, pale Irish skin, that always looked stretched to the breaking point. She thought of her father and the bruised translucency of his hands and arms before he died. She bet Gina's father looked like George Clooney.

As Gina walked away and promised to call her as soon as she had more information, she, too, told her to get some sleep. Told her to go home. Maggie supposed she was right. She'd been up for nearly two days now, and her eyelids had that heavy feeling she used to get when Emma was a baby. Plus, she was getting weepy over moisturized skin and how strangers' fathers aged better than her own. A sure sign that she needed to rest, to calm that mind of hers down.

"Maggie." Gina stopped, called over her shoulder. "You know the reason they didn't find Frank's killer right away? The reason they interrogated you, asking you those stupid questions? That was my fault."

Maggie sighed. "I have always believed it was all your fault. Every piece of it."

"I deserve that, I know, but specifically, I didn't do the right thing. I didn't grab my weapon and run after the perp. I should have, and I didn't."

"I'm sure you told Moriarty that. I'm sure

he's forgiven you for screwing up."

"I did. He did. But I did it for a good reason."

Maggie blinked. "To stay with Frank."

"Yes."

"So he wouldn't die alone."

"Yes."

Maggie couldn't believe they were both standing here, on a college campus, twenty feet away from each other, discussing Frank's last moments, and both of them appeared to be dry-eyed. She understood her own lack of tears but not Salt's.

"If you expect me to thank you for that, I'm not sure I can."

"I'm not asking you to. I'm apologizing for the unnecessary interrogation."

Maggie knew this technique — gain their trust with a confession, then wait for a confession in return. But she wasn't falling for it. They had a job to do.

"Okay then," Maggie said and continued to walk. "Wait," she said suddenly. "I did find one weird thing on the phone."

"What's that?"

"Well, someone told Kaplan Emma had a boyfriend, but when he interviewed the guy, he said they worked together on the paper, but that's all."

"Okay. And?"

"And she never mentioned a boyfriend to me. But there was a contact on her phone that said 'Future Husband.' "

"Future husband? When you called the number, who did you get?"

"I haven't called it."

"Well," Salt said, walking back toward her. "What are we waiting for?"

TWENTY-TWO

EMMA

Emma didn't know if it was growing up with a mother who was a hairdresser or her own worldview, but she'd always believed that if her hair was clean, trimmed, and styled, that was all she needed to look good. Hair was more than half the battle, and if her hair worked, the clothes and makeup didn't matter so much. As a result, she'd never really paid much attention to the rest. Her mom cut her hair in angled layers like the photos she showed her on Instagram and taught her how to blow-dry it and style it in beachy waves and put it into a bun in the cutest, fastest way imaginable. So her hair was always on point.

At her high school, almost everyone played sports and didn't wear much makeup to school. Their selfies and videos were more playful, fun, not posed. But suddenly, at college, everyone cared about everything; the world revolved around going out and looking good. Even girls who ran track and wore sweats to class could turn it up a notch at night. Emma hadn't caught up. And maybe, just maybe, if she looked a little bit more like Fiona, Fiona would talk to her more. So she went to CVS and bought mascara, eye shadow, lip gloss, and blush. She had to guess at the colors but thought she'd come close. Even if it didn't work with Fiona, she needed to look more worldly if she had any hope of getting inside that club. She went home and watched YouTube videos about cat eyes and contouring and decided that the people who did this for a living were insane, even though they were probably rich. Emma didn't know anyone who made videos in their rooms on any topic, or at least no one who confessed to doing so.

When she was done, she looked in the mirror and decided she looked pretty good. Not better, just older. She was going to pay a visit to her valet friend and see if the club was open. See if they might be taking job applications. She could be a hostess. She could help them with their social media. She could bus tables. She could wash dishes. She didn't have to become a sugar baby to learn what was happening. She just needed to get in the door. She couldn't count on Fiona making an overture to her like she had to Taylor. Couldn't count on her confiding in her or even, if she was brave enough, taking her there or introducing her to one of her "daddy dates." She'd have to pursue all angles until one of them opened up.

And later, when she got back, she was going to follow Professor Grady. She was already pretty certain he took the train to work, didn't drive — she'd seen the SEPTA pass hanging around his neck with his school ID. Two lanyards, which clicked together as he walked around the room, handing back tests. She could almost imagine following him by that sound, like the tags and collar on a dog, like the halyards of boats, a kind of elocution. Did he even know this happened? Did it not bother him, listening to himself walk, like squeaky shoes or creaky knees? *Oh well,* she thought; if she wrote the story, this would be an interesting detail. That he wasn't as quiet, as under the radar as he thought. He had a tell, just like everyone else.

She skipped her late morning class, figuring she'd just do the reading again and catch up later. Maybe she could borrow someone's notes, maybe not. As long as she kept up on the reading and turned in her papers, she'd be fine.

Emma took the train downtown, getting off at Suburban Station, and walked south. She'd chosen the same dress she had worn last time, to jog the valet's memory. She'd heard Taylor say that about auditions, that you should always wear the same thing to the callback as you did to the first audition.

She approached the private club from the cross street, not ready to go past Beck's quite yet. She'd timed it to be there just after eleven, when she thought the manager would be there but not the staff. The fewer, the better, she believed, until she figured out what exactly was going on there. And until she figured out what exactly she was doing with it all, which could, she thought ruefully, take a bit longer than she anticipated. She'd never written a story that required tracking down sources or lying to get answers. She knew she could ask Jason for help — and knew that she should, at some point — but she wanted to have a solid outline at least, a plan and a couple of paragraphs, before she did.

The building looked old and vaguely English in style to her eye, like a pub. It reminded her of buildings she'd seen on family visits to New York City or Boston, where her cousins lived; the opposite of skyscrapers, she'd said when she was a little girl, and her mother had laughed. Back then, she'd thought there were only houses and skyscrapers, and then suddenly she knew there were others, these in-betweens. The mullions of the divided-light windows had been painted a glossy black. Velvet curtains, a shade somewhere between maroon and brown that her mother would have called cordovan, kept prying eyes out. No curtain, though, on the top half of the locked door, which she wasn't quite tall enough to see in properly. She jumped a few times, noticed a light on toward the back, perhaps near the stairs. She could make out the shapes of tables, the curve of a bar. She thought she heard the low buzz of music, but it could have been coming from somewhere else.

She took a deep breath and knocked, waited. Nothing. A firmer knock, three times in a row, and when she heard footsteps, her heart started to pound. A series of electronic beeps, then the click of a dead bolt, and the door opened.

"Oh," the man said, startled. "You're not the new bartender."

"I could be," she said quickly.

"You could be?"

"I'm a fast learner."

"Good for you," he said, and though he hadn't said it with malice, hadn't said it with anything more than a kind of fatherly teasing, she felt it then, the line of red creeping across her face. She hoped it looked like sunburn. "And bad for him, because he's late, and I hate people who are late. What can I do for you?"

He looked to be around forty, though Emma thought every guy who wasn't her age appeared to be forty.

"Well, I'm not late," she said.

He laughed loudly. "Thank God," he replied. "You're too young for that."

She was disappointed twice. One, she didn't understand the joke. And two, he'd called her young.

"I'm looking for a job."

"I don't hire high school kids."

Her eyes widened. "I'm in college," she said slowly and only a tad defensively. And then, horror — did makeup make her look younger instead of older? Like she was sitting at her mom's vanity, trying on her makeup?

"Oh, okay. Freshman?"

"Yes," she said, deciding that if she told some truths and some lies, the lies would sound a bit better.

"Are you eighteen?"

"Yes."

"Okay, then you can put in an application, in case we have any openings. Which we don't. Unless the bartender doesn't show up. In which case we do. But bartenders have to be twenty-one."

"Okay, well, I —"

"You have hostessing experience? I can't stand one of our hostesses. She manages to look right at you and yet somehow, psychologically, on the inside, she's rolling her eyes. You know?"

"Yes," she said. "Sort of."

"Yes, sort of, you know that kind of girl, or yes, sort of, you have hostessed?"

"Both. One, my roommate is an actress, so she acts polite, but there's disdain just below the surface. Two, I was the receptionist at a busy hair salon, which is a lot like hostessing."

He blinked. "To your first point, that's precisely the reason I don't hire actresses or models. I don't trust them. To your second point — food versus hair. Interesting leap. But mostly female clientele, I assume, at the salon? Our customers are mostly men."

Yeah, she wanted to scream, *and I know exactly why.*

"Meat eaters. Bourbon drinkers. Wine snobs."

"I know the type," she said carefully.

"Of course you do," he replied. "They're impossible to avoid."

The sun was rising overhead, making him squint. He had crinkles around his eyes and mouth, but they weren't dry and sad, like her father's had been. His seemed to be happier, to point up. And she thought, once again, that her father might have been depressed. Not just unhappy, not just trapped. The night he died, she was ashamed to admit, she had wondered if he had taken the gun and shot himself, and Salt had just said it was a drive-by shooting to save his pension and his reputation. No one saw the sadness in her father the way Emma had. But what did it help to think this or to know this? It didn't, so when the thoughts trickled in, she brushed them away, always.

"Can I . . . come in maybe? To fill out the application?"

"What? Oh crap, yes, of course. I'm Sam, by the way," he said, putting out his hand.

"Emma," she replied with just a second's hesitation. "But some people call me Mary. Long story."

"Okay, Emma-slash-Mary. Enter."

He turned on the lights over the bar, and the bottles glowed, bounced off the mirrored surface behind them. She couldn't help noticing there were a lot of other mirrors, too, above some of the tables, tucked into small corners. There were candles on all the tables, and she imagined it would be beautiful, all those candles, reflecting back. But also — all those men looking at the girls from all angles. She felt bile rising in her throat. How could Fiona do this? How could she stand it?

"Could I," she said, looking up from the paper and pen, "possibly use the ladies' room?"

"Sure thing," he said. "It's downstairs. Let me check the light, though. People keep unscrewing the bulb. Pretty dangerous in high heels."

She followed him toward the back. He turned on the light and ushered her through with one arm. A steep set of stairs pitched down toward a lounge area with two velvet sofas. Well, now she understood. Unscrew the lightbulb, screw the girl? She thought of Fiona in her cherry-red shoes, tumbling down the stairs. She thought of a dozen Fionas, falling like dominos, because some idiot needed to grind one out before he got home. She glanced at the plush sofa, a dark turquoise, curved arms, beautiful, really, but she didn't want to look too closely. Like everything else, beautiful at a distance, but the truth was trickier up close.

The women's bathroom had a carved red-and-beige cameo hanging on the door. The bathroom was large, with a sink that would have looked like a trough if it hadn't been gilt-edged. Velvet curtains draped the high, street-level window. A vanity in the corner lined with candles, a wood-framed mirror, a velvet settee. Velvet, gold, candles, mirrors. The whole effect was heavy and sexy, like somewhere an aging rock star would stage a photo shoot with a famous photographer. The thought struck her suddenly — was this how old-fashioned bordellos looked? Had they thoughtfully designed it to look like what it basically was? The idea of it, the straightforward intention, turned her stomach.

She sniffed the air, curious. The bathroom didn't smell like a bathroom — no disinfectant, no bleach. Neither did it smell like bathrooms in clubs — no hair spray, no perfume, nothing covering up anything. It smelled instead of matches, of bonfire. She picked up one of the candles, sniffed, looked at the bottom. Wood smoke, it said. Well, that explained it. She wondered if old bordellos had wood fires to keep the scantily clad women warm, if someone had researched that. She wondered briefly how exactly you would put a smell like that in a candle. Crushed wood chips? Ashes? Then she took a minute and jotted it all down, made notes. Another detail for a corner of a story that wasn't ready to be told. Not yet.

She slipped back into the corridor and, on an impulse, opened the door to the men's room. Empty. She stepped in cautiously. It was almost exactly the same as the ladies' room, except for one detail — a round tray of condoms, fanned out carefully, artfully, like blossoms. The packaging, burgundy and brown foil, the colors alternating. The restaurant's logo and location were stamped on them in gold. *Ridiculous,* she thought; if you didn't know what it meant, you'd wonder why they said London Philadelphia. As if that was a city-state of some kind or the only two locations of all the condoms in the world. She thought of all the old dirty hands that had touched this tray and dropped it. Ewww. Then with the edge of one fingernail, she tucked it back into formation, so Sam wouldn't have to do that, too.

There was another door beyond the men's room, past the sofas, but it was locked. Upstairs, she heard a door open and close, low voices. Then, footsteps clattered overhead, so she hurried back up to see who it was. Another man had arrived, but he wasn't the bartender. Unless the bartender wore a FedEx uniform and wheeled a hand truck.

"You one of the new girls?" he asked her amiably.

"No," she said, hoping it hadn't been too quick, too filled with disgust.

"She's applying to be a hostess," Sam said. "So don't tell her how mean I am."

The FedEx guy laughed. "Nicest guy on my route. Don't let him fool you."

Emma smiled. It was hard to square Sam's personality with the reality of his business. He was friendly without a drop of smarmy. His eyes stayed on her eyes, never travelled elsewhere. She didn't get even the slightest creepy vibe from him, and that unsettled her further. *Stop liking him, Emma. You need to be impartial!*

She finished her application while he tinkered behind the bar, turning bottles to face forward, wiping invisible crumbs and droplets of water off surfaces. He seemed to like people, genuinely. So, how, exactly, had he gotten into a business that could hurt people? She hadn't actually thought there was the slightest chance of getting a job — this was just a ploy to get inside, look

215

around, ask questions. She'd been expecting a class-A, alpha-male asshole, all business, who would take one look at her and decide her tits weren't big enough to be worth his time.

"So you're the owner? Or the manager?"

"I am merely the day manager. A peon in the scheme of things."

"But you're not open for lunch."

"Very observant of you, since there are no people here eating chopped salads. You ever notice how much men love chopped salads? They just love to shovel it in."

She blinked. Did he even know how that sounded? In a place like this?

"A lot happens during the day. Deliveries, prep, cleaning, hiring. So I handle the day, and someone else handles the night. I own another restaurant, and I spend most evenings there. Now I've told you everything. We could go on a game show called *How Well Do You Know Your Boss?* and you would win."

"You seem pretty invested for someone who doesn't own the place."

"Well, I love the person who owns it. And I owe the person who owns it my life."

"Your wife?"

"My brother. You have siblings, Emma-slash-Mary?"

"No."

"Ah, well, then you might not understand. Listen to me," he laughed. "Blathering to you like you're a bartender. Where else you looking for a job? I could recommend you."

She shrugged. "Anyone with a sign up."

"I didn't have a sign up," he said quietly.

"Well, I was walking right by. And it looks like such a nice place."

He sighed. "Yeah, it does. You know why?"

"Why?"

"Because it is."

"Unless you roll your eyes at the day manager?"

"Exactly."

She said goodbye, and he said he'd be in touch if he could figure out a way to fire the other girl, but that was a secret, not to say that to anybody, and she promised. He said he wasn't sure it was legal to fire someone for the way their eyes moved when he wasn't looking. She smiled and shook his hand before she left. As she walked down the street toward the valet at Beck's, she decided that Sam Beck reminded her of her softball coach in third grade. Friendly. Good with young people. Honest. It made her wonder what his brother had done that made him justify doing what he did — even though he claimed to walk away every night and worry about something else. How good a liar, how good an actor did he have to be to sleep soundly every night?

As she approached the entrance to the store, one of the valets sprang up from his folding chair, smiling broadly.

"Hey, it's you!" Michael said.

"You forgot my name," she said, pouting.

"Mary," he said. "Mary of the yellow dress."

She smiled; she knew wearing the same thing had been a good idea.

"But you look fancier today."

Yes, she thought. No Converse, actual grown-ass woman heels.

"Yeah, well, you got to step it up once in a while."

"So what's up, Miss Mary?"

"I need your help."

"Okay."

"Can we talk somewhere? Can you take a break?"

"Not formally," he said. "But do you want to help me park the next Maserati?"

"Yes," she said. "I totally do."

TWENTY-THREE

MAGGIE

Gina had insisted on calling the number herself, and Maggie reluctantly let her, understanding her position. First, Maggie was sleep deprived and not thinking clearly. Second, she could be locked up for just the actions of one evening alone. In a few hours, she'd already contributed to the delinquency of a minor and tampered with evidence. Could she really be trusted to interview someone this important, or would she try to threaten him, spew hate, and make it a trifecta?

It was a whole lot of discussion considering the phone call went straight to voicemail, a voicemail that said, "This is J. Leave a message." Of course, everyone knew how infrequently young people even listened to their messages. But a text from Gina's phone identifying herself as a police officer got no response either. Whoever he was, he was asleep, as any normal person should be. Maggie told her that the editor's name was Jason, so this could be him. And of course, it could be a thousand other people, too.

Gina promised to follow up, hailed Maggie a cab, and agreed to call her the next day. Maggie went home, texted Chloe that she'd be out a few more days, then opened her laptop, intending to set up a Facebook page that looked like the poster, but when she logged on, she saw that Sarah Franco had already done this, sent it to her three thousand friends, and tagged the communications directors of their former high school, grade school, and college to help spread the word. Grateful and defeated, Maggie lay back on the sofa thinking about what else needed to be done, and in the doing, or the undoing, her body fell asleep.

She woke abruptly, arms flailing, to loud knocking and hard yellow light. She looked at her phone — 1:00. In the afternoon? How was that even possible? She wiped her eyes with the heel of her hand and went to the door, looked through the peephole.

Gina. She had on the same clothes as the night before, and her hair didn't look any cleaner, but Maggie knew better than to start comparisons when she'd slept in her mascara on a sofa. She let her in.

"Good, you slept."

"Yeah," she said.

"Sorry to wake you."

"No, I'm glad you did. I have to think about maybe posting a reward. I —"

"Hold off on that. I have some news."

"Did the boy call you back?"

"Yes, but that's not really the news."

"Do you mind if I make some coffee first? Do you want some?"

"No, I have to go home and sleep as soon as I leave here."

"Sleep?"

"Yeah, I just got off my shift. Not much action this morning, thank God."

Maggie tried to process this. Gina had been working while she was sleeping? She measured grounds, poured water, then waited for it to brew. They stood together awkwardly while the water heated, trickled down across the grounds, not speaking. They were not going to be people who ever got to small talk.

Gina didn't look nearly as tired as another person would have after being up all night. Frank was like that, too; Maggie used to call him Camel for his ability to go without food and water and sleep for long periods of time. As if he weren't quite human, mortal. Those were the people who should be cops and spies. Those were the people who won reality shows where they were castaways without clothes or food. Frank could have won. Maybe Gina, too. *Great,* she thought; *they are exactly alike. Maybe I'll grow to hate her, too. Oh right, wait. I already hate her. A woman I hate is helping me now, staying up all night because she feels guilty. Because she owes me. Because she's human after all.*

"So Kaplan's agreed to dust for fingerprints, get her phone records and the surveillance tapes from outside the dorm. He refused the rest, but that's pretty good for now."

"Wait, what? How did you do that? Did you go to his captain?"

"No. Going to someone's captain is like committing treason."

"How then?"

"Simple. I told him you were an old friend of mine."

"And he believed this?"

"I think it kind of turned him on."

"Jesus."

"I'm kidding, Maggie."

"Oh."

"I simply pointed out that interviewing the editor of a college newspaper, an editor known for his investigative reporting, regarding a missing member of his staff without trying really, really hard to solve that crime might be a very bad move."

"Well, that makes more sense. Good. Thank you."

"I'll call you tomorrow if I know more, okay?"

"Okay."

"I just wanted to . . . make sure you were all right."

Maggie tried to process this for a second. Guilt? Humanity? Part of her job?

"So, wait a minute. What did Future Husband say when he called you back?"

"He said he'd already been interviewed by the police, thank you very much, and goodbye."

"Wait, what?"

"Yup. I figure unless Kaplan got very industrious suddenly, that Future Husband must be Editor Boy. He said his piece; he knows his rights. His daddy is probably a lawyer."

"And he had nothing more to add to whatever he told Kaplan?"

"Well, he did remind me that as a quote unquote journalist, he couldn't reveal his sources to the police."

Maggie's heart dropped in her chest. "So

this has to do with a story? With a source?"

"Sounded that way to me."

"He's hiding something."

"Could be. Or he's seen too many Robert Redford movies."

"So now what?"

"We wait for the fingerprints and the tapes and the roommates to be interviewed. Today, you go meet with the Take Back the Night group. And maybe we should start reading the *Semper Sun*. Maybe there are some reporters there less principled than Editor Boy. Maybe he'll crack eventually. Who knows?"

"That's all?"

"That's plenty, Maggie. You'll know more later, and we can go from there. Okay?"

"Okay."

"One more thing."

"What's that?"

"I promised Kaplan that if you stole the phone, I could steal it back from you."

"He knows it's gone?"

"Of course he knows it's gone. He's a dick, not an idiot."

"Tomorrow."

"Tomorrow?"

"Yeah, he can have it tomorrow."

"Okay, then promise you won't do anything crazy today."

"You're just saying that because you want the phone."

Gina smiled, and Maggie realized it was the first time she'd seen her teeth. White and even, they were small, like Chiclets. *Endearing* was the word that popped into her mind. She thought suddenly of the trick Father Mike had taught her a long time ago. When someone angers you, wrongs you, crosses you, picture them as a child. Innocent. Feel empathy for their younger self. At that moment, small teeth flashing bright, Maggie could easily see Gina as a little girl, doing her chores, dancing, twirling in her room, never the girl in the neighborhood who shoplifted or hit someone, always the one mediating, understanding.

"Maggie, are you okay? You look like you went into a fugue state or something."

"I'm fine," she said and walked her to the door.

When Gina left, Maggie took out the phone and synced it to her iTunes so she'd have all her daughter's contacts. There weren't that many; she could easily phone them all in a couple days' time. But she knew something was off with this. Kids prided themselves for being connected, for having as many friends as possible. Sarah Franco had three thousand Facebook friends and almost that many Instagram followers. Maggie's Facebook contacts were automatically added to her phone; it drove her crazy, scrolling through them, that she hadn't figured out how to remove them. But her daughter had neither Facebook or Instagram on this phone and only forty-one contacts in total. Scrolling through, she saw many of them were emails, not phone numbers. How small was this circle? Another thing that bothered her — some of them seemed to have nicknames or code names, and some of them didn't. *Future Husband. Baseball Coach. DadBod. Mr. Maserati. Prince of Suburbia.* And way down in the *V*s, *Valet to the Stars.* Were they all connected?

She held on to the phone like a talisman, trying to feel its energy. *What were you doing, Emma? What were you hiding? And where the hell are you now?*

She poured a cup of coffee, added cream. Considered adding Baileys like her mother used to but didn't. The coffee tasted delicious, and she took a few more sips, waiting for it to do its magic, to wake her all the way up, to make everything clearer, better, more hopeful. How many cups would it take?

She warmed her hands on the mug like

the world's smallest bonfire. Outside, the leaves on the small trees lining the sidewalk had turned gold, orange. Soon, they would fall, and the morning would bring the sound of rakes, brooms. The seasons were changing, and somewhere, her child was changing, and she had no idea what was happening. She held her daughter's life in pieces, clues, ribbons that didn't braid together. Not yet, anyway. She put down her cup.

Maybe Future Husband wouldn't reveal his sources to a cop. They'd made an error there. But would he to a grieving mother? If she met him in person, would he be able to look Emma's mother in the eye and not tell her where she was? He couldn't be that heartless. No. He was a boy. He was someone's son. He had a mother.

She looked at the phone, Emma's phone. *He'd think it was her,* she thought suddenly. And then, a moment later, her finger slipped, and she hit FaceTime. Her own face on the phone scared her, always, that shock of bad lighting and smudged mascara. *Fine,* she thought. *Maybe I'll scare him, too.*

An almost instant connection. And there he was. Dirty-blond hair. Glasses. A serious look on his face.

"Hi," she said.

"Whoa," he said in surprise. "You're her

mother."

"Yes."

He nodded slowly. "I . . . see the resemblance." He took a deep breath, rubbed his face.

She saw stubble there, and he didn't look like the stubble type. No, he'd been up late. He looked older than she'd expected, wearier. He had the look of a parent, a mix of fear, guilt. *Good,* she thought. *Maybe he is scared.*

"You're the editor of the paper," Maggie said.

"Yes, yes I am."

"Look, I read a newspaper every day. I get it. I understand how important it is to publish stories. I get why you are protecting someone from the cops."

He nodded.

"Her father was a cop, and he died last year. Did you know that? I am not a cop. I am her mother, and she is all I have left of my family. Just her. So I–I need to know where she is, Jason. If you don't want me to tell anyone, I won't. But I need to know."

She'd done what Frank had always told her victims needed to do with their attackers: humanize themselves. Share the details, the backstory. Paint a picture. Did this work on noncriminals too? It had been reflexive,

228

desperate, as desperate as if Jason had cornered her and taken out a knife.

He took off his glasses, cleaned them on the hem of his shirt. She could see that they were a little crooked. His shirt, a button-down so wrinkled, it looked like he'd slept in it. His hands, not as soft looking as she expected. They were ruddy, not smooth. Like he did more than typing with them. A worn Band-Aid on the tip of one index finger, a bit dirty at the edges, like it had been stretched too many times and he didn't have another one.

"Mrs. O'Farrell, I really think that Emma is okay. I do. I believe that she is protecting herself right now. And that's why she is . . . not easily found."

"That's not saying very much," she said. "That's not saying anything."

"I know it's not concrete. I know it's not what you want to hear."

"Can we meet?" she said suddenly.

"Meet?"

"I can ask you questions, and you can give me hints," she said. "You wouldn't have to compromise your integrity. No one would know."

"I don't know if that's a good idea. I don't —"

"Emma has code names on her phone,"

Maggie blurted out.

"Code names?"

"Could they be related to whatever she's working on?"

He took another deep breath, then nodded. "Could be."

"It could be her way of keeping them anonymous, keeping them safe, right?"

"Yes, it could be. Easily."

She nodded. "So can you at least tell me what the story is about? So I can start piecing this together?"

"I'm not sure what shape the story is taking."

"Is it drugs?"

"Look, Mrs. O'Farrell, this is —"

"This is what?"

"This is not helping."

"No shit it's not helping! You are not helping me very much at all, Jason. What would your mother say about that, huh? About not helping another mother?"

"I have to go, but I promise —"

"You promise what?"

"If I hear from her, I'll tell her to get in touch."

"If? I would really like to hear a when, not an if."

"Okay, when."

"All right. By the way, are you sleeping

with her?"

"What? No!" His eyes narrowed, then closed, as if he couldn't bear to picture what she was describing.

"Hooking up, sexiling, whatever you want to call it?"

"No, no. I swear to you, no."

"Promise?"

"I promise. But in return, I'd like you to promise . . . to be careful with those phone numbers."

"Careful?"

"Yes, because if they get spooked —"

"What? They'll stop talking? You'll lose your story?"

He was silent then. "No, I meant for Emma's sake."

"You know what I think? I think you'd better keep in touch with me," she said. "About this story. I'll text you my number. The police are taking this phone."

He sighed, didn't answer.

"Unless you'd like to explain to me, and the police, why your number was listed in Emma's phone under 'Future Husband.' I'm sure you know how the police think it's always the boyfriend, right?"

"Wait — what? What did you say?"

The blush extended all the way to his hairline, and she knew then that she had made a mistake. He didn't know how Emma felt. She had betrayed her daughter, and she felt nauseous suddenly, like she'd shown a boy Emma's diary, her artsy scribblings of their commingled names. And she thought of her daughter and her terrible, red-cheeked, Irish blush. Was she somewhere, right now, blushing in horror, in embarrassment at what her mother had done? Maggie felt ill all over again. She didn't know what she was doing. Was she making things worse? And what did she know about this boy and Emma? Absolutely nothing. She thought she could make him scared enough to talk? But what if she'd just made him angry enough to snap? Or scared him away from a girl who was right for him?

When they hung up, she sat there and tried to decide what she should do before she went to campus. Her life was divided now, like a commuting student, between two worlds. She didn't trust herself to know what to do with the information in her hands. She knew she should just turn the phone over and call it a day. Yes, she thought she could solve everything, but she could also ruin everything.

She took a deep breath and decided to call the most innocuous code name on the list. She decided to call *Valet to the Stars.*

TWENTY-FOUR

EMMA

Emma thought she could probably count on one hand the types of cars she had been in. Where she lived, everybody's parents drove the same ones and didn't think about the others too much. Subaru wagons. Honda minivans. A Prius here and there. So many white Lexuses or Acura SUVs, she'd lost count. Occasionally, a Range Rover or Tesla showed up at a soccer game, and the boys were excited by that. She supposed if you were a gearhead, the suburbs of Philadelphia were a very disappointing place to grow up, because no one flaunted their wealth with cars. Maybe there were Porsches and Mercedes convertibles tucked into garages for occasional use, but she didn't see them, and the Ferrari dealership on the edge of town always looked like the set of a movie, clean and sparkling and empty of people.

But this car that she'd slid inside now was unquestionably different. No extra room in the front seat, it enveloped her, hugged her, the way she imagined a race car might. The softest leather seats, different from leather in other cars. The dashboard and its instruments unusual, too, more like an airplane.

"Wow," she said.

"I know, right?" Michael said. "Some days, I have the best job in the world."

The main lot was across the street and didn't involve much driving. But he explained that there was an overflow lot several blocks away, and he sometimes brought the nicer cars there just to have a chance to drive them longer. Plus the guys who oversaw that lot loved cars, guarded them with their lives. He said the guy across the street sometimes fell asleep in his chair out of boredom.

"So if I want to steal a car, I should go to the lot across the street?" she said.

"Ooh, a girl car thief. I love it."

"Don't be sexist, Michael."

"Sorry."

"Maybe my dad taught me how to hot-wire."

"Or your mom," he said, winking.

"That's better."

He went the long way, to the farthest lot,

and predictably, the two men in charge of it fawned over the car, running their hands across the curves appreciatively, asking if Michael needed it washed or detailed, if it needed gas, anything extra. Michael said no, handed over the keys.

"You don't lock it?" she whispered.

"Don't tell anyone, but sometimes we leave the keys inside, too. Depends how busy we are. Can't be locking and unlocking all day long. Unless the tip is huge. But forget about cars, right? It's a nice day for a walk."

She smiled. It was a nice day — cool but not windy. Not that feeling that winter was on the way, threatening.

"You wouldn't rather spend all your time inside a car?"

"Maybe half the time. I'm studying to be a high-performance mechanic," he said proudly.

"Sounds fancy."

"It pays, like, crazy amounts of money. More than you can make with a lot of college degrees. No offense."

"None taken. I get it. I do."

"I figure being a valet is a good way to network for my next job."

"Makes total sense. But I was wondering, maybe, related to that, to networking, that you could help me with something?" she said.

"So you're not just flirting with me because my future as a mechanic is so bright? Damn." He smiled.

She laughed. There was something incredibly easy and welcoming about him, and she thought that it was probably a shame that he hadn't gone to college. A nice guy like this was a rarity and the reason you sometimes saw beautiful girls with lanky, ordinary-looking boys. Because they were attentive and nice.

"But back to your question, sure, if I can help, I will," he replied, and she didn't doubt him. Everything about him was earnest, born to be helpful. She knew, too, that people like him were also born to be taken advantage of. Had he figured that out yet?

"So," he continued, "do you need help buying a car or something?"

"No. Listen, I know we don't really know each other, but I sense you can keep a secret."

"Oh, I can," he said. "Like a vault. You can ask my brothers and sisters. My poor parents," he sighed.

"Good. Well, I'm investigating something, and I need help."

"Look, if this means borrowing a car, I can't —"

"No, no, nothing like that. I need . . . people. Sources."

"You want me to keep my eyes open, search a glove box, something like that?"

"Well, that might be helpful, too," she said, "but mostly I'm wondering if you know anyone who goes to that club, London . . . and if anyone who goes there and leaves their car with you . . . if you might have noticed anything about them."

"Like what?"

"Like maybe they seem . . . regretful. Or guilty. Maybe they used to go and stopped? But still visit the store?"

He stopped on the sidewalk, as if he couldn't think and walk at the same time.

"Whoa," he said slowly.

"I know it's a lot to ask, to process —"

"No, I'm just thinking for a second. About this situation."

"I know you don't approve of what's happening there, so —"

"No, no I do not. I got a sister, you know?"

"Yes."

"So, are you trying to close them or something? For, like, health violations? Are you a cop?"

"I'm a reporter," she said, whispering, as

if she didn't quite believe it herself. But something about saying it out loud, practicing it, made her swell with pride.

"Wow," he said. "I knew you were smart. I sensed that right away."

"So I need a man who's been there and is unhappy about it. Maybe he hates the owner, maybe he hates himself? Someone who was tricked by a girl or lost all his money or feels guilty about the girls being young. I need someone . . . disenchanted."

"But, like, off the record?"

"Well, on or off, either one is good for now."

"Disenchanted is a very nice word. Very descriptive," he said.

"Thank you."

"You should use that in the story."

"I'll consider it."

"You know, there is someone. I haven't seen him in a while, but he used to go over there on Wednesday nights. One time, he came to Beck's first, with a new haircut, you know, spiked up like Alec Baldwin's. Then he went in the store and got all dressed up. He got a new shirt and tie and a jacket to go with his jeans, and he asked me to put his old clothes in his trunk before I parked the car. He even had on new cologne. I remember that because I told him he smelled like a million bucks, and he asked me if it was too much and I told him no. He had a present wrapped up with him, too. Pink ribbon. It was like, I don't know, like watching someone go to prom, you know? Then later that night, instead of coming back with a girl, he came back alone. He said, 'I'm an old fool, Michael.' And I'm like, 'What's wrong, Mr. M?' And he said, 'It's true, you know. Money cannot buy you happiness or friendship or love. Remember that.' "

"Wow. Have you seen him since?"

"Couple times, but only in the store, far as I know."

"He sounds perfect. Do you know his name or where he works?"

"His first name is Andrew," he said. "Last name starts with an *M,* because that's what he asked me to call him. I don't know his last name. I guess if that's important, I could look for his registration? In the glove box? I think maybe he's retired. Or maybe just a consultant. Something part-time, you know. He sits on a board, I know that. But all these guys do. I always thought it was because they were guilty, you know? Like if they did some good somewhere for free, it would make up for something bad they did for money."

Emma paused and took that in for a moment. It struck her as both wise and cynical, and Michael didn't really seem like either of those things. It made her wonder about his father, his mother. If he was quoting them. If they were good people, and he was a good son.

"Oh, and one more thing. I know he's a widower. That's why, you know, he ended up going there. He was lonely. I remember him buying a new suit for the funeral. Cancer."

"It sounds like you've been a good friend to him," she said.

"That's funny you should say that. I told my mom once that's what I try to do. Be the friend they know they can trust with their car."

"I love that sentiment."

"I mean, wealthy peoples' cars are one of the most valuable things they own, after their home or their, you know, watch. Some of those guys, man, those watches are worth more than my parents' house, that's for sure."

They were nearly back at the store, and Emma realized she'd been walking slowly, extending their time together.

She said she'd try to find this customer on her own, but if she couldn't and Michael ran into him, would he be able to mention it, gently, to him? And he said sure, he could. "I know you'll take good care of him, just like me with his car."

"I like the way you look at things."

"Well, you're easy to talk to, Mary."

"One more thing," she said. "Please don't be mad, but . . . my name isn't Mary."

"Wow," he said. "What is it?"

"I don't think I should tell you quite yet. For both of our sakes."

"Wow. That's some heavy shit. Pardon my French."

"Yeah, maybe I'm being paranoid, but I don't want you to get in any trouble."

"Okay, so . . . you're working undercover."

"I guess."

"Well, you know what that means?"

"What?"

"We're under the covers together now."

She laughed, and he laughed, too, a kind of giggle that reminded her of a child, like someone she'd known forever.

TWENTY-FIVE

MAGGIE

Maggie was disappointed. The last number she'd allowed herself to call had reached a business, not a person. She'd foolishly chosen the one number that actually was what Emma said it was — a valet service. Still, she waited for the recorded message to finish — *If you need valet service for an upcoming event, feel free to text us anytime. If you need more information about rates or hours of service, visit mrvalet.com* — and followed the instructions.

She looked at the website and found that MR not only meant mister, but the founder's name, Michael Redmond. Clever. There were testimonials from CEOs, the mayor, even the former governor, and a few photos of cars being buffed, keys being handed over, and a nameplate on a uniform with the logo. But no faces. That meant, she thought, that the owner was young. Too young to inspire confidence on a website, because who wanted a kid driving their expensive car? A kid who'd probably never seen a stick shift or parallel parked without a backup camera?

The website said to text him, so she texted him, saying she needed help with an event. This was technically true. There would be a search for Emma and a gathering of people to help. *That's an event,* she thought. Then added "in the city." And then "a fundraiser." She'd have to raise some money for a reward, right?

She thought of Frank suddenly, laughing at her because she couldn't tell a lie, even a white one, without crossing herself and confessing on Sunday. She contorted the truth regularly to make up for this, and he thought it was ridiculous. As a cop, she knew, he had had to lie to people all the time. For their own protection, he used to say. But really, it had been for his. That was what being a cop was all about — living to serve another day. If you had to tell a lie, fool someone, use someone? That was part of the job. Once you realized that and accepted it, it made everything clearer. But Maggie was different from her husband. She was a blurter, a truth teller. She could not be a cop, ever.

He texted her back within minutes. Friendly. Asked date and time, if she wanted him to reserve it. Said he could hold the slot for twenty-four hours and could discuss details at 5:00 p.m.

Can we talk now? she texted back.

Sorry, on a job.

She signed off, accepted his terms. What choice did she have? And who wouldn't reward someone for staying focused on the job at hand?

She got in the shower, washed her hair, put it up in a topknot. The salon was quiet downstairs, no water running, no blow-dryer. Midafternoon during the week was always slow, post lunch hour, before happy hour. She expected to find Chloe playing Candy Crush, but when she opened the door, she was dusting, wiping down surfaces. *God bless her,* she thought and then laughed to herself. She probably heard her coming downstairs.

Chloe immediately ran to her, hugged her, asked her if she needed help. Maggie told her that keeping the salon open was more than enough help. She showed her the posters, asked her to post some around town, and maybe at the high school. Chloe nodded, said of course. Then Maggie told her about the Facebook page and asked her to share it.

"You got it," she said. "Have you done any ads yet?"

"Ads?"

"Yeah, Facebook ads from the page? Asking for leads?"

Maggie shook her head, professed ignorance. Chloe told her that this was the newest thing, targeting people on Facebook. She could wait until there was surveillance video and a reward, and she could spend a little money and target the whole university. It costs almost nothing, Chloe added.

"But are kids even on Facebook anymore?" Maggie asked.

"Sometimes. They post stuff for their parents or in albums. Plus you want teachers, faculty, and staff, right? Those people are on for sure. I mean, there's a hospital there, a security center, thousands of employees. And you want kids' parents. They'll ask, be nosy. They'll want to help. I can do it for you, set it up."

"You're a genius, Chloe."

"No, I'm not," she said and sighed. "I'm a single thirty-year-old woman with too much time on her hands who reads all the *People* magazines in the salon cover to cover."

Chloe was being modest. She was kind and funny, and the customers loved her like

245

a big sister. And she had great hair she was always tinkering with — a blond, wavy bob with highlights in the summer, strawberry-blond when she was feeling low, sometimes caramel and gold in winter. Half the girls who came in requested the same exact look for themselves. Maggie believed Chloe would leave her one day to start her own salon; Chloe believed she was going to meet Mr. Right, get married, and never work again.

As she drove to campus, Maggie went over all the conversations she'd had, tallied what she knew. All in all, she felt a little better and wondered if that was real or just her body's need to calm down.

Maybe Valet Boy worked in the city. Maybe he'd agree to meet her. Maybe he was just a kid Emma knew from school and this was his number and it all meant nothing. Maybe she'd thrown a charity event for one of those organizations she'd signed up for the first day of school. What were they? Maggie tried to remember. Those days, such an exciting blur. How she'd tried to gather all of it in, the roommates, the parents, the hallways, the excitement. What an idiot she'd been, not remembering the right things.

She parked in the main lot, paying with

her credit card perfunctorily. Then it hit her — the debit card. She had access to Emma's account. She could check the activity, withdrawals, payments. She didn't need the police to do this. But she was a "go to the branch" person, not an online person. But she had no online account set up. *Chloe could help with that,* she thought; she did all the banking for the salon.

She walked to the cafeteria, where Sarah had said she'd meet her in front of the fountain. Sarah was there first, one of those kids who was always on time. She hugged her, asked her if there was any news, and Maggie told her about the dorm room being processed and surveillance video being pulled. Sarah nodded her approval and then said the Take Back the Night girls were meeting in a conference room at the computer center to distribute everything and to talk about next steps.

"Some of them have experience with this kind of thing," she said.

"What do you mean? Have other girls gone missing here?"

"No, I mean in their past. Two of them have sisters who —"

"Oh my God," Maggie said, holding up her hand. "Don't tell me. Seriously."

"Okay," Sarah said. "The important thing

was, they've been through this process before and can help."

"Great," she said. "In the group, do they have an advisor?"

"Yes, Dr. Woodruff. But she's mostly just on call and is the liaison to the college administration. She takes the heat for us, basically."

"Heat? What kind of heat?"

"Like when we run a rapist off campus and his parents complain that #MeToo is ruining boys' reputations."

"There's a rapist here?"

"Mrs. O'Farrell, there are rapists on every college campus in America. People just don't know about them. They don't put that in the brochures and the videos."

"A rapist," she repeated. "Here? This semester?"

"First week of school."

"Wow."

"Tell me about it. We signed up and thought we'd just sit around talking about replacing lights on walking paths and coordinating rides home from parties and then boom. Major event."

"And that boy is gone?"

"Oh, no, he's back," she sighed.

"What dorm? What's his name?"

"Darcy McLaren. Lives off campus."

"Darcy?"

"I know. Doesn't suit him at all. But he's not connected to Emma. I doubt it anyway. He's on probation, has a curfew. Probably has an ankle monitor."

"Could that . . . could that have been the story she was working on, though? That sounds controversial."

"I don't think so. She knows I'm with the group. She would have asked me about that."

"Right. You're probably right."

"But wait, didn't the people at the newspaper say what she was working on? I know she wasn't technically on staff —"

"What do you mean?"

"I mean, they told her to look for a story."

"Well, she apparently found one, and they won't tell me what it is."

"That has to be illegal. Right?"

"Wrong. They won't reveal their sources."

"That's fucked up. Pardon my language."

"No, I agree. It's very fucked up."

"I think one of the girls who's meeting with us is from the paper. We'll ask her what's up."

They walked the block to the computer building, and Maggie was struck, yet again, by how separate everyone looked from one another — the earbuds in, the backpacks on. In their own worlds. Flocks of boys who weren't together, just moving in the same direction. Heads down, hair in their eyes. Pretty girls not making eye contact, unpretty girls not either, no one smiling, no one frowning, faces set. Only a few in pairs, talking, interacting. But mostly, a crowd full of what looked like lonely people. How did anyone connect under these circumstances? How did anyone know anyone? Alone and sober by day and then let loose, drunk, by night? And what were they listening to all the time in their heads? Who wanted that much music? Who needed a perpetual soundtrack to their lives?

Sometimes when Maggie got home from the salon, she wanted to scrub the day's Sonos out of her mind; she wanted silence, white noise. She wanted nothing, nothing. Empty nest, empty bed, empty air. Why did people want to fill it? She just wanted it gone, so she could rest. So she could be. Now, she'd gotten her horrible wish. There was nothing at home for her now. Nothing.

Inside, on the second floor. A group of perhaps ten girls waiting around a large table, all on their phones. They looked almost identical in their postures, and Maggie resisted the urge to treat them all like she'd treat Emma and tell them to sit up straight.

One of the girls at the end lifted her eyes slowly as Maggie and Sarah walked in. She nodded solemnly, and suddenly Maggie's heart lifted. The blond girl from the party. The girl with the shoes. Maggie smiled at her, a small smile, a smile that wouldn't embarrass her, wouldn't let her know how happy it made her that someone had listened to her. Someone had actually heard.

Sarah greeted them all, introduced Maggie, and distributed a sign-up sheet. Someone needed to organize a search, as soon as the police could narrow some things down, give them direction. Everyone needed to distribute posters and sign up for certain areas to be covered. Someone needed to be in charge of social media follow-up or distributing video if they got a description of a suspect. Maggie listened as Sarah and an older student, Liz, informed the group calmly. Maggie was there to answer any questions, they said. They didn't say that Maggie was there because she had no life and didn't trust the police. Didn't say that Emma was her only child, her only hope, her only hobby. Didn't say that being here was the only productive, organized thing she'd done since the police knocked on her door and that she'd just been desperately bouncing between dorms, parties, stolen phones, and calling people she didn't know to find out more of what she didn't know. Only one girl in this room knew how desperate she could be. Until the door opened and another girl walked in.

"I'm sooo sorry I'm late," she said breezily. "I'm one of Emma's roommates, and we're all so grateful for your help. They wanted to be here, too, but I'm representing the dorm. Anything I can do, anything at all. I'm here to help," she smiled broadly, her teeth glistening.

Ten thousand dollars of orthodontia, the smile of a model, the smile of an actress.

Taylor.

TWENTY-SIX

EMMA

Emma didn't mind that she'd wasted three evenings in a row following a man who was doing absolutely nothing wrong or odd or unusual — he was merely taking the train home to the suburbs. Three times, she'd watched him not get off at Suburban Station, not get off at Thirtieth Street either. Three times, she'd hoped he'd get off at one of the right stops to walk to the club, which was located between those stations, and three times, she'd been disappointed. She'd waited until the last possible second, then jumped off with the gaggle of other college students and Amtrak travelers switching at Thirtieth Street. She did not want to be stuck on his train line and pay for another ticket back to campus.

She knew Professor Grady was heading out to Wayne, where he lived, to mow his tidy lawn or rake the leaves that were starting to fall now or relax in the huge renovated space she'd seen on Google Maps. No, she was becoming used to the wasted time and effort. What she minded was paying for the train tickets. She hated wasting the money and hated that she cared about it, thought about it. Sometimes she felt like she was the only girl on campus with limited spending money that she'd earned herself. Everyone else got money transferred every month from their parents. They called it an allowance, as if they were five years old and buying gum.

Emma knew Maggie would send her money for anything she needed if she ran out. Books, fine. New shoes, gloves, a charger for her laptop, anything like that, anything with a name, Maggie would pay for. But not just a random ask. She wasn't built that way. It defied the way her family worked, and Emma wasn't going to start changing that now and become one of those girls who whined and begged and said everything was sooo expensive, even though it was. Ubers, public transportation, bike rentals, food, and yes, alcohol — all cost more than she expected. Not to mention Magic Markers or crepe paper or poster board, things other girls bought from the school store without a moment's thought whenever they needed to decorate or celebrate. And sweatshirts and sweat pants, purchased whenever theirs were ripped or vomited on or too nasty to deal with. In the garbage bag, out the door. No one took care of anything. The same girls who carefully recycled cans and wouldn't drink from a plastic straw, like, ever, because it hurts the animals, threw away their stained clothes in a dumpster whenever vomit or blood touched them. Emma was stunned the first time she'd seen this, Taylor drunk, wobbly, hitting her chin against the table and then vomiting. The blood and vomit mingling at the top of her sweatshirt, staining the fuzzy embroidered *S* of *Semper.* Fiona yanking her clothes off her, wadding them up, putting them in the trash. Emma wanted to ask her how she'd gotten through life with her period. Had she thrown away every pair of underwear she'd soiled?

Later the next day, she'd fished out that sweatshirt, holding her nose. She'd rinsed it in the sink, rubbed the stain with a bar of soap, then thrown it into a hot water wash cycle with another load of clothes. All the stains came out; all the school colors stayed true. She'd dried it, folded it, and put it in Taylor's room before the other girls had even woken up. But Taylor hadn't even noticed.

The small ministrations that had made Emma beloved to Sarah Franco and other kids she knew in high school meant nothing to her college friends. It hadn't taken too many instances before she got the message and vowed, *No more. I'm done taking care of you assholes.* The last time, when they'd been at a party and all had too much to drink except her (she'd wisely started throwing her last few shots of vodka into the soil of a plant), on the walk home, she'd dug into her small cross-body purse and doled out Advil to everyone.

"Thanks, Mom," Annie had said, and they'd all laughed except Emma. No one wants to be the mommy in college. They want to be a hot girl or a powerful woman. To hop from child to mother was the absolute worst, and Emma vowed to be more careful from then on. She would try to fit in without taking care of anyone. No, she would only take care of herself.

She switched platforms, going down one escalator, across the main concourse, weaving through a thick throng of commuters. Coming to Thirtieth Street always meant a weird confluence of people — travelers from the airport switching trains, lost, clueless,

256

not knowing where they were going; commuters, hurrying, working on laptops, reading materials for their meetings the next day; and students, since this was the stop for Drexel and Penn. Emma didn't look out of place here, but then the mix of types, of locals and out-of-towners, meant no one did. And that was why, as she finally got to the up escalator, brushing elbows, avoiding luggage slung on people's shoulders, that at first she didn't think twice about the man in the beige windbreaker on the platform off to her left. She sensed him more than she saw him, smelled something familiar — cologne? the woody pulp of old books? — then turned abruptly, jostling a woman standing too close behind her, apologizing. Below her, the man darted away, behind a partition, then gone. Brown hair, beige jacket, and she wasn't sure precisely what he looked like. But he was wearing exactly what Professor Grady had been wearing. Had he been watching her? And jumped off at Thirtieth Street, too, to follow her?

There was no path to get up the escalator faster; no one was walking up the left or moving to the right. Too many people. When she finally got to the top, she ran back down the stairs, back to the concourse. She looked left, right, scanning, her mind chanting *beige beige beige* like a mantra. She'd never seen so much black, blue, and red in her life.

She crossed, ran up the platform where she'd originally jumped off. If he'd been heading back to his home, that's where he'd be. But she heard the train as the stairs rose, and running didn't help. The faster she ran, the more the train seemed to accelerate, pulling out of the station. She stood, staring at the back end of it, half expecting his face to appear, half wishing she'd been wrong. She was just being jumpy, she thought. She was just a number in the lecture hall to him. She might be onto him, but he, she was certain, had no idea who she was.

Her heart rate slowed finally, and she headed back to her platform to wait. She sat on the metal bench and waited for the next train. This platform was full of students, all going the same direction. She didn't recognize anyone, and no one noticed her looking, glancing around. She sighed. Why couldn't it be a male student she needed to follow instead of a grown man? That would be a piece of cake. She thought of the easy obliviousness that propelled her roommates through the world — leaving digital clues, inviting attention. Professor Grady sure as hell didn't show up on any

Snap Map, that was certain.

She boarded the train and rode back. She was the only person in the car without earbuds in, and she found herself cocooned in the buzzy, tinny sounds of their leaking music. She wondered what they could and couldn't hear with all that in their heads. Would they hear her scream or laugh or speak? She smiled at the thought of acting crazy and being ignored. Then she realized she *was* going a bit stir-crazy. She thought of her father saying once that police work was ninety percent waiting, ten percent listening. She felt that now and wondered how her father, with his constantly jiggling legs, itching to get up and go, handled it. He wasn't built for it yet managed to do it; she, more motherly and patient, should be better at it. She just needed to cut herself a break and give it more time.

But how much time? Emma walked back to her dorm, trying not to think about her homework and her laundry and all the things she wasn't doing while she was out chasing theories that weren't playing out the way she wanted them to. She didn't have months to let her theories play out. Her story had to come together, or she had to let it go, work on something else. She could almost hear Jason telling her that. And if following her professor wasn't working, she needed to switch tactics. She could watch the club, not the professor. Who knows who else she'd see? All she needed was a car to wait and watch in. Or a job as a hostess, waiting for him to come in the door.

She texted Michael and asked him if he could ever "borrow" a car for a night.

She texted Sam Beck and offered to work a shift for free.

Then a call came in, making her jump, and it wasn't from either of them. It was Jason. She was so excited, she almost declined the call, fumbling while trying to answer. She finally picked up, and he asked her if she could update him on her progress. Asked if she was somewhere private, somewhere she could talk.

"In a minute I will be," she said. There were students all around her, and all she could think of was finding a door to lock. She ran into her dorm, up the stairs. No one was in the kitchen, Fiona wasn't in her room, but she went into the bathroom anyway, locked the door, and, just for good measure, ran the water in the shower full force. She told Jason about Fiona and the account at the store. She told him about the valet trying to get her a good source. She told him about Sam Beck and trying to get a job as a hostess. She told him about Professor Grady being a former patron of the earlier club and the over-the-top renovations on his house. She said it all in a rush, and he didn't say *slow down,* didn't say *wow, good work,* didn't say anything. For a second, she thought he'd hung up, that they'd lost their connection and she'd have to explain all over again. In those seconds, all her fears came forward. She realized she didn't know him either, that he was a stranger, that phones have recording devices, that his father could be a patron of the university, for God's sake, and she felt about as vulnerable as she had on the train platform. She wished she could see his face. Not just because it was a pleasant face, not just because she wanted to see him, but because, her father's words about listening aside, she realized she wasn't good at it. She needed to watch, to see, to know if someone was lying or angry or interested or fascinated. For her, it was all about movement and body language.

Finally, he spoke. "Are you . . . in a hot tub?"

"No, I'm in the shower," she replied quickly, then promptly wanted to curl up and die. Would he picture her naked now? Jesus! "I mean, I'm near the shower." Then

"Wait, is there a hot tub on campus?"

"There's a Jacuzzi in the gym."

Ah, the gym. Another place she wasn't going while she was chasing the story.

"Okay, so, Emma, you're definitely onto something here. But unless you nail down a source and get more facts, figures, dates, you can't write anything. You need to find more girls to talk or become one of the women yourself. I mean forget working as a hostess. You need to go on one of those dates and prove what actually happens."

She exhaled loudly. "I don't think I can do that."

"I know it's scary as fuck, but you either have to find a girl to talk or become a girl, or else the story isn't about the girls, it's about the men."

"No." She shook her head violently. "Jason, it's not about the girls or the men, don't you see? The story is about the school!"

"I know that's what you think it's about, Emma, but —"

"No, I know. I know it."

"Well, knowing it and proving it are two different things. And we can't print it until you prove it."

The knock on the door was loud.

"I gotta go."

"Okay, keep me in the loop."

"Are you almost through? I need the shower," Annie called.

Emma hung up the phone, turned off the water, and wrapped her head in a towel.

"Going out tonight?" she asked Annie breezily as she passed by.

"Possibly," Annie replied. "You?"

"I have homework due."

She laughed. The same laugh that had charmed Emma so on move-in day, a child-like laugh that rose and fell over something silly Morgan had said. She thought she could be friends with someone who laughed like that. But now it sounded hollow, forced.

"Okay, Mommy," Annie said, and as she turned away, Emma felt all the red in her skin, rising, burning.

She went to her room, shut the door, and started going through Fiona's things. *Fuck them,* she thought. *I'm not doing this for them. I'm doing it for me.*

TWENTY-SEVEN

MAGGIE

The summer before, when Emma was helping her at the salon with ads and social media, Maggie, Chloe, and Emma had gotten into a discussion about mean girls. Maggie had told them about Beth Flaherty's slumber party in high school, when she'd been tricked into putting a yogurt and honey mask on her face and then they'd whistled for Beth's two large dogs, who came bounding down the stairs, jumping on her, licking frantically. She was certain they were going to bite her face off, and the screams she emitted would have brought anyone else's parents running, but Beth's parents were drunk at a block party. Maggie had never recovered her social status with a few of those girls, who ate yogurt in front of her tauntingly at the cafeteria for years. Then Chloe had talked about being the last girl to get her period in high school and her friends coming in to class wearing tampons as earrings and necklaces. And Emma had not been surprised or even appalled. She had calmly told them how Sloane Adams had created a fake Instagram account and pretended to be a boy flirting with a girl in their class who had Down syndrome. Set up a date and everything, then broke the girl's heart and recorded it all on video.

"Okay, you win," Chloe had said. "That's some CIA-level shit right there."

"You never told me about that," Maggie had said, frowning.

"I'm telling you now," Emma had replied.

That interaction encapsulated their relationship. Emma would always answer a question; Emma would always come clean. But it would be on her terms. It was like living with someone on time delay; Maggie never knew when her daughter would hold on to something or how long she'd choose to cling to it, enjoying the secret or processing its meaning before she casually tossed it to her mother. Maggie thought of that now as she looked around the table at these girls who barely knew her daughter. What were their motives? What were they capable of?

As the girls signed up and took stacks of posters and colorful thumbtacks, Maggie took a deep breath and approached Taylor.

"How nice of you to come," she said evenly.

"Oh gosh, of course. Anything for Emma."

"I assume you've already spoken to the police?"

"Well, I wasn't much help. I haven't seen her in days."

"So let me get this straight — now that you're upright and sober — you'd do anything for her but not worry that you hadn't seen her for days?"

Taylor's eyes narrowed so slightly that she probably thought Maggie wouldn't notice. But Maggie was used to looking at women and girls, used to the micromovements they made in the mirror when they looked at their hair and tried to decide if they loved it or hated it or wanted to have Botox or liposuction. She was used to strangers not telling her the truth with anything but the tiny flickers of movement in their faces. Was that women's intuition? Or just being a good hairdresser?

"Oh, Emma was always in and out," Taylor said. "So busy. We never knew where she was."

"Really?"

"Really," she said and smiled.

Because that was the exact thing Emma had told Maggie about her roommates. That they were busy and didn't spend much time in the dorm. But would saying that now, spitting it into Taylor's face, betray her daughter? She thought so, so she said nothing. At the time, Emma's comment had made Maggie happy. That her only child, used to quiet if not peace, had plenty of alone time to think and study. But now she wondered if she'd been foolish.

"So when she moved all her stuff out of Fiona's room, that didn't faze you?"

"Well, we figured she just needed her stuff. A girl needs her things, right?"

Taylor cocked her head jauntily, and the move was so obvious, so calculated, it made Maggie sure of one thing. Taylor was a terrible actress. She would never work in this town or any town, let alone New York or LA.

Maggie took the posters from Taylor's hand. "We had plenty of volunteers show up before you," she said. "But thank you anyway." She didn't want to waste the posters. She could practically picture Taylor walking around the corner and throwing them into recycling.

"Wait, what? But I want to help."

"Oh, I think you've done enough already."

Taylor took a deep breath, offered another fake smile, and left.

As Maggie worked her way around the room, handing out posters, thanking the girls, one of the girls asked her if she'd checked with health services.

"No, I don't think so. Why?"

"Sometimes girls leave school abruptly because they're having a health crisis."

"A health crisis?"

"Yes. You know, a complicated problem or an embarrassing problem? Something they're ashamed of, maybe? Related to health?"

Maggie offered her a tight smile. How many ways could this poor girl try to say something awful without saying it?

"I think she'd come to me with that," Maggie replied.

"Maybe," the girl shrugged. "But it's worth asking. And she was — is — Catholic, right?"

"Yes," Maggie said. "Yes, she is. And I'll check, thank you."

When they were finished, she called Kaplan and was surprised when he picked up the phone.

"I was just about to call you," he said.

"Really? Why?"

"Well, you called me, so you go first."

"I was wondering if you'd contacted the health center on campus."

"I have," he said.

"Oh," she said.

"Sorry to take away the pleasure of you yelling at me."

"Well, what did you find out?"

"Emma made an appointment last week but didn't show up."

"An appointment for what?"

"She didn't say."

"She didn't say, or they wouldn't tell you?"

"Judging from the intelligence of the person I spoke to, it's hard to answer. But there are HIPAA laws protecting patients. So we don't know if she needed a flu shot or a shrink."

"She had a flu shot."

"Okay."

"So . . . why were you calling me?"

"We got partial handprints in Emma's room that didn't belong to one of the girls."

"But that could mean anything, right? It could mean a party."

"If there had been a party, there would have been multiple handprints and finger-prints. And the, uh, position of these prints would indicate an intimacy."

"You're talking in code," Maggie said with a sigh.

"Above the bed," he said simply.

"Oh."

"They're not in the database, though. And there was no DNA on any of the sheets."

"So you have nothing," she said simply.

"Spoken like a cop's wife."

"Widow."

"Well, there is one thing," he said.

"Which is?"

"The reason I called it a partial and not a full was that one of the fingerprints was missing."

"And the other ones were there?"

"Yes. So we might be looking for someone with an amputated finger or a finger in a splint."

Maggie's breath caught in her throat. "What about a Band-Aid?" she asked.

TWENTY-EIGHT

EMMA

Like lots of only children, Emma had gone through a phase of wanting a sibling. Specifically a sister. And impossibly, she kept asking for an older sister. Maggie had carefully explained, without going into too much detail, that that wasn't the way things worked. Emma hadn't been happy about that. She'd seen the difference in her friends' homes: the babies crying, the toddlers grabbing at necklaces, biting fingers. But the older kids were useful. They doubled the toys, doubled the clothes, halved the blame. So a few years later, when Emma finally understood the biology of what her mother had been trying to tell her, she started a small campaign for them to adopt, or at least borrow, an older girl. She tried to be subtle yet forceful. She left Big Brothers Big Sisters literature around the house. Emma casually mentioned famous actors and singers who had been adopted. Her parents tolerated the behavior but didn't overreact. It's possible they laughed at her alone at night in the privacy of the kitchen, when they sometimes shared a snack when Frank came home from his shift. But it wasn't until high school that Emma overheard the truth from Maggie's sister, Aunt Kate. They were at a confirmation for one of Kate's children, and in the kitchen, Kate had told another woman how hard these celebrations were for her sister. There had been miscarriages, half a dozen, maybe more, before they'd simply given up on the idea. Maggie's body and mind couldn't take any more, and she took birth control pills, church be damned. The friend had nodded and said she didn't blame her. "I'd like to see how the pope holds up after six miscarriages," she'd said.

Emma had stood in the doorway, stunned. How had she been so insensitive, so unaware? How her mom must have been in pain, real pain, so many times and she had never noticed. Her mom, who noticed every sigh, every groan. Who kissed her forehead, checking for fever at the slightest flush in her cheeks, who smoothed every stray hair on her head. Her mom who noticed everything. Emma, who noticed nothing.

She thought of all these things as she tore through Fiona's half of the room. Opening drawers, rifling through clothes, looking for . . . what, exactly? Mementoes? Love letters from the men? That was ridiculous. No one kept those things anymore. Or did they? She had no sisters, so she didn't really know what girls held on to and what they threw away. What was normal? What wasn't?

In addition to these deficits, Emma wasn't very good at being deceitful, at sneaking, at hiding. She had no small witness, no companion who could turn on her. And that was probably the reason she'd forgotten to lock the door. So she didn't hear the cue of a key turning. She missed the soft sweep of an unlocked door opening and the tiptoe of Fiona walking down to her room, high heels in her hand, because at last, her feet were killing her.

"What the fuck are you doing?" Fiona said calmly, a little too calmly, from the doorway.

"I . . . lost my necklace," Emma said dumbly.

"And you thought I would steal your necklace?"

Fiona touched her own neck as she said it, which was adorned by an elaborate gold bib, studded with colorful stones that picked up the aqua of her dress.

Emma's only necklaces were a cross and a small pearl pendant.

"No, I thought it got mixed in. By accident."

"Uh huh. Sure. You know, Emma, if you want to borrow my clothes for a special occasion or something, you could have tried asking instead of stealing."

"I'm not stealing." Emma felt her skin going pink, hot.

"Oh, you're not? So then you're one of those girls who gets off on other girls' underwear?"

"No."

"Well, you could have asked. If that's your thing, then that's your thing. I'm not judging you. Not like you constantly judge me."

"I don't judge you."

"Please. All your condescending innocent questions at night. Not all of us grow up with silver spoons in our mouths like Taylor. Some of us need to earn money."

"I'm not, I mean —"

"There's no shame in needing to earn money, Emma."

"I never said there was."

"And just because I don't want to wash people's fucking hair all day only to end up so poor, I need a scholarship for my daughter —"

"Wait," Emma said. "Are you kidding me right now? Now who's being judgmental?"

"Well, at least I'm not a thief. What would your mommy think about you stealing? You planning to sell something on eBay, huh, thief?"

The shove to her shoulder caught her by surprise. Fiona was surprisingly strong, and Emma nearly fell back against the bed. The look on Fiona's face was different than she'd ever seen, contorted.

"Fiona, I'm sorry. I shouldn't have touched your dresser. I should have asked. I —"

"Woulda shoulda coulda. Well, it's too late now. You broke the dorm code. And you have to pay the price."

Fiona picked up the phone and started to text.

"No, please, I'm sorry. Please don't call the RA. I —"

Fiona laughed and shook her head like she was a dog, shaking off unwanted water. Quickly, easily, instinctively.

"Oh, Emma," she said. "I would never trust our dipshit RA with this information. I am summoning a more appropriate tribunal to try to decide what to do."

"Tribunal?"

"Oh, I'm sorry. I meant your other roommates. I didn't mean to use such a big word. I guess Jason hasn't taught you that one yet?"

Twenty-Nine

MAGGIE

When Valet to the Stars was finally available to speak, it was five o'clock. Maggie had asked to meet him in person, and he was reluctant, said he only had an hour break. But she needed to look him in the eye. She needed to make sure he had all his fingers. Maggie knew better than to try to drive downtown at rush hour, so she took the subway and walked. It had been years, five at least, since she'd been on public transportation. She'd almost forgotten the damp, warm cloud that always enveloped you while waiting on the platform. The weird combination of smells — sweat and urine, perfume and oil — that melded in the air. That it could still be so warm belowground in the fall that your scalp could throw sweat and your knees could buckle if you didn't sit down. The lights on the cars so bright, they could be used to torture prisoners. Maggie had grown soft. This was what living in the suburbs could do to you. The comfort of her own vehicle parked outside her door. All her walking now confined to her salon. Weeks would go by before she even remembered the world outside her door, much less the world she used to inhabit downtown.

She walked, swaying, toward a seat near the middle of the car. But as she was about to sit, she realized the car was filled with students, and she had a clutch of posters in her purse. She jostled between all the young people who were standing, asking if they'd seen Emma, forcing them to pull their earbuds out and answer, most of them shaking their heads. A few said she looked familiar. A few took the poster and said they'd ask around. There were kind people in the world, Maggie reminded herself. There were observant people, too, she knew, nosy people, people who worried and noticed and worried some more. In South Philly, where she'd grown up, there were plenty of people like that, keeping watch on the block. Where were those people now? *All I need is one,* she thought. *Just one.*

Mr. Valet had asked to meet at a pizza place near Chestnut Street. It was the kind of hole-in-the-wall that sold slices and sodas and nothing else. How they could afford their rent at those prices was an equation Maggie couldn't solve without a conspiracy theory involving drugs or the mafia. When she went inside, she was relieved to see that the men making pies spoke Greek, but less relieved when she saw that Michael looked to be Italian. *An Italian kid from South Philly who loves cars,* she thought immediately. *Here's hoping he also loves his mother.*

"Thank you for meeting with me," she said and sank into a red plastic chair.

"Thank you for being patient." Two pizza crusts lingered on a paper plate in front of him, and he wiped his hands on a tiny napkin, then extended one to shake. All his fingers completely intact.

She shook his hand, looked into his large, doe-like eyes, and told the story she'd practiced in her head, just to see what he'd do.

"My daughter is missing, and I need to create a fund-raiser for the reward," she said in a rush.

"Oh gosh," he said. "Do you need me to donate my services, then? Because depending on the day, I can work it myself and do that."

The tears sprang to her eyes. This unexpected kindness. This earnestness. His mouth dropped open a tiny bit at the sight of her tears, and he hastily offered her a napkin. She took it, dabbing her eyes, breathing in its lingering, familiar scent of oregano and tomato. This boy could not be a suspect. Not a psychopath, not a stranger, not part of a car theft ring Emma had uncovered on campus. No. No, no, no. She knew it in her bones. And she knew, just as suddenly, that she couldn't lie to him. Not him. Not today.

"I'm very sorry, Michael," she continued. "There actually may or may not be a fund-raiser, I'm not precisely sure. I just, um . . ."

He waited, nodded. Didn't leave, didn't demand an answer, didn't ask why she was wasting his time on the only break he got between 7:00 a.m. and 11:00 p.m.

"There's just a lot of confusion around her disappearance, and I found some names I didn't recognize in her phone. And yours was one of them. And I wondered if you worked together somehow or how you might have crossed paths. Or if you might have seen her heading somewhere."

She trailed off, blew her nose into the napkin.

"What's your daughter's name?"

"Emma," she said. "Emma O'Farrell."

He shrugged. "I don't know her."

"Maybe you met at a bar, forgot her name?"

"No, no, I don't drink."

"You don't drink?"

"Well, sometimes I'll toast at a wedding, but otherwise, no. She probably was planning an event and called the company? Or intended to. That's probably why."

"She was a college student."

"I do plenty of college events. Lots of colleges in the area with high-rolling donors. They tip really well."

"I bet they do," she said, smiling. He was one of those young men who still had the little boy in him — eager, wide eyes shining through. Easy to imagine him playing with Matchbox cars, pretending to rev their engines, running them up and down the kitchen counter to his mother's chagrin.

"Could you just take a look?" she said as she fumbled in her purse for the envelope of posters. "Maybe it'll jog something?"

She held the paper out toward him, just as he'd offered her the napkin, but he didn't take it. It was still in the air, moving, when he whispered, "Mary. Oh no."

"Mary?"

"She didn't tell me her real name. She was trying to be all cool, and then she confessed that it wasn't her real name, but she never told me. Emma? It's Emma?"

"Yes."

"Wow, that fits her totally. Better than Mary."

"Mary is my mother's name," Maggie said.

"Oh, no offense."

"None taken."

"She, um . . . We met up a few times. We had dinner the last time."

"When was this?"

"Last Wednesday."

"Wednesday," she repeated. "Okay. You're sure?"

"Yeah, because that's the day I work late at the store."

"Store?"

"Beck's, on Chestnut," he said. "I have a regular contract with them," he added proudly.

Maggie had never been to the store but knew it by reputation. An expensive men's store with a small women's department, too. They were known for impeccable service and tailoring that catered to Philadelphia's elite. And apparently provided valet parking.

"Did she work there? At the store?"

Maggie was embarrassed that she didn't know. Had her daughter taken a job?

Needed money? Wanted clothes? She thought of Emma's roommates, the casual way they dressed, with shirts tucked in the front just so and designer flannel shirts tied around their skinny jeans. Those clothes could cost a fortune, she knew. Once, she'd complimented a girl at the salon on her plaid shirt, and she'd said she bought it at a boutique around the corner. Maggie went there to try it on, and it was $189. Soft, beautiful, perfectly draped, but still. She'd taken it off quickly, before she got used to it.

"No, she was doing research."

"For a class?"

"No, for a story."

There it was again. The goddamned story. The story that hadn't been written. The story with notes in a backpack that wasn't in her room. The story only Emma knew.

"Please, Michael," she said with a sigh, "do you know what the story was about?"

"Yes. It was a secret, though, so you can't tell anyone."

"Well, I might have to tell the police," she said.

"But they won't tell, like, the public, right? Or the school?"

"No. I highly doubt it. But why? Why does that matter?"

"Well, at first, I thought it was because it's a scoop."

"A scoop?"

"Yeah, an exclusive? She didn't want anyone else at school to write it."

"Well, that hardly seems important now."

"I agree. But then I saw that she didn't trust the school. She thought maybe they were in on it."

"Whoa," Maggie said. "You've got to back up a bit."

"Okay," he said. He told her everything he knew — about the private club, the escorts, the comings and goings of cars that arrived with men and left with men and girls. That Emma had wanted to interview the girls but was having trouble finding one to go on the record. That she had tried to get a job there as a hostess, that she liked the manager and trusted him, but that Michael had told her he thought that was a bad idea, too dangerous. But that her editor thought it was a good idea. Maggie had nodded her assent; Michael had a good head on his shoulders. And she thought, once again, that she wanted to murder the editor with her bare hands.

"So, where did you come in?" she asked when he took a break. "How did you help her?"

"Well, first, she wanted to use our cars for surveillance."

"Surveillance?" Maggie took in a sharp breath. She thought of Frank, of his brothers and father, of the long history of police work in his family. And she thought that if, at the end of all this, Emma got the crime-solving bug and left school to join the force, she might actually become physically ill. She said a prayer not just for her daughter's safety but for her sanity. She'd seen first-hand how the chase was a kind of drug. The adrenaline of the first hunch, then the slow gathering, the momentum, leading to the shining, throbbing confidence of knowing. Then it came again, the cherry on top — the swagger of justice. That's what fed a cop. Not donuts. Being right. Knowing, proving, solving.

"Yeah," he said. "But I talked her out of that. I wasn't sure what it would prove except identifying people. And what was she going to do then, run their license plates, track them down, and blackmail them until they talked to her? It sounded like a bad strategy."

"Well, it's a good strategy for a cop with a gun and force behind him, but a bad strategy for a kid with a pen."

"Agree, one hundred percent. So I found

a guy for her to interview. Former member. Nice guy. Thought he'd give her all the detail she needed."

"Did your guy have all ten fingers?"

"Excuse me?"

"The cops want to interview someone who might be missing a finger."

"Whoa," he said. "Like *The Fugitive.* The one-armed man. 'I did not kill my wife.' 'I don't care!' "

Maggie smiled back. Her skin almost cracked going into position; it felt like the first time she had smiled in a year.

"My husband always said Tommy Lee Jones's character did care. He was just tired, and it didn't matter at that moment. It was his job to capture him."

"I agree with that assessment."

"You like movies," she said.

He nodded. "I do. That's the first thing I thought when your daughter approached me, that it sounded like a movie."

It was a relief to be sitting in a warm diner, the scent of dough bubbling in a hot oven, talking about movies with someone. She felt her shoulders soften downward, settling in like resting wings. Maybe she didn't have to be charging ahead every second to find Emma, not resting, not eating. Maybe Maggie would find her by what happened

286

here, in the in-between.

"So," he said, "fingers. Yes. I can picture his hands on his steering wheel. All ten of them. I remember now because he had a deep tan and a little white stripe where he'd taken his wedding ring off."

"Oh boy," she said.

"No, it wasn't like that. He was a widow. He was lonely. It was his friend's idea."

"Every bad idea is always someone's friend's idea, isn't it?"

"You sound like my mother," he said and smiled. "But I know Mary — I mean Emma? She came up with this idea herself. She put the pieces together. No one handed it to her."

"Yeah, the part of me that isn't angry and isn't terrified? That part of me is a little proud," Maggie said ruefully.

"Here's the guy's name and phone number," Michael said, digging out his phone. "You ready?"

"Wait, did he drive a Maserati by chance?"

"Yes."

"I have that number already, I think. Unless there's another guy with that car."

"There's only two other people you might want to talk to," he said. "The guy who manages the place? Sam? She interviewed with him as a hostess. He didn't have any openings, but get this — she actually liked him."

"Great," she said. "A charming pimp finds out she's onto him."

"Maybe. Maybe not. I sensed she had pretty good taste in people. Also there was one of her professors she thought was involved. She wasn't sure. She just was worried about it. I don't know his name, though."

"Okay. What about — did you get the sense she had a boyfriend? She didn't tell me, and I've gotten conflicting reports. Maybe it was just someone she was hooking up with? Maybe it was casual, and she didn't want to say."

"I . . . don't think she's the hooking-up type, to be honest."

"Look, we raised her in the church, but I'm a realist, a modern woman. Also, she had an appointment at the health clinic she didn't keep. She could be pregnant and afraid to tell me, and —"

"No. That is not what is happening."

"How do you know?"

"It's a little weird, and I don't mean to embarrass you."

"Embarrass me? Trust me, Michael, the things I've done in the last few days? What I've stooped to? I'm miles beyond embarrassment."

"When we were talking about trying to go undercover and, you know, act like one of those sugar babies, like her editor wanted her to?"

"Yes?"

"Well, she thought it would be weird for her because she was, you know, a virgin."

"Really?" Maggie felt a sliver of pride. There had been a couple of boys in high school Emma had "dated" for a few months, and Maggie had always wondered. Wondered how it progressed, wondered why it ended exactly.

"Oh man, she blushed, like neon pink when she told me. I felt so bad for her. Like she'd never told anybody, and here she'd told someone she hardly knew."

"I think that's the whole point, though," Maggie said. "If you happen to be a virgin, you use that information to kind of hold back men you hardly know. You tell lots of people."

He blinked. "Well, I don't think that she — I wasn't coming on to her or anything. I don't think that's why she told me. She just needed to talk, I think."

"Maybe."

"Yeah, she said she had a tiny bit of PTSD about sex, because once, she'd walked in on her fa—"

"Wow." Maggie cut him off. "Whoa, whoa, whoa, I didn't know. Oh my goodness. She never told me. I never saw her! She didn't make a peep!"

"Well, you were kinda busy," he said with a small laugh. "Yeah," he said. "Sex can be traumatizing when you're young. Looks kind of angry."

"Yes," she said, and she thought of Frank then, his swagger extending to the bedroom sometimes. Convincing her. Cajoling. Some would say manipulating, but he would never think so. He'd just think he was being charming. That was the problem with charm, when it spilled over the edge of sweet and became just another tool to have exactly what you wanted all the time.

"Wow. Well, Michael, you've been very helpful. I really appreciate it." As they stood to leave, she touched his arm. "You used the phrase 'go undercover.' Do you think maybe she's doing that now? We're all worried that someone took her or that someone found out, but maybe, could she be disguised or pretending or —"

"It's hard to say. I wish I knew her better," he said wistfully.

She saw it in his eyes. The missed connections, the if-onlys. The things that kept you up at night about the one who got away. The strange position of liking a girl, knowing her only a little, yet sensing multitudes.

She wanted to know, suddenly, of how they met, what she looked like, what she was wearing. She knew if she asked Michael, asked him right now, he would remember every detail, down to the color of Emma's shoes. She also knew, if she asked, how desperately sad it would feel. Like she was asking for a last glimpse. Like he was painting the last portrait of a ghost. She swallowed it down, this morbid impulse to know. She had to stop thinking these thoughts. They weren't helping. She'd seen them on TV, these crazy mothers who insisted they'd know if their daughter was dead. Saying they felt her life force. That they knew she was out there, breathing somewhere, and that if they could just reach the person who'd taken her, they could talk him into giving her back. And here Maggie was, one of them. One of them thinking the exact same thing. *I know she's alive. I know it.* Was she the exception to the rule or the rule?

"But if I had to guess, based on my hunch? I think she's hiding."

"Hiding?"

"Hiding and watching."

"Without her phone?"

"I know your generation thinks we're addicted to them and all, but the real question is, did she leave her computer behind?"

"No."

"Well, then," he said. "She's writing."

"She's writing," she repeated dumbly.

Of course she was. She was working on a story; that much everyone agreed on. She was somewhere, hiding and writing and waiting for all of it to come together. And writing could take a while, couldn't it? There could be more to the story. People she needed to interview who didn't know she was missing. Places she needed to investigate. A new thought struck Maggie with almost a physical blow — did she need to travel somewhere to talk to someone? Was something happening in another city? And couldn't they check Emma's debit card to help them figure that out?

A text buzzed on her phone. Kaplan, asking to meet in an hour.

She excused herself from Michael, saying she needed to go, but agreed to keep in touch. She held out her hand to shake his goodbye, and he opened his arms instead.

Those young arms, spread out with the warmth and compassion of an older man, were like a benediction to her. How long had it been, she thought, as she leaned in to him, since someone had hugged her without her offering, without her opening her arms first?

THIRTY

EMMA

Emma couldn't help thinking, weirdly, of history books and Bibles. The photos and drawings and diary accounts she'd seen of tarring and feathering. Of stoning women. Of throwing witches into the sea to see if they'd drown. The rituals of history, of the church, the sins of the past, and now, here she was, in a circle. Judge and jury of mean girls staring back at her. Guilty and not guilty at the same time. But who could see that, other than her? By keeping this all to herself, close to the vest, she had no allies.

She sat in her own living room in a butterfly chair that was only comfortable if you were drunk or five years old, surrounded not by rocks to be thrown or matches to burn her at the stake but by empty, red Solo cups, a few spent Juul pods, and a stack of brown, recycled napkins they'd stolen from Starbucks instead of buying some. The knives stayed in the drawers. The scissors remained in their desks. No weapons, and yet she felt the threat. The threat was beyond the physical. These girls wanted to ruin her life, not her body.

"So, in Saudi Arabia," Fiona said to the group, "they cut off people's hands for stealing."

"I didn't steal anything," Emma said hotly. "Check my pockets. Check my desk."

She knew only one thing for certain: none of these girls were stupid enough to cut off her hand. In fact, all her assumptions about their intelligence levels were starting to shift. It was possible that every one of them was smarter than she'd assumed, grades aside. That was the thing — grades were a terrible measure of intelligence. Emma's father used to say that whenever she got a B. But then she'd always think, *does that mean my A means nothing? Does that mean all my hard work doesn't matter to you?*

"You didn't steal because I walked in on you before you had found something you wanted."

"No."

"If you weren't stealing her stuff," Annie said, "then what were you doing?"

"Maybe she has a panty fetish," Taylor said. "It's a thing."

Was that supposed to be a lifeline? If Emma presented herself at that moment as a lesbian panty eater, was she in the clear?

"Ew," Morgan said.

"Well, whatever you were doing, it ends tonight."

"Okay."

"We can't trust you anymore."

"Look," Emma said nervously, "I was just snooping. I don't have sisters. I never had a roommate." She looked at Taylor imploringly, eyes widening. She was the smartest, the most reasonable. Would she please just stand up to Fiona?

"You never went to camp?" Annie said, and Emma thought, of course that's her reference. Didn't everyone go to camp? Didn't everyone sleep in a tent and sing around the campfire?

"No, Annie. Camp costs quite a bit of money."

"It does?" Annie looked at Morgan, who shrugged. And there was the least intelligent of the group.

The glance Taylor gave Annie, with just a whiff of derision, spoke volumes. They weren't that united, this group. Taylor wasn't really like any of them. She just liked drama, Emma thought. And if that was the case, maybe Emma could make her come

around. Wasn't an explosive story the ulti-
mate drama? Wouldn't Taylor love to be
Deep Throat if she got the chance?

"Well, I don't want you in my room
anymore," Fiona said.

"Well, we're not switching," Morgan
added. "We don't want her either."

Emma thought about offering to transfer
to another dorm, but that wouldn't help her
with her story. But if they told the RA she
was stealing, she'd be expelled.

"Give me your room key," Fiona said.

"Where am I supposed to sleep?"

"You can keep the key to the main door,
and you are welcome to stay on the couch.
Where we can see you."

"What about my stuff?"

"Well, turnabout's fair play, right?"

"What?"

"We'll go through it and decide what you
can keep. Starting with your phone."

"My phone?" Emma thought of the two
phones in her backpack, which glowed in
her mind as if being x-rayed, as if they were
bombs.

Fiona put out her hand, wiggling her
fingers impatiently, like there was an electric
current in them, jangling. She was always in
a hurry, on her own schedule. Tapping her
foot outside the bathroom, gritting her teeth

waiting for their turquoise Keurig to brew. Emma decided to take her time.

Emma unzipped the backpack carefully, listening to the sound, enjoying it just a little. She loved knowing the burner phone was in a separate pocket, hidden by a book and her laptop. The value of an old backpack — no one knew its tricks. No one wanted to touch it. And no one expected little Emma O'Farrell to have anything to hide.

She dug around for her iPhone as if she didn't know precisely where it was. She brandished it slowly, a bit dramatically, as if she couldn't bear to part with it.

The look on Fiona's face transformed her. She didn't look pretty anymore. Her features were pointed. Without bronzer and contour, she had no cheekbones. Her eyes were set too close together, and when she squinted, as she did at Emma's phone, they almost looked cross-eyed. Were these thoughts true revelation or retaliation? Was it Emma's brain's way of getting back at her, seeing her clearly, judging her? Maybe.

Her mother used to say it derisively about people on the covers of magazines or on TV: *She's all hair. She's nothing without that hair.* For who would know that better than her mother, who saw women at their most vulnerable, hair darker and wet and flat against their heads like animals? Their features either fell away or stood out. The hair protected them, shiny and glinting, catching the eye first. You had to look more closely to see what a person was actually made of. Now Emma actually looked. And now she saw how right her mother was. Fiona was nothing without that hair and those high heels. She was just a scrawny, pinched girl with long legs, doing the best she could, using what she had. Legs and hair, legs and hair. Emma almost felt sorry for her. How far could one person travel with only two assets?

They left her on the couch, and she could hear them behind the door in her room, opening drawers, laughing. Shoes hit the ground. Hangers swung. Were they trying on her clothes? Taking pictures? She didn't know whether they were laughing at her clothes or the few contacts and photos left on her phone, and she didn't particularly want to know. It almost seemed like performance art, the way Taylor followed and Annie and Morgan trailed behind. A show. A production. Borrowed clothes, posing, like something they'd do at summer camp. Emma thought of the first girl at school who'd worn a bra in third grade. A chubby girl named Amber, a dark, greasy girl who didn't match the magic of that name. The boys had found out, had bribed a girl to ferret the bra out during gym class when they were swimming. They'd looped it over Amber's locker, and she had to go the whole day without it until she found it, breasts swinging, her small nipples poking from beneath her white polo shirt. Was that all her roommates were doing now? Some version of that? She didn't know. But she had a feeling she wouldn't have to wait long to find out.

She tried to settle in on the small, stiff, cotton-covered sofa. She listened to the flat notes of her roommates' laughter down the hall, the only music now. She thought of Cara Stevens, working at the *Inquirer*, in an office filled with books and files and silence. Her bosses hadn't supported what she was doing. But at least they weren't trying on her clothes and making her sleep on a sofa. And if Cara's peers were laughing at her and thinking she was an idiot, at least they weren't doing it in front of her, within earshot. There was something to be said for people doing things behind your back. Sometimes, you just didn't want to know.

THIRTY-ONE

MAGGIE

It was a long walk from Eighteenth and Chestnut to the precinct, but the weather was cool, and the trees to the north, lining the parkway, were starting to turn colors, and Maggie decided she needed the air. She would cut over to Broad Street eventually, when the neighborhood turned more transitional, but for now, she just looked at the stores, the window boxes outside the restaurants, the trees dotting the sidewalk in heavy planters. There were other people walking in a city, always, moving through their lives like nothing was the matter. Frank used to take long walks, trying to puzzle out his cases, walking through their suburban neighborhood, the only person without a dog or a stroller or a cigarette. Everyone walks now, for their health, but for many years in Ardmore, no one did unless they had a reason. And Frank's reasons were all internal and more numerous than Maggie had bargained for. Did he call Salt during those walks or just think of her? Maggie had suspected a girlfriend existed before she knew; Frank had started going to the gym, had bought new underwear. Weren't those the classic signs? Once she'd caught him using her eye cream, dotting it on the creases that appeared at the corners of his eyes, and she'd laughed at him, told him that he should have started twenty years ago, wearing sunscreen. That nothing could help him now, it was too late. She felt sick, thinking of those words. How right she'd been.

But now, angry as she was, she missed her husband deeply. Not because he knew better what to do — she'd learned plenty over the years after all — but because he'd go off the playbook. A mother going crazy with grief is a harridan, easy to dismiss. But a father? A cop? He was a vigilante, not to be crossed. Frank would know the exact moment to take that editor kid and twist a rep tie around his neck until he gave up his so-called sources. Frank would handcuff those roommates in a squad car for jaywalking and refuse to allow them a phone call until they confessed. Frank would make it happen. Only a slightly dirty cop, an old-school cop, could make it happen. Not Kaplan. Going by the book took time. And who had time?

Maggie cut over to Broad Street, passing a church, a school. The bell in the tower chimed as she walked by, and she wondered if Emma had thought to go to church for solace, for moral protection, for guidance. It was hard to imagine her doing so. That was what Maggie and her sister had often done as young girls, turned to quiet prayer, to reflection to guide them. Now, girls did yoga and used meditation apps. They paid money to go somewhere and float in water or nap on clean sheets. And why? When the filtered light from stained glass was there for free on nearly every corner?

Above Broad Street, Maggie passed the downsized offices of the *Inquirer,* an upscale barbecue place across from an old-school diner, a mix of new and old in this area of the city. She smiled, thinking of Frank's hatred of craft beer and artisanal burgers, his Philly accent tripping over the word *artisanal.*

By the time she reached the front door of the precinct, she was almost calm. Her blood pressure, which had seemed to do nothing but rise since she'd gotten that first visit at the salon, had settled down a bit.

Walking had calmed her, just like Frank. So she should have been ready for whatever Kaplan had to say, but the look on his face as he came up to greet her was grim.

"There have been a few developments," he said.

"Oh no," she said, her hand going up to her chest. Had her long walk been the last moment of peace she would ever find? She knew "development" could be a euphemism. Was it code for "finding a body"?

"It's okay. It's nothing definitive. But let's go to the video room."

"Video," she said dumbly.

"Are you okay? Do you need water?" He said it clinically, like a nurse, but she tried not to hold that against him.

Behind him, Salt came up and took her arm. "It's okay. Take a deep breath."

"Did you find —"

"No, no, no. We got the security camera footage back, among other things. It's going to help. We're getting closer."

"It doesn't show —"

"No."

Kaplan shot Salt a look Maggie didn't understand. Was she contradicting him? Was she just saying whatever needed to be said to calm her down and keep her from fainting?

304

Salt guided her to a room, set her down in a chair, then sat down next to her.

"You're wondering if there's violence or worried that there's blood or something you can't handle seeing," she said calmly, and Maggie swallowed hard and gave a small nod. "And there isn't. It's helpful, though, so let's go through it together and talk about it, okay?"

"Okay," she said. She drank the water they gave her.

"Unless you don't want to look? We can just describe it, but we thought you'd —"

"Yes, yes, I want to see it."

A technician came in, sat at the computer. A box of tissues nestled next to him, and that scared her, too. It all scared her. She knew some crimes were solved solely on the basis of security footage. People forgot the cameras were there. People thought they were in disguise. People were stupid, and cameras were smart.

Maggie thought of her mother, telling her and her sister to be strong at her grandmother's funeral. She always said the best way to stop crying was to pretend you were drinking something through a straw and holding it in. It had worked, but it also meant she and her sister had walked around the funeral home with pursed lips all day. It was one thing for a girl to cry over a death and another for a mother to cry over evidence. She didn't want to be that woman, but she was that woman. She was that girl, and now she was that woman, scared and sad with a reservoir full of unshed tears.

They said the first view they had was outside Lenape Library. There was footage that was clearly Emma, arriving late morning, leaving before dinner, almost every day. The times were slightly different, but nothing else. She looked pretty, clean, neatly dressed. Completely normal except she wasn't smiling. She didn't look unhappy exactly, but the word *businesslike* occurred to Maggie. That, and though she passed lots of clusters of kids, she was always alone, with her backpack. The inside camera showed she walked past the tables of study groups and went to the computer area.

"We have this same basic footage for almost two weeks. It coincides with the date of her second meeting with the editor and ends the day before she is reported missing. So we're confident that Sarah Franco got the timeline right. And while it's reassuring to see her looking perfectly fine, it was initially worrisome, because she has a clear routine and schedule. If anyone wanted to follow her, it was easy to know where she would be."

"Do you see any evidence of anyone following her?"

"No," Kaplan said with a sigh. "We've been through it thoroughly and don't see anyone behaving suspiciously. And no one who repeats any of the days."

"Which is good," Salt added.

"It could be interpreted that way," Kaplan said. "Bad for the investigation maybe, but good for her welfare."

Maggie thought perhaps that was all she could ask for. Not that she could know or that they could all figure it out. It didn't have to make sense. As long as Emma was alive, it could make no sense. She'd have to remember that, to fight the urge to put the pieces together. The pieces didn't matter. Only her daughter did.

"We wonder if she's not working on her own laptop because she's doing something private, for the story she is researching. It seems a little cautious, but that's what people who are hiding something do."

Maggie nodded. That made sense to her. And the fact that that's what criminals also did to cover their tracks wasn't lost on her either. She knew Kaplan had to be thinking that, too. She also knew journalists sometimes broke laws to pursue stories, but they weren't usually freshmen in college.

"There is also no log-in under her name, but there is under Sarah Franco's. Do you think the two friends might have had a beef?"

"No, no —"

"Okay, maybe they were working together?"

"No, that's probably just being secretive again. She needed to log in with someone else's info."

"Okay, one more thing. This also might be because her laptop was stolen or damaged."

"No," Maggie said. "If she needed it repaired or replaced, she would have called me. We have AppleCare."

Salt and Kaplan exchanged another look, and Salt began to speak. Maggie saw what was happening now, a version of good cop/bad cop. Boy cop/girl cop. Salt stepped in whenever there was something difficult to explain or deliver. Like she was interpreting. Like she was giving Maggie the mom version. But what did she know, this woman without children? It was both helpful and irritating at the same time.

"Well, we ask because there's another video we're concerned about. We thought you might have some insight into it."

"Okay," she said slowly.

"It's outside the trash bins in your daughter's dorm."

"Oh God," Maggie said.

Salt patted her arm. "You can do this," she said. "It's okay, I promise."

The tech pressed more buttons, then sat back. Three girls taking the trash out. Fiona, Taylor, Morgan.

"Those appear to be your daughter's roommates."

"Yes," she said. "Everyone but Annie."

Fiona carried a large black garbage bag, the others, smaller shopping bags.

The girls were laughing, lighthearted. Not the grim faces of someone who had committed a crime. Not the nervous glances of someone afraid to be caught.

"The bag looks light," Maggie said with relief. Not a body. Not parts of a body. Even these girls weren't stupid enough to dispose of a person in their dorm hallway and laugh while they were doing it. They were idiots; they weren't killers.

"Yes," Kaplan replied. "We think it's your daughter's clothes."

"Why?"

"Go in on that tote bag," he said to the tech.

The picture sprang to life, detailed. She

could see the fibers, if not the correct colors, of the plaid sleeve.

"Same pattern she was wearing at the library," he said.

"Is it?"

"We think so. Go back."

The technician went back to the Tuesday footage from the library. Plaid shirt. Brown and green. Tucked in the front, loose in the back. The tails lifted in the breeze.

"She loved that shirt," Maggie said simply. "Loves," she corrected. "Loves."

She remembered Emma buying it, bringing it home. It was soft, rayon, purchased on sale at American Eagle, and Maggie had worried that it had to be dry-cleaned. She worried Emma would take it to college, shrink it in an old-fashioned laundromat on high heat. That she'd forget, be in a hurry, not take care of it. That someone would steal it and throw it away because she loved it? Yes, it was safe to say that had never occurred to her.

"Of course, it might be a coincidence," Kaplan said.

"No, I don't think so." Maggie said. For once, she and Kaplan agreed. "We found her room empty."

"Yes. And her roommates said they had no idea why."

She turned to Kaplan. "How stupid are they? Do they not see the cameras? How did girls this dumb get accepted at college?"

Kaplan smiled. A rare sight. "If there's one thing you learn quick, being a cop, it's that people are never as smart as they think they are. Never. Especially kids."

"So what is this? Is this theft? Is it tampering with evidence?"

"It's taking out the trash," Kaplan replied. "At least that's what they're going to say."

"So, the bigger issue," Salt said haltingly, "is if they'd throw away her favorite shirt as a prank and take her phone, which was in Fiona's drawer, what's to keep them from taking her computer?"

"Especially," Kaplan added, "if it was important to her. If she was, in fact, working on a story that mattered to her, and they knew that."

"Wait, did you say 'prank'?"

They were silent. It had been a bad choice of words.

"Is that really what you think this is? Stealing her stuff and throwing it away?"

"It doesn't matter yet what we think," Kaplan said. "It matters what we can prove and identify."

"Have you checked the other garbage

bins? In the other dorms? Or the dump-sters?"

"We're doing that," he replied.

"I think," Maggie said, "not that it really matters, that in that library footage, her laptop is in her backpack. And some of that is time-stamped after this, right?"

They went back to the other footage. Maggie pointed to the backpack, how the edges sank down, heavier.

"That could be a book," Kaplan said.

"A book as big as a laptop? No, Maggie's right," Salt said.

He sighed deeply, as if he didn't like be-ing told by two different women someone else was right. Maggie was used to that from Frank; that rankled a cop more than any-thing, finding out they were wrong. It was what bothered the force the most about cold cases, new DNA techniques. That someone would sweep in later and tell them they were wrong. Because being right was what a cop was all about.

"We also retrieved some deleted images from her phone," Kaplan said.

Maggie didn't think it was possible for the blood in her veins to actually go cold, but she swore she felt it turn. Didn't Kaplan re-alize that his measured tones and vague sentences were more ominous than being enthusiastic and direct? She wouldn't be nearly as frightened if he would just be himself. And then, a more chilling thought — maybe he was. Maybe this measured man was all there was to him. Maybe he wasn't covering anything, wasn't holding anything back. He was what he appeared to be.

"What type of images?"

She was prepared for his answer, or so she thought. She had never caught Emma or her friends doing anything sexual or aggressive with a camera, but you can't parent a girl, go all the way through high school with her or, God forbid, middle school without hearing the stories. Of videos passed around boy to boy. Of girls playing strip poker over Skype to a whole team of football players. You didn't have to go to the same parties or even be in the same room to have something terrible happen to a girl. And it all began on the phone.

"Well," Salt said, taking in a deep breath. "It seems one of her roommates stole more than Emma's clothes."

"Just tell me," Maggie said firmly. "Did she hurt her?"

"Only her pride," Salt said. "Remember the partial handprint above the bed?"

"Yes."

"Fiona had a visitor, filmed it, and shared

313

a screen grab of that video with Emma."

She pulled a photo out of a file. It was taken from a height, above the bed on the right side of the room. A naked boy, on top of Fiona, his hands against the wall for leverage. A boy with one finger bandaged.

"Jason," Kaplan said.

"Future Husband," Salt said.

"Oh my God," Maggie said.

"We're bringing her in for questioning," Salt said.

"No," Maggie said.

"No?"

"You need to talk to him," she said.

THIRTY-TWO

EMMA

They gave her back her phone, three pairs of underwear, two pairs of jeans, two worn T-shirts she usually wore to bed, and an oversized cardigan sweater everyone else thought was ratty but that she loved. With the weather turning colder and frost on the grass, that was actually the best thing they could have done. She was certain they thought it was fashion punishment, but it was an accidental act of cozy kindness. She also found a dark-green jacket in the hall closet that they'd forgotten to search, so she was set until it snowed. She thought they'd locked the rest in her room, but she wasn't sure, or maybe they'd divided the cutest things among them or sold it all on eBay or burned it in a pyre while chanting her name. She didn't know, and on some level, she didn't care. She was mortified at first, embarrassed by her stupidity, then flat-out afraid. Afraid they'd tell the RA, afraid they'd tell everyone, that they'd use it against her somehow. But then, she saw the mistake they'd made.

She missed her flannel shirt and her long yellow dress that was as comfortable as pajamas, but other than that, she wasn't that attached to anything. They'd made a critical error, thinking she was like they were. That she cared about clothing and jewelry, how she looked. Of course they would think that, these shallow girls who thought sex work was harnessing their own power. Fiona and her merry band of followers.

There was something freeing about fitting everything into a backpack. It was like living in a tiny house or traveling through Europe. You pared down, and then you could go anywhere. The couch was just the beginning.

Because she didn't intend to stay on the couch for long. She would find Jason, and he would help her find refuge while she was writing the piece and interviewing Mr. Maserati. He probably lived off campus, in an apartment, with a bunch of other guys. They'd have no room for her, but they'd know other people. Senior girls who were too smart for the kind of bullshit she was going through.

Emma was looking forward to meeting with Mr. Maserati later that night and seeing Michael afterward. He'd suggested going out for a late supper, and she'd said no, warning him that she was going to be casually dressed, and he'd countered with pizza or a burger, and she'd laughed and said maybe. That kid did not take no for an answer, which reminded her, in a weird way, of her dad. All the more reason to keep him at a distance. She was at college, and she had to be focused on people there.

She'd called Jason and left a message, told him she had an update for him, and he'd texted her back a few hours later and agreed to meet in the journalism building.

She was starving, so she went to the dining hall first and ate a bagel with cream cheese, just half, in case he wanted to grab a meal with her. Something to tide her over either way.

As she sat down, a short girl with a tight head of black curls pulled into a ponytail, a girl she recognized vaguely from one of her classes, walked by with a shirt tied around her waist. Emma's shirt. Brown-and-green plaid.

"Hey," she called out, and the girl turned. "I don't mean to be weird, but did a girl give you that shirt?"

"My boyfriend found it in a dumpster," she said. "He does work-study as a janitor."

"Yeah, it's actually my shirt."

"What? Are you sure, or are you just doing random walkabouts to get shirts?"

"I'm in your history class. I've worn it, like, a thousand times."

The girl blinked at her, considering, and Emma blinked back. Was this girl truly poor and more worthy of the shirt? Should she back off or press on?

"Then why did you throw it out?"

"Someone else did. My roommates are assholes."

The girl cocked her head, sizing her up. Then she untied the sleeves and handed it over. "It needs to be washed. It smells like Chinese food."

"Wow, thanks for understanding."

"My roommates are assholes, too."

"Freshman?"

"Sophomore, and you know what that means."

"Yeah, it means it's not going to get better."

"Hey, you have any classes in the liberal arts building?"

"Yeah, why?"

"You ever see the bathroom on the first floor, in the back? There's, like, a shower in

318

there. And a sofa. The teachers use it because it's near their lounge, but no one's there later. In case you need an escape valve."

"Thank you."

"College sucks," she said, and Emma smiled.

She watched the girl walk away and imagined telling her mom about this encounter. She knew exactly what good old Maggie would say. *Did you get her name and number? You could make a date for coffee, or maybe file paperwork to become roommates somewhere else? She sounds like someone with character. Someone who would be a true friend.* And she would have to explain that meeting your new BFF in the cafeteria was not a thing. The world did not work like that. Not with friends, not with boyfriends. The world was not a romantic comedy.

Emma finished her bagel and put the shirt in her backpack. It did smell vaguely of peanut sauce and red pepper, which wasn't entirely unpleasant. Funny how things that were gross and dirty could actually be not terrible if you didn't think about them too hard. She remembered a boy she knew in high school, Keegan, who had moved away. That's what he'd said about a hoagie-eating contest. That at some point you stopped

319

thinking about what you were doing and you just did it. That it was the thinking that would get you, not the doing. Life advice from a stoner. *Thank you, Keegan,* she thought.

Still, all things considered, she wondered if she shouldn't throw in a load of wash and leave it there, come back in a while to dry it, but quickly realized she couldn't afford to do things like that now. What if someone stole all the clothes she had left?

She checked for seeds in her teeth, then swiped on some lipstick, the lone pale gloss that had been in her backpack. She didn't want to look like she was trying too hard. She wanted to look cute, yes, but serious and professional. She knew she often looked serious even when she wasn't, because her whole life, people had been asking her what she was thinking about when she wasn't even thinking, wasn't worried. But professional? That was hard to achieve when you were young. When you were young and carrying all your possessions on your back like a snail.

She strode up the stairs to the journalism building, trying to feel confident. She had a story and a purpose and her favorite shirt, if nothing else. Her backpack was heavier than normal with all her clothes in it, but it wasn't more than she could handle.

When she stepped off the elevator, Jason glanced up from his desk as if he was aware of her. Aware or wary? She didn't really like the look on his face, the way he wasn't making clear eye contact when he greeted her. He led her to an empty conference room with only a sliver of a glass panel and shut the door. She remembered, at that precise moment, her father telling her that classroom doors didn't used to have glass. They used to be solid and stayed open most of the time, but when they were shut, they were shut. If a teacher needed to change clothes or argue with his wife on the phone, he could do it behind that door. But he could also do other things, and that's why, he told his daughter, when she headed off to seventh grade with her brand-new bra, they mandated the glass. Emma hadn't parsed his meaning precisely at that moment. But a few stories from older girls, a few slumber parties, a few bad romance novels later, and she understood perfectly.

Jason swallowed hard, a hangover kind of swallow, like there was bile in his throat. She knew that swallow, associated it with alcohol and boys. Still, she didn't hold it against him. He was human, wasn't he? But his glasses were smeared, too. His face had a film on it, as if he'd been working too hard in an overheated room. Or as if he'd been up all night and hadn't bothered to wash his face. He looked beautiful and terrible at the same time.

"Emily," he sighed.

"It's Emma," she said quietly.

"I'm sorry. There are so many Emilys and Emmas and Emmys on campus. Carolines and Carolyns. It's impossible."

"Maybe you need a life proofreader."

He blinked, took a deep breath. "That's funny."

"Yeah, well."

"Anyway, do you have anything yet? Because —"

She interrupted him. She told him breathlessly about Sam Beck and the free shift she offered to work, that she was sure Fiona was recruiting girls, that there were free condoms in the bathroom at London, that they owned a store that gave free clothes to girls, that she was meeting with a former patron that very evening, and that she was certain she'd been followed when she —

He held up a hand. A hand that reminded her of a professor, of a dad. Of every boy and every man who just didn't want to hear it anymore.

"So you have nothing more."

"No, I'm meeting the guy, I told you —"

"Former patron? Not current. And you don't have the hostess job, let alone posing as an escort yourself. And you don't have a girl on record. You don't have proof of recruitment. Did you even interview a psychologist? Did you talk to a gynecologist about STDs?"

"Wait, what? No, those would be general, and you told me to be specific —"

"Concrete. You need to be concrete. And you have nothing. So look for another story."

"No, I —"

"Look for another story, Emma, or get your name off the list for the paper. There are plenty of other girls dying to write for me."

"Are you hungover?" she blurted out.

"What?"

"You look . . . like crap," she said.

"Not that it's any of your business, but I've been working all night on another story. A story with documented, on-the-record sources and photographs that support it. A real story."

She blinked. She was trying to decide if she hated him. She was trying to decide if he was a true asshole or just someone who was under a lot of pressure who turned into an asshole when he was hungover and needed Advil and a cheesesteak, like a normal boy. *Just go eat some meat,* she thought. *Call me after you've scarfed down a sausage pizza and a Coke.*

"You have three days to bring me something different, or you're off the team."

"Fine," she said, standing up and hoisting her backpack against one shoulder. Forget looking cute but serious. No more cute for him. "Maybe the person who's following me will abduct me. That'll make a great story. How about that?"

"Emma," he said, like he'd already known her name and had said it a million times this same way, the way everyone said it when they were disgusted with her, when they were tired of her shit, when they thought they were right and she was wrong, exhaled it with a long, drawn-out sigh — but she was gone by then. His sigh was just a bad, sour breeze, a whiff of beer breath that followed her out.

She was almost at the library when the text came in from Fiona. She had to squint to believe what she was seeing. The photo, a bit blurry and dark but unmistakable. "Whose Future Husband?" it said beneath it.

Well, she thought, *look at this. Here's a*

photo that supports a story, Jason. A real story, a dark story, if not exactly the one she thought she was chasing.

She put her head in her hands and blinked back the tears. How stupid. How trite. Not that he would act this way. But that she had. Stupid, guileless Emma. What a freshman fucking move. How totally JV could she get, thinking he might actually like her.

THIRTY-THREE

MAGGIE

Go home and sleep, they kept saying to her. As if that was possible. As if that was preferable. Maggie swore that every time she heard those words, this time at the precinct, her feet grew heavier, locked her into place, wouldn't allow her to. Telling a worried mother to sleep as she stood in the sticky, damp hallway outside the detective's waiting room was the stupidest thing a cop could do. There had been so much soda spilled on that floor, so much mud, so much blood, that the linoleum had turned into another surface altogether. It was hard for leather soles or sneakers or any kind of shoe to even slide on it. *If you want people to leave,* she wanted to scream, *if you want people to go home and sleep, why do you make your floors like flypaper? You want to catch criminals but get rid of all the crying relatives?*

So she became part of a classic tableau, a nimbus of cliché surrounding her everywhere she went. The crying mother who didn't want to sleep in case she missed something. The mother who didn't want to go home, because she wanted to work the case herself.

Finally, they'd said something foolish. *What if your daughter comes home? Don't you want to be there?* And she'd wanted to scream and claw Salt's eyes out. Because she knew Emma wasn't going to come home, no matter how much sense it made. So as she lay awake on the sofa, trying to close her eyes and just rest — for that was all she hoped for, rest, not sleep — she kept asking herself why. Why, if Emma's roommates were bothering her, why, if she was scared and had nowhere to go, why didn't she just come back home to her mother? Salt had brought it up precisely because it made sense, made sense to anyone who thought about it for two seconds.

Emma could write her story at home. She could commute to class, not easily, not quickly, but she could have. Maggie would have made her favorite dinners — chicken parmigiana, shrimp scampi — the things she asked for on her birthday. She would have proofread for her, rubbed her shoulders when she worked all night, racing against her deadline. All Emma had had to do was tell her what was happening, and Maggie would have supported her. But Emma was stubborn; yes, she could be as stubborn as Frank when she wanted to be. Teachers called it determination and perseverance, and while it helped her push through difficult subjects and long projects, Maggie knew that's all it was — pure Irish stubbornness, as her mother would say. The world's best and worst trait, depending on what you applied it to. But still, Emma was also practical, pragmatic. So all Maggie could come up with, the only thing that made sense as she stared at her own ceiling, as if the brushstrokes of paint and the shadows from the reading lamp would point the way, was that Emma was almost finished. That she could see the endgame and just needed a few more days. If she'd been an inch away from something, so close she could taste it, she would stick it out. But what was that final piece?

Maggie replayed her conversation at the precinct again and again, projecting it across her eyelids as she lay down, rewinding it back and forth. What had she missed?

Maggie had given the police Mr. Maserati's phone number, but Kaplan said they'd already called him. They'd called everyone in Emma's phone, every single contact, he'd claimed.

"Everyone?" she'd said incredulously. That meant he was either lying to her or he had more manpower assigned; that other cops were canvassing, following up. But Michael hadn't said a thing about being contacted by the police. Michael, the Valet to the Stars? Mr. Honest? Mr. From the Old Neighborhood? Wouldn't he have told her if the cops had called him already? Or was he playing her, too?

"Are you also going door to door in the dorm?"

"Yes."

She'd sat there, not sure what to believe. Where was her surveillance footage? Where were the angles that showed the police doing exactly what Kaplan said they were doing, searching every darkened penumbra of this sprawling campus?

"Have you spoken to her professors?"

"There weren't any professors in her phone," Kaplan had said.

"That's not what I asked."

"We did an initial ask, yes."

"You have to realize," Salt said softly, "the classes at a school this size number in the hundreds. It's the first semester, and —"

"Are you telling me she hadn't been going to class at all?"

"Perhaps. Or —"

"Or what? You're telling me her own professors didn't recognize her picture?"

"It's early still. There are a lot of new faces."

"Is that what they said? Was that their excuse?"

She thought of what Michael had told her, that Emma thought the school was in on it. The moment they'd shown her that awful photo of the Idiot Editor, the Future Philandering Husband, she'd assumed that was what Michael meant. But if the editor of the paper was someone involved with the scandal, wouldn't there be a way to go over his head? There had to be a teacher advising them. Was that what Emma meant?

Maggie picked her way back over their conversation and all the pieces of evidence. All the assumptions that Emma might be missing, kidnapped, killed, suicidal. The worst thoughts coming first. But what if it was simpler? Why would her daughter hide? What would she be close to proving? If she was close to finding a school official involved, she might not feel safe at the school. But who? A janitor, a security guard? A teacher? Maggie thought of the security guard and the RA she'd met the first night. The ones with keys. The thought took her breath away, and she sat up, convinced she had to go there immediately and hunt them down.

They were low level; they wouldn't add much to the scandal of Emma's story. College boys and college minimum wage workers having sex with girls in dorms? The thought made her sick, but it was hardly novel. It had to have happened a million times before. And even if there was payment involved — again, this did not surprise Maggie or shock her. There were rumors of boys paying girls for sex at high schools, for God's sake. But still, *those guys had keys.* They could get to Emma or any of the girls, the same way her roommates could get to her. Had Salt or Kaplan thought of that?

Maggie took a quick shower, dressed in clean jeans and a sweater, went downstairs. A couple hours' rest would have to be enough. The thought of having a direction, a purpose, refreshed her more than sleep.

The drive was brief in the middle of the day; traffic was light, and even the trucks, which often drove too quickly for the narrow Schuylkill Expressway, seemed to be going slower, allowing her quick passage.

She parked on the edge of campus in a

two-hour spot. She did intend to leave, she thought as she closed the door. As she put quarters in the meter, she thought of her fingerprints lingering there, the timer telling a story, the meter reader surveying her car's color. She thought of everything she did now, everything that happened, as evidence, a clue, motivation. There was a kind of buzzing low voice, a running monologue inside her, an awareness that wasn't there before — it told her she was leaving DNA. It reminded her that she had a license plate, that she drove the same route, that she had a distinctive, long-legged gait with a size 8 footprint. Her tics, her traits, her peccadilloes, left their mark as much as anyone's. And she realized suddenly that this was cop awareness. Vigilance. Knowledge. Something inside them, like a heart murmur or tinnitus, they couldn't shake.

Was that why so many of them drank, did drugs, caroused? To make this horrible stain of an underlay recede? She walked fast, passing students, heading for Emma's dorm. She'd start there. She'd find the RA, the janitor; even if they wouldn't talk to her, she'd look them in the eye. Sometimes that told you more than words, especially when they were kids. Maggie had always been good at knowing when children were lying, if not necessarily husbands. Oh, the clues were there with Frank, too, she had to admit, but she had ignored them. Ignored them because they were too much for her to deal with.

As she approached the dorm, a small group of students gathered by one of the buildings north of it, standing on the steps, blocking the entrance. A class outside? She didn't see a teacher. A college tour? She didn't see any parents. As she walked closer, more students approached that building, and the buzz of their conversation grew louder. She detoured, curious. As she approached the bottom of the stairs and peered through the bodies, a blue uniform stood sentry, a cop, hand on holster. She forced her way up, elbowing students, shouting for them to let her through. The group jostled, shook, as she went to him.

"What's going on?"

"Police investigation," he answered. Was the rule book, all the procedures, imprinted on his tongue? Crime tape wove through the door handles, crisscrossing back and forth. One of the windows was cracked, and that was the only thing that calmed her. A break-in? A rock thrown? Would that prevent them from letting students in? Would they call a rock a police investigation?

The drone of an ambulance behind her, the shadow of flashing lights casting red and blue tints across the pale faces of the crowd.

"Did you find a body?" she asked the cop, and he ignored her. As if she were a reporter, a pest. The kids behind her, milling about, looking not for gossip or scandal but something to take a photo of. Something for their Instagram story that showed they had witnessed something in their boring crush of a day. She thought of these kids, these babies, finding her daughter's body. A stream of them walking past, thinking it was someone sleeping off the night before, until a biology major finally bent down and looked at it more closely, poked at it like a lab specimen, like something they would put under a microscope later.

She asked again, louder. Nothing. She wanted to reach for the cop's arm, shake him. But she knew better than to touch or grab any part of a cop. That was how things went wrong, always. A touch, a look, a sudden move. When a person was on edge, those small things flashed larger, cut deeper, than they did to civilians. Everything little meant something big to a cop.

She didn't feel the phone vibrating in her purse; the leather satchel, the small packet of Kleenex, the wallet, the fingerless gloves, all absorbed its message. Before she saw that summons, she felt a hand on her own shoulder and turned. Salt and Kaplan. Where had they come from? Were they going inside?

"Did someone find a body?"

"No."

"What's in the building? What's going on?"

"You didn't get our message?"

She looked between their faces. So they were a *they* now? Salt was his partner, finally aligned with someone else, now that Frank was gone and her medical leave was up? Was this official? She set the small shock of that thought aside; it didn't matter much at this very moment. After all, Frank was dead. His partner having another partner didn't make him more dead, did it?

"I didn't hear my phone. I —"

"It's okay," Salt said. "Let's go somewhere quieter to talk."

Blue gloves hung out of Kaplan's pocket, a sure sign that he'd been inside, looking at something.

"What did you find? What did they find?"

"Let's go ins—"

"No!" she cried. "Stop moving me around, trying to get the conditions right. The conditions are never gonna be right again, okay? I won't be sitting down, I won't be well rested, I will not ever be calm! So just tell me. Tell me now. Tell me right now."

"We found something unusual in the first-floor bathroom."

"What do you mean unusual?"

"It appears to be hair," Kaplan said.

"In the sink, you mean? Strands? Are they Emma's color? Are they —"

"Not exactly."

"Not exactly what?"

"Not exactly strands, not exactly in the sink," Salt said.

Maggie's mouth dropped open. Were these two kidding her right now? Was this how they communicated with the whole world, hiding half the information, not telling people what they needed to know, when they needed to know it?

"Well, what exactly and where exactly were they then, for Christ's sake!"

Salt took a deep breath and looked at Kaplan. He closed his mouth. They didn't know what to say, how to tell her? What the hell had they found that they had no words for it? A life-size voodoo doll with her daughter's scalp on top?

Maggie broke away, ran. Her purse flapped against her hip, weighing her down, but she was still fast, still track-team wiry enough to beat them back to the steps. She heard them behind her, the slap of Kaplan's shoes, the rustle of rayon fabric between Salt's thighs. She took that as a sign, as a victory. She may have been older, but Maggie ran quietly, as fast people often do. She was a breeze, and they were thunder behind her, trying to catch up but too heavy and earthbound.

Finally, she felt Kaplan's arm on hers, touching her in a way she wasn't allowed to touch him.

"Let me go," she cried. "I need to see!"

"Maggie," he said. "We can't just let you roam the campus."

"I won't touch anything. You know I won't."

"I don't think you understand."

"You're damned right I don't!" Her face contorted, twisted in a way she knew was ugly, pinched, and she did not care. Mock a grieving mother, take a photo of her at her worst, and she will say nothing. Nothing at all. It was like giving birth; who cared what you looked like when you had a job to do?

"Maggie, we have some camera footage of someone following you," he whispered.

"What? Who?"

"We don't know. A man or boy. Can't tell. A hoodie, a hat. Dark clothes."

She sighed and shrugged. "Oh well."

Their faces, so blank.

"You don't really think I care, do you? Let him grab me. Let him try. Maybe then he'll take me to Emma! At least someone will!"

"Maggie —"

"Maggie what? 'Maggie, calm down?' 'Maggie, pull yourself together?' 'Maggie, let us do our jobs?' 'Maggie, shut the fuck up and go home?' What? My daughter is out there somewhere, and you two fuckers are talking in code and in circles! Be concrete for God's sake!"

"Okay, okay," he said. "We'll take you inside. Come on."

He spoke to the cop guarding the door, then handed her a pair of gloves, and the three of them walked in together.

"According to people in the building, this is one of the biggest public bathrooms on campus, and it has a shower. It's also one of the least frequently used bathrooms, because it's kind of dark and hidden. Janitor said he barely has to clean it. Usually a few female teachers who work nearby and go for runs on campus rinse off here, that's all."

Maggie blinked. That was a lot of concrete information, but somehow, she doubted it was relevant. Emma didn't run for exercise.

She was fast, like Maggie and Frank, but she hated track, hated the boredom of going around in circles. The one thing Maggie didn't have to worry about was her daughter being abducted while running.

"Do you have video?" she said, looking up. She was trained to look everywhere now, up, down, around. Part of her thought this vigilance would never go away.

"No, camera's broken."

"How convenient."

"Janitor called us when he found this bag," he said, pointing to a dark-green trash bag. "Said it was unusual, out of character, and when he picked it up, he heard a clink and thought there might be a gun in it."

"Was there?"

"No. Scissors. Heavy, old-fashioned scissors." He took them out and held them aloft. "Recognize them?"

She shook her head. She'd sent her daughter to college with a pale-green, rubber-handled pair leftover from high school.

"They're not hair-cutting scissors?"

"God no," she replied. "These are old, cheap kitchen shears. They're not even sharp."

"How can you tell?"

She shrugged. "I can. So . . . the hair was in with the scissors then? Someone trimmed their own hair?"

"Yes, or changed someone else's appearance."

"Because . . ."

"Well, we can only speculate."

She swallowed hard. She could speculate a bit too easily.

They opened the bag and pulled out a huge cascade of hair. Brown with gold and red highlights in equal measure. Titian, it was called in the past, in the Nancy Drew days, in the days when people didn't say caramel or coffee with cream. She took off her glove and touched it, quickly, before they could tell her no. Silky and smooth, just the right shampoo and product applied. Tears ran down her cheeks.

"It's Emma's," she said.

"We'll have the forensics back in a few days."

"Don't waste your time," she said, wiping her face.

"What?"

"There's no need to test it. It's hers."

"Well, we have to be s—"

"Sure? You have to be sure? I'm sure, okay? Put that in your report. Write down that her mother, the hairdresser, is certain it's Emma's hair," she said. "I've brushed and cut and styled that hair a thousand times, a million times. It's my daughter's hair. My baby girl's. No one else's."

They were silent. They stood together in the world's smallest, most confined circle, in the college's biggest bathroom, pondering everything it might mean.

"Maybe she just wanted a change," Salt said. "A new look for her new school, her new year." She sounded like a mother now, an older sister, a best friend. She was trying to help, but Maggie just shook her head and gave a small laugh.

"My daughter would never cut her hair with these dull scissors." She paused, and they all took that in, too. What that had to mean. That someone else had done the cutting? That she'd been forced?

"There's no real sign of a struggle." Kaplan pointed at the floor, walls. Porcelain tile, floral wallpaper. This was probably the oldest building on campus, built for another time, when roommates didn't try to torture roommates and men didn't pay young girls to be their babies, sugar or not. No, this old-fashioned room looked almost pristine, but he kept on. "We found no fingernails, no skin, no —"

Maggie held up her hand. Enough. Because Maggie wasn't done with her sentence. Maggie had just stopped to take a breath, not leave an opening for a cop to fill with bullshit.

"She would never have done it," she said, shaking her head. "Unless . . . she was in a hurry. Unless she was desperate and in a hurry," she added.

And she was beginning to be certain, dead certain, that's exactly what Emma was.

THIRTY-FOUR

EMMA

Emma wasn't huge on regrets or reflection; her parents had substituted hard work and church for those things. *Bury whatever you're feeling, and then if you can't stop feeling it, ask God to take it away.* She thought of the big story about the thousands of priests abusing children in the city, how they'd asked the kids to gargle with holy water afterward. It was the cure-all, the world's largest Band-Aid. But she found herself, as she grew up, being drawn to other things when she was feeling low. Music. Videos. Quotes. She still felt calm when she walked past stained-glass windows. She liked hearing the church bells peal outside her dorm every Sunday. But she didn't feel the pull anymore.

Like many young girls, she believed in a different kind of fresh start. She believed that New Year's resolutions could wipe a slate clean; when she was feeling lonely, she read her horoscope in the *Cut* and felt inspired, guided. One good memoir from someone young she admired was more helpful than the small Bible her mother had smuggled into her suitcase the night before move-in. She believed that a new school year with sharpened pencils and brand-new notebooks brought a kind of forgiveness. You could remake yourself every September and every January, do a reset, a cleanse, a makeover.

But as she sat in the library, drinking her last coffee for the day, a substitute for dinner, and struggled to memorize all the questions she had for Mr. Maserati in an effort to let them flow effortlessly off her tongue (because it was one thing to write down his answers in a notebook, but it was another thing to read the questions from it — childish, student-y, unprepared), she felt the regret, the lack of friendship. If she had become friends with Taylor first, if she'd gotten to her before Fiona, would it all have played out differently? Taylor would help her learn her lines. Taylor would practice with her. Taylor would give her tips. But she shook her head vigorously, as if she could make it go away. These thoughts were not helping. Because the truth was, Taylor would be much better at interviewing people, at digging out their secrets. Taylor could playact the role of reporter, from the wardrobe down to the language, and thinking about how she'd do it and how she'd do it so very well was only making Emma feel like she couldn't.

And now, her wool blazer, her dresses, her grown-up, block-heeled shoes, the ones her mother had insisted on her buying — they couldn't help her either. Now it was jeans, boots, makeup. Now it was wear your glasses, not your contacts, so you at least look smart if not old. She'd cried an actual river over her own stupidity the night before. She'd failed the most basic college entrance test of all — finding one fucking friend in her own dorm. How stupid. How embarrassing. She'd misjudged the one boy/man she thought held the key to her future. She'd blown it completely, but she was not going to blow the rest of it.

Before she met Mr. Maserati, her plan was to stash her backpack with Michael, so at least she didn't have that fat, navy-blue flag that screamed *student* flying on her shoulders. At least she wouldn't have the weight of all her remaining possessions dragging her down. She would carry her notebook, pen, and burner phone, that's all.

She walked to the subway, the light more liquid than it was in August or September, the air heavier, frosty. It would be almost dark when she got back, but her coat was in her backpack. She had all she needed, she repeated to herself as she waited on the platform for the next car. She was stripped of all the artifice, and she was just going to have to be her smartest self and get what she needed to get.

The train pulled up, and she got on. The cars heading south were not even half full at this time of day. Students weren't going anywhere now; this was rush hour, but only for people headed in the opposite direction, going away from the city. When she got out at Suburban Station, there was a crush of commuters jostling to get on. Men in suits with loosened ties. Women carrying tote bags that pulled on one shoulder, their laptops and Kindles and exercise clothes and water bottles weighing them down. She knew that a bag like that meant you had somehow graduated; someday, she'd have one and shoulder other burdens, but she dismissed this thought quickly. She was only a freshman. She had time. No one would expect her to be like those women, not even Mr. Maserati. The thought relaxed her, and she felt positive as she stepped off the train.

Then, as she turned toward the escalator, a wash of déjà vu. The last time she'd been on the train, trying to follow Professor Grady. That terrible feeling, that shadow that fell across her mind — that someone was trailing her, too. She craned her neck, saw nothing. But she heard. She was on full alert now: sounds, colors, motion. She raced past the escalator, took the stairs two at a time. Well behind her, someone matched her pace. Did she dare look back? No. She ran instead, turned right at the top of the escalator, then pressed herself up against the wall. Watching. Waiting. She expected the same flash of beige jacket she'd seen before, and when it didn't come, she felt stupid. He probably had several jackets. He could be in a jean jacket, a blazer, anything. There had been no one on the platform at school; wherever he got on, it wasn't with her. She didn't even know what he looked like! She watched six men exit the escalator and stairs, moving straight ahead, not stopping, not glancing around them to see where she'd gone. She waited five minutes until no one was coming up; people were only going down. She took a deep breath, climbed the next set of stairs, up to the sidewalk, and kept going.

On the way to the store, she changed her

route several times, switched direction, ducked into a few shops, testing herself. Nothing. No one. No one out of the ordinary anyway. No eye contact. *Okay,* she thought, *okay.*

When she got to Beck's, Michael wasn't at the valet stand, and the other boy working there said he was just delivering a car. She waited with him awkwardly, not talking, and finally, Michael rounded the corner. He smiled as he approached, then looked at his watch.

"He'll be here soon," he said.

"I'm early, I know."

"You look nice," he said.

"Thank you."

"But not too nice, which is good."

She laughed. If someone else had said it, she might have taken it the wrong way or been confused, but she knew what he meant. After all, she didn't know this man, and Michael didn't really either, did he? The worst thing would be for him to take her the wrong way. For a lonely, widowed man to misread her intentions.

A few minutes later, the car they were waiting for pulled in. A navy-blue convertible. Curves in these sports cars always reminded Emma a little of a cat about to pounce. She didn't really know the differences between a Porsche and a Ferrari and a Maserati; how often did she see one? Pretty much never. Still, she was glad that it wasn't red. She wasn't sure she could trust a man who had buried his wife and then immediately bought a red convertible.

He opened his door, stood up, handed Michael the keys, and shook her hand firmly, with a small, tense smile, and suddenly, she was afraid. Not afraid of him, exactly; he looked perfectly ordinary, a pleasant-faced man with salt-and-pepper hair, a round belly straining the buttons of his white oxford shirt, a navy blazer over that, and blue jeans that looked as if they'd been ironed or dry-cleaned. She made a mental note of all that. It wouldn't be nice to write things down now, before they'd spoken. He'd know she was writing notes about his appearance. No, she was afraid to go out in public with him. How it would look. Who might overhear. How not-private it would be. The lack of privacy made it safe in a way, but it would hold him back, surely. He would be more forthcoming with no one else around. She clearly had not thought this through, and now there were only a couple of options: go somewhere private, like a hotel room (a hard no), or go for a drive.

"Hey, how about we just drive around a little?" she said suddenly.

"Ah, you like my car," he said with a broad smile.

"Well," she said, "it is nice, but I was thinking . . . it would be quieter than a restaurant."

"A convertible is not quiet," he laughed, and Michael joined him.

Great. She'd just arrived, and she'd said something stupid.

"Well, relaxing? Easier to talk."

"My wife always said men talk best when they're driving and looking straight ahead," he said. "So they don't have to make eye contact!"

Michael laughed again, and she liked that, the way he included him. And she liked that he had mentioned his wife. Get that out in the open, don't hide the fact that she existed or that she was dead. Make it okay to talk about by mentioning it first. Or was that just a technique to make her feel at ease?

Michael winked and told him he would miss taking care of the car but that he should drop Emma back at the valet when they were finished.

"Do I have a curfew?" he joked.

"Make good decisions," Michael sing-songed, then laughed.

When he closed Emma's door, he patted it and nodded, as if he knew it was all okay and she was going to be in good hands.

It was a bit loud, interviewing someone in a convertible, and she wished she had her coat and not just her sweater, but he answered her questions directly, didn't hesitate or tell her he wasn't comfortable, any of the things she'd imagined he might say when she asked him if he'd been on dates with more than one girl (yes) and if he had had sex with any of them (yes), if he used condoms (yes), and even after she asked him if the age differential between him, his wife (she'd read the obit; she was a year younger than he was), and the girls bothered him (yes). "That bothered me quite a bit," he said. "I was very taken aback on my first visit. I had assumed these would be women, in their thirties or even forties. Not their twenties. Not —"

"Their teens?"

"Well, I never knew that for certain, but yes. I got the impression there were some eighteen- and nineteen-year-olds there. I tried to gravitate toward the older-looking ladies."

"But it's hard to tell how old women are," she added. "The makeup, the hair."

"Don't I know it," he sighed. "But usually

after a few dull and one-sided conversations, you know when you're dealing with someone too young. Someone who never read a newspaper, someone who doesn't know certain words or phrases. And then there are the ones who chew gum constantly. And the things that they drank! Ugh. Ice cubes in their wine, things like that."

"Do you have any daughters?"

She knew the answer, that he had sons, but she wanted to make him just the tiniest bit uncomfortable. She wanted, she realized, watching him squirm, for him to feel a bit punished.

"No, I don't think I could have gone there at all if I did. And if your next question is would I want them in this line of work, the answer is a definite no. Of course not. But it would make a better story if I had a daughter, wouldn't it?"

He suggested driving down to the river, along Boathouse Row. It was a lovely night, and the lights on the boathouses would be twinkling with the fall leaves in the background. She said fine, probably too quickly, without enough thought. He was taking her somewhere you'd take someone on a date, and that was probably not a good idea. He was a lonely man with a young girl on a soft autumn night. But Michael knew where she was and probably knew the license plate number of the car.

"It says on some of the sugar daddy websites that there is a screening process," she said. "Did you ever register on a site and go through that process?"

"No, that's not . . . my style. I'm a total technophobe. My friend told me about the club."

"So there is no screening process at the club?"

"Well, someone has to recommend you."

"Ah," she said. "Did you spend all your time talking to women at the club, or did you get to know some of the men, too?"

"Oh, there were nervous conversations at the bar, kind of small talk, while we were all sizing up the girls."

"Introductions?"

"Yes. Although I've since learned that many didn't use their real names."

"The men or the girls?"

"Both, apparently."

"Well, the men were probably married."

"Some of them. But many, I was relieved to hear, were divorced or widowed, like me. But you know what they say about that."

"No, no I do not."

"That men can't be alone?"

"At my age," she said with a tight smile,

"all they want to do is be alone. Speaking of age, would you estimate the other men were usually around your age or younger?"

"Most I would say were slightly younger. And thinner!"

He laughed, and she laughed, too. This man liked to state the obvious, that was for sure.

"What about full names? Or professions?"

"Sometimes. None that really registered, though. We weren't there to network."

"Other than restaurant workers, did anyone seem to be in charge, like an event planner or —"

"Yes, there was someone kind of wrangling us. Moving us from the bar to the restaurant, suggesting certain girls."

"Man or woman?"

"Man."

"Suggesting how?"

"Like, 'that girl over there is a little shy. But she's very nice once she feels comfortable.' That kind of thing."

"Did he also speak to the girls?"

"Not really, now that you mention it. It was as if he already knew them."

"So did you get the sense he was in charge of the girls? Working with them, like a —"

"Like a pimp? Is that what you were going to say?"

354

"I don't think I've ever said that word in my life," she said quietly.

"Well, you're young," he said. "Sorry for getting testy. I guess, see, the whole thing is, most of the guys there have convinced themselves that words like 'pimp' and 'prostitute' and even 'escort' do not apply to their situation."

"I know, it's just friends introducing friends," she said.

"That's what it says on their business card."

"Actually, not anymore."

"Well, maybe Sam has knocked some sense into his brother."

"Sam Beck?"

"Yeah, he's trying to get his brother to run a legitimate restaurant with good food and beautiful hostesses, but not, you know."

"Friends seeking friends."

"Exactly."

"Do you know both of the brothers?"

"Just casually. Not well."

"Then how do you know of their business plan?"

"I know someone who plays squash with Sam."

"Have you seen any evidence of tension between them, disagreements?"

"Not personally."

"But your squash partner has?"

"Not in so many words."

"Are you a customer of the store?"

"Yes," he said. "Although you're supposed to know that from my stylish, understated clothes."

"Sorry," she said and smiled. "I'm not really up on men's fashion. Or . . . fashion. So, were there materials advertising the club at the store? Brochures, flyers —"

"Yes, in the bathrooms, but look, if you don't mind me saying this . . . this is not how I expected the interview to go."

"Really? What did you expect?"

"I expected you to ask if I fell in love, if I had regrets. But you're very focused on facts."

Concrete, she thought to herself with a smile.

"Well, facts anchor a news story," she said. "And feelings make it more of a feature story."

"That's a good way to put it."

She nodded. She had to admit that she liked this man. She imagined meeting him again on his turf. Seeing his home, the pictures of his wife, his bedroom, still showing the feminine touch. And she could see the bedroom of one of the girls, too, filled with Mardi Gras beads and shot glasses as she perched in a chair in a short skirt. *Wow,* she thought. *You're seeing it now. You're envisioning the photos accompanying the story, bold and graphic, award-winning.*

"Okay, I need to say something off the record and slightly crazy."

Her eyes widened. "Okay."

"I think someone is following us."

She turned around. Behind them, a white SUV, maybe an Acura? She wasn't sure. She wasn't good with cars or clothes or things.

"Not him," he said. "A few cars back. A silver sedan."

"How long?"

"I think he's been there since Chestnut Street, and he keeps speeding up and slowing down."

"Maybe it's an unmarked cop car? Patrolling?" It was a little desolate on these river-hugging roads once you went under the bridge. Like a lot of frontage roads, these were less populated, darker, and the business above the water tending toward the industrial.

"I don't think so. The car is too nice. An Audi, I think, not sure."

"Did you see who was driving it?"

"A man, no passenger. Looked like he was balding or had a high forehead."

The breath tightened in Emma's throat. A

silver Audi in the driveway on Google Earth. Balding just a little, at the hairline.

"Was he wearing a beige coat by chance?"

"Well, it was definitely light, not dark. I know that much. Pretty observant for an old guy, huh?"

She took a deep breath.

"Okay, so you have a jealous ex-boyfriend? Something like that? Should we call the poli—"

"No. I wish it were that simple."

"Well, I could pull over, see if we're right or not."

"I don't think that's a good idea."

"Is this guy you're worried about armed?"

"I doubt it, but I don't know, actually. I just think he's trying to intimidate me."

"A gun is certainly intimidating."

"So is following someone."

"Well, I could just speed up," he said. "Following a Maserati in an Audi is not quite a fair fight. I'm a good driver, but this is a very tight road. Might be scary."

"I'd rather get a better look at the car," she said.

He said he'd wait until there was shoulder, up ahead. He put on his flashers and pulled to the right. They waited in tense silence, as if they were being overheard, not just watched. The white SUV passed. A second car, black, two-door. The gray car slowed, as if it was thinking. The car approached slowly, and the slower it went, the faster Emma's heart beat.

"Maybe this was a mistake. I never thought he'd actually —"

"Duck down," he said.

"What?"

"Get close to the floor."

Just as they crouched down, the other car lurched, brakes screeching. U-turn.

He lifted his head. "Dammit! That was so strange! Should we follow?" he said.

"No," she said, pulling herself up on her seat. "I can't make out the license plate."

"Me either. All I saw was a Semper sticker in the rear window."

"Are you sure?"

"Of course I'm sure. I'm an alum."

Emma felt her heart thumping too loud in the cage of her ribs. So loud you could mistake it for something even worse. Like footsteps. Like all of it, catching up to her.

THIRTY-FIVE

MAGGIE

Maggie had handled so much hair in her life — smooth, matted, tangled, snipped, discarded — that it settled into her, into all the open places. Ears, mouth. Sometimes, when she wore a low-cut shirt, she'd find a dusting of small blond clippings nestled in the bottom of her bra cups. It always snuck its way in. It was probably in her lungs, her kidneys, her stomach. It was part of the background of her life, like crumbs were for chefs. But that didn't diminish the potential for hair to still hold power. It came from the top, after all, the head. Everyone always said it was "just hair" — diminished it, took its importance away just because it could regenerate, keep going. They weren't looking at it the right way. A hairstyle could change everything. The way the light caught it, making it shine? That could blind you, change you. Still, she had to look at the flip side. That hair was changed and thrown away every day. That people blithely hacked off their own bangs, plucked the errant grays, twisted it into taut braids to get it out of their way. Hair was nothing and everything. It meant the world, or it was just a coincidence.

For that reason, it was easy to stay strong and focused and not to break down. It could mean nothing, right?

But when Sarah Franco ran up breathlessly, saying she'd talked to Chloe and finished the Facebook videos, Maggie was not prepared. She didn't imagine she'd have two people next to her as witnesses, two people she hardly knew. But she was glad they were there. Glad because they grabbed her arms before her knees buckled.

"I did a couple of them," Sarah said.

The video had white bars across it with words that matched the voice-over. She told them she'd done that intentionally, because so many people watch on mute. This way, she said, they won't miss critical information.

Do you know Emma O'Farrell?

Could you be the key to finding her?

Emma is from Semper University, and formerly Lower Merion High School.

5 feet 4 inches, 110 pounds. Brown hair and

green eyes.

Last seen on campus, leaving the library. Wednesday, October 15.

If you have any information, please call Philadelphia Police.

But none of those things made Maggie feel faint. No. It was the video footage of Emma leaving the library. The footage that showed her alone, in the dark. The footage that showed her shoulders slumping under her backpack. The footage of her face in shadow, a hoodie pulled over her head, obscuring her hair, which may or may not have been there. Where was Emma's hair?

Suddenly, her legs failed her. Crumpled like two badly designed buildings, and it was only Salt and Kaplan that kept her from hitting concrete, hard.

"Oh my God," Sarah said. "I'm so sorry. I thought it was a good thing. I thought —"

"It *is* a good thing," Salt said. "They're very professionally done. I'm sure they'll help. The photograph at the end is very clear."

"Yes," Maggie said softly. "Thank you, Sarah."

"You know what?" Salt said. "You've had a helluva day. I live close by, near the *Inquirer* building. How about we go there and rest for a few hours?"

Maggie closed her eyes and nodded. It was finally catching up to her. They walked to Salt's car, and she buckled Maggie in, like a child, and Maggie let her.

The apartment building was old and grand and enormous, with rococo trim, Philadelphia by way of Florida. Maggie remembered reading about the renovations and the amenities. She was surprised Salt could afford it, but when she saw how small it was, she decided it couldn't be that much.

Very little furniture, all modern. No animals, no plants. Typical of a cop, nothing that needed tending. Salt told her to lie down on the couch and covered her feet with an afghan. Salt told her she'd set the alarm for an hour and a half, if that was okay? Did it seem like enough time? Maggie nodded. She fell into a dreamless sleep and didn't think about all the time her husband might have spent in that apartment, whether he'd sat in the very same spot, drank from the glass, done God knows what. She didn't think about those things because she was finally, at last, too damned tired to think. Her legs shook, as if they had to let it out, and that's the last thing she remembered before she fell asleep, her legs shaking like they were rocking the rest of her body to sleep.

The chime of the alarm woke her before she knew it. She blinked her eyes open, turned it off, and took a sip of water from the glass she'd had earlier. Salt wasn't in the room. Maggie didn't hear her, so she stood, stretched, and took a few steps down the hallway to listen. Had Salt left? Was she alone? She assumed she was and started down the hallway toward the bathroom, passing two doors, one shut, one ajar.

She peered into the first one, open a few inches.

"Hello?" she called. No answer.

The master bedroom. Clothes hung on a mahogany valet by the bed. Jacket, shirt, empty holster. *Like a man,* she thought. Bed made, smooth and flat, a dark printed bedspread with no extraneous pillows, no extra comforter folded at the foot of the bed. Pale-blue walls, no shelves or artwork. Twin lamps mounted on either side of the bed. She blinked. Was that where they slept? Did Frank sleep on the right, nearest the door, like he did at home? Or did he flip it around, do the opposite? She walked over and sat on the right side of the bed. She didn't feel him here; she'd been raised to believe in the afterlife and that the energy of a soul could remain. But she didn't feel Frank here. Not his scent, of lime soap and astringent shaving cream. Not his energy, either, the way his certainty and strength changed the air, taking up more than his share of space. No, Frank was not lingering here.

Like the living room, there was nothing fancy or decorative; everything had a use. Neat. Militaristic. She had a feeling if she opened the closet, she'd find shoe trees, cedar panels. But no Frank. Because Salt didn't need him, didn't mourn him like Maggie did. She was pretty certain of that.

Back in the hallway, she thought she heard something outside in the corridor, perhaps in another apartment. She called out, "Gina?" No answer, no Salt. Had she gone out for a walk or errand?

She knocked lightly on the second door, listened for a response, got none. She pushed open the door, expecting to find clutter or closet, but inside saw neither. A second room, windowless, set up like a small office. Less streamlined, less tidy than the rest of the apartment, but not by much. A few papers scattered. A stack of books on the floor. Photographs by Ansel Adams. A biography of Margaret Thatcher. Mindy Kaling's memoir. Field guide to butterflies. No fiction. That was extra, she supposed, not needed. She had a feeling Gina Colletti didn't watch television either.

A shelf of diplomas, high school, community college, the police academy. And one faded photo, unframed, curling. Salt's family? As she leaned over to pick it up, she was struck by two things. One, it was dusty and darker around the edges, like it used to be in a frame. And two, it wasn't Gina's family; it was Maggie's. Frank and Emma, standing in front of a tree. Emma looked to be around nine or ten. There was more foliage in the background and a tall kiosk. A historical park? The Philadelphia Zoo? Maggie's heart felt heavier in her chest. What this could mean. What this couldn't possibly mean. A piece of evidence that could prove someone's guilt of another crime, a worse one.

Salt's footsteps in her own hallway weren't particularly light, but Maggie heard them too late.

"Maggie, are you —"

"Am I what?" Maggie said, turning around. "Am I snooping?"

"No, that's not —"

The room was too quiet now. There was nothing to hear, no ticking clock, no open window letting in the traffic on the street, no heater turning on and off. Just two women breathing hard, weighing the mo-

ment. Just eyes landing on the same photograph.

"You knew her," Maggie said simply. "You
knew Emma."

"I was his partner. There were work
picnics. There were —"

"You weren't his partner then."

"Frank and I . . . knew each other a long
time, Maggie," she said quietly.

"How long?"

"It wasn't like that. We were friends in the
beginning. We —"

"Friends? Take my daughter to the zoo
kind of friends?"

"I liked the photo. It was from his desk. I
took it when he died. I'm sorry —"

"I don't believe you."

"Okay, I knew her. Not like you know her,
but —"

"Not like I know her?! Not like I know
her? Of course you fucking don't know her
like I know her. I'm her mother! I gave birth
to her, twenty-eight hours of torture, and I
walked the floors with her when she had
colic, and I worked two jobs to pay for her
Catholic school, me. Not you. Me."

"I know."

"I can't believe," she said, sniffing back
tears, anger, snot, fury, "how stupid I am.
How blind."

"Maggie, you didn't really think —"

"What? What didn't I really think?"

"You didn't really think I was doing all this for you?"

She said it gently, but it fell like a sucker punch. Maggie felt her bones breaking, blood moving, the way she looked and felt forever changed. Yes, she believed that when push came to shove, one woman would help another. One woman would rise above the crowd of men who didn't get it and men who didn't see and help another woman.

She believed it, stupidly, and she supposed Emma had, too. And that was where they'd both gone wrong.

"I have to go," she said, and Salt didn't argue. Maggie handed her the photo back. "You can have him," she said simply. "You can keep him."

THIRTY-SIX

EMMA

As they drove back to Michael's valet, Mr. Maserati answered a few more questions, and the Audi didn't show up again. If he was following them still, he was doing a better job of it. She didn't share her concerns with Mr. Maserati; she didn't share them with Michael, either. The only person she shared them with was Cara Stevens, who she called from the cab on the way home. She'd picked up her backpack and gone to the lobby of the Latham Hotel and gotten into a good old-fashioned cab, with a privacy screen and a hinged window for money and change. As if anyone used money anymore.

Her mother would be so happy about this. Her mother, who was always railing against the idiocy of Uber and Lyft, who thought riding with strangers was the stupidest thing a young girl could do, was always defending cab drivers, with their unions and medallions. "Cabs are dirty," Emma would say. "And they're scary." *They are guaranteed to have no criminal records, and their cars are licensed and inspected,* her mother would parry. *They are the opposite of scary.*

"Are you sure?" Cara Stevens had asked, and that was where Emma had faltered. She felt like an idiot when she said she was pretty sure. Grady was the professor on Cara's list. He was her professor. She'd seen a similar car in the driveway when she'd checked Google Earth. And there was a university decal on the car. Cara had told her to back off, to lie low. She said Emma was in a classic conundrum on an investigative story: there were too many people who didn't want their involvement made public and not enough people who did. Cara said she needed a few more who did, who supported the truth coming out, to balance those who didn't.

"Like who?" Emma asked.

"Like a teacher who knows what Grady is up to. Like a disgruntled sugar baby, not just a daddy. Hey, was Fiona in his class?"

"She was originally," she said. "She transferred out."

"Maybe you should quietly look for other girls in his class, then. Or other girls in your dorm. She didn't turn Taylor, but maybe she reached out to others?"

Emma thought about this. She'd totally forgotten about her revelation that the girls in her dorm seemed hotter than others. She'd dismissed that as paranoia, coincidence. What about the other girls in Grady's classes?

"None of the girls I've met seem unhappy about anything. People are just a little too happy. Also, Sam Beck, who runs the club, is actually super nice."

"All pimps are nice, Emma. Their charm is what separates them from common criminals."

"Well, Fiona doesn't seem ashamed, and our roommates, who know about her, don't either. They called me judgmental. People aren't that concerned about sex work, I guess. Some women find it empowering."

"Well, I doubt their parents or the board of trustees or any hotshot alumni with a big charitable gift to give would agree with that kind of campus empowerment. There has to be some girl who came to her senses. And all you need, really, is one on the record. Like Mr. Maserati."

Emma thought of how girls often went out in clusters. Fiona didn't go out as often, but sometimes. And never alone. Everyone had other friends; who were they, really? If she could figure it out, maybe she could convince them to talk. She thought of Samantha, the girl from their hall who she'd seen shopping at the B boutique. Had they recruited her, maybe? And how could she get her to talk — threaten to tell her parents, boyfriends?

"But in the meantime, lie low. Stop going to Beck's, stop trying to follow the men. The men are dangerous, Emma."

"And the girls are not?" She sighed. "My roommates completely turned on me."

"Because you made mistakes. You shouldn't have gone through their stuff. That was not the way to do it. That's what journalists do in the movies but not in real life."

"Okay."

"So just stop," Cara said. "I'll talk to a few people still at the *Inquirer,* see if they know anything new about these guys, if they can help. But in the meantime? Stop. Observe. Try to rest. Let the story come to you."

Emma repeated those words to herself as she paid the cabbie. That was what Jason had said, too. She could let the story come, but how the hell was she going to rest on that stiff sofa while her roommates threw away her stuff?

She headed for her dorm, because it was better than sleeping in a classroom or hiding on the floor in the library. She knew better than to go to her RA, who would either try to mediate things or tell her to fill out paperwork for a transfer. And transferring only took her away from Fiona — and if there was anything else to get out of Fiona, Emma needed to stay close. She thought about asking Sarah Franco if she could crash with her, but that was her backup plan. She might need her more later than she did right now, and the thought of explaining all this to someone else was exhausting, defeating, and, let's face it, embarrassing. To some degree, she'd screwed up at almost everything — being a roommate, being a reporter, being a student, being hot enough for Jason. What else was she going to screw up?

And if she was being totally honest? She knew Sarah would simply tell her to stop. Stop the story, go to the housing board with a complaint, transfer schools, whatever. Going to Sarah would be almost as bad as going to her mother.

So for now, sofa. As she approached the door, her RA came out, held the door for someone behind him. She held her breath, ducked behind a shrub. Fiona.

She came out, and he lit a cigarette for her. She looked up and down the street, as if waiting for someone else. He looked at his watch, pointed in the opposite direction. A pair of boys in blazers walked up to her, and they all shook hands. *Great,* she thought. Now she's available on campus. For three-ways? One of the boys reached in his pocket and held an envelope aloft. Manilla, the kind that closed with metal clasps. But Fiona didn't take it. The RA did.

Oh boy. Part of the story had just come to her. She almost laughed. And she wondered why on earth she hadn't seen it before. Good old Tim. Always on call. Knew everybody. Had a key to everyone's room in case they wanted to kick out their roommate or use someone else's bunk bed for sex transactions.

Right under her nose. Right down the hall. But then, she'd slept in a bed next to a paid escort for two months and thought she just liked to be clean at night, so what did she know? Chasing after people and it was here, right here all along.

She waited until Fiona left with the boys. Her high heels, her short stride, her struggling just a little to keep up, them holding back just a little to be nice.

She watched them go off into the night like this was all completely normal, being dressed up and going somewhere for paid group sex. A fraternity? Probably. A wealthy fraternity. Something about the blazers just screamed fraternity to her. Now that was an angle she hadn't considered. She made a mental note to research Professor Grady, the Beck Brothers, and Mr. Maserati to see if there was any overlap. Maybe this was just as much about Greek life as it was about Semper.

But she couldn't move, couldn't leave, until Tim Trenton did. She watched him watching Fiona walk away. He lit a cigarette, too, completely breaking the rules of having to be two hundred feet away from a building before doing so. *Tsk, tsk.* Still, she supposed he could be watching after Fiona in a brotherly way. Not just a meal ticket way.

He turned right, away from her, headed off in the general direction of the gym, and based on how he was dressed, in long shorts and a long-sleeved T-shirt, she supposed he could be going there. Impossible to know, since boys wore shorts to class, to go out to bars, to walk in the snow. And yes, he was a senior, but in her mind, in those shorts, he was still a boy. Still an asshole, good-for-nothing college boy.

She knew this time of night, the gym would be packed. No treadmills available, a wait for every machine except the recumbent bike, which carried a kind of shame around it. Only injured people used that. And only pussies who hated cardio used the treadmill. Real runners, she knew, ran outside, except when it was pitch-dark or pouring rain. Then, reluctantly, they made do at the gym. You could tell who they were from how fast they ran and how grim their faces were.

There was a whole section in the welcome packet about the dangers of running in a city school at night. Was there any parent who hadn't pointed that out to their daughter? They all held tight to their beliefs of the real danger, of city criminals ringing the campus, breaching the lines. Nowhere in the brochure was there mention of how laws, bones, and hearts could be broken on campus. No, nothing.

Tim walked a hundred feet, then stopped. She thought he was taking a phone call, but no. He patted his pockets as if he'd lost something. Even in the low light, she could see the pulsing yellow of the tiger head logo on his gray shirt. Semper Sabres. The menacing teeth. The narrowed eyes of a predator. A warning to the other teams.

Her feet were getting damp. The sprinklers must have been on earlier. She took a step to the left and forward, trying to hit drier ground, and something snapped. A twig. An acorn. A pigeon cooed near her elbow, suddenly aloft, and she shrieked. What the hell was a pigeon doing here at dusk? Didn't birds, like, sleep?

He turned left in her direction, squinting. Crack, coo, yelp. Small sounds that added up. She had no idea how visible she actually was from that angle. Dark jeans and shirt. She turned her face away, gave him only a view of her backpack, and started to walk. A breeze blew up, lifting her hair, blowing it back. She passed under a security light, and it went on with her motion. She blinked beneath the light, felt the heat on her hair, illuminating her.

"Emma?" he called out, and she could have frozen, could have circled back to talk to him, to accuse him, to ask him what the hell he was doing. But no. She walked faster, as fast as she could without running, straight to the liberal arts center. A class or meeting running late on the second floor, lights on. The door was still open. She took a pair of scissors from one of the classrooms and headed to the large, empty, well-lit bathroom. It was easy enough to stop fol-

lowing the men. But she needed to make
sure they'd stop following her.

THIRTY-SEVEN

MAGGIE

Maggie stood outside Salt's apartment building, looking one way, then the other. A crossroads. In one direction, home, rest. In the other, school, her daughter. But it was time to consider that Emma was not there anymore. Someone had taken her, was hiding her. Her hair was gone, her appearance changed. Why? And by whom? Frank had always told Maggie, when she worried about their daughter being out late or traveling in a car, that being forced into prostitution, sold into sexual slavery was a rare occurrence. He'd said it simply didn't happen to white girls in their zip code. He'd told her to worry about the preppy boys in Emma's class maybe, but not about a van stealing her off the street. But Maggie knew it happened in the United States. She'd seen the stories, the articles, the shows. Who else would take those scissors to Emma's hair?

Who else would change her appearance? Emma was an eighteen-year-old college virgin who looked years younger. Maggie had to consider this possibility even as she heard Frank's voice from the grave telling her she was nuts. She knew these trafficked girls often went to truck stops, to houses where they were held, or motels where the owners turned a blind eye. She would research nearby motels. She would go to the truck stops on the turnpike. It was time to get those flyers off campus and out into the world.

She was texting Sarah Franco to see if she could help her with that when the call came in from Kaplan.

"Hope I didn't wake you."

"You didn't, and you know I don't care if you do."

"Just keeping you in the loop on something."

"What's that?"

"The gentleman in Emma's phone named Mr. Maserati?"

"Yes," Maggie said. "She was interviewing him."

"So they both say."

"Did he give you any reason to believe that wasn't true?"

"Not really. He struck me as a nice guy.

Straight shooter. Around your age, I would guess."

"Great. Maybe I'll date him after all this is over."

"He gave us a couple leads we're trying to verify."

"Such as?"

"That there might be video of her outside London, which is a private supper club where escorts are known to work. We pulled the video from across the street, and she's on it. So I have to ask —"

"My daughter was not an escort!"

"Well, she's meeting with an older guy. She's on camera —"

"She was writing a story."

"Well, maybe the story went too far, and she —"

"No. That can't be it."

"He also said that during their interview, they were followed by someone."

"Did he describe that someone?"

"Vaguely. Balding, wearing a light jacket. But he gave me plenty of detail on the car. Make, model, color. A new Audi, gray."

"License plate?"

"Spoken like a cop's wife."

"That's a compliment, I suppose."

"No license plate, but there was a Semper decal."

"A student?" *Dear God,* she thought, *are we living in a world where kids bring new Audis to campus?*

"Actually, we're thinking faculty or alumni, based on the description."

"Alumni could take forever."

"Yes, but we got a hit in the faculty lot. Two Audis, the attendants say. Both gray. One a couple years older than the other. And the witness was adamant, this was a brand-new car. Car guys, you know?"

"Yes," Maggie said, although she didn't know, didn't know at all. But she thought of Michael, his knowledge, his specificity. So she could imagine.

"Well, this is delicate but — our guy was worried that this was a jealousy situation."

"What?"

"I know this is truly awkward, but is there any possibility that Emma was involved with one of her teachers? Because the new Audi is reg—"

"No," she said automatically. "Jesus, Mary, and Joseph, do you have any theories that actually make sense? Anything that doesn't insult my intelligence and ruin my daughter's reputation?"

"Video doesn't lie."

"Well, video doesn't explain either!"

"How about her psychology teacher?

Someone persuasive, who understands the way the mind wo—"

"No! You have it all wrong. Did you lift any prints off those scissors yet? And check them against faculty? Because I th—"

"With all due respect —"

"You know, whenever anyone says that to a woman, it means the opposite. It means no actual respect. None at all."

"Maggie, we're on the same side here."

"Grady, that's the psychology prof's name, right?"

She pictured her daughter's class schedule in her head, pinned to the bulletin board. She'd put it there so she could envision Emma moving through her day, yawning in an early morning class, enjoying her lunch, going to the library for a free period.

"Actually, the car was registered to his wife."

"Same last name?"

"Look, we are interviewing him this afternoon. We are on it. You do not need to think any harder about this. I just wanted your perspective on the possibility of the relationship —"

"There is no possibility of a relationship! This has to be connected to the story!"

"Well, the editor says the story was killed. Not enough sources to make it a story."

"The editor who was fucking one of the girls in the story?"

"I don't know if she's in the story."

"You're absolutely right. You don't know a damn thing."

THIRTY-EIGHT

EMMA

Emma wasn't sure what made her do it, exactly. Maybe it was another sleepless night on the dorm sofa, a night in which exactly none of her roommates even came home. She woke up whenever she heard a noise in the hall, thinking they were coming in. Slumber-party vigilant, in case they wrote *bitch* on her face with Sharpie or waxed one of her eyebrows off, the crap you saw on YouTube. But no. Five beds, all remaining empty, locked up and unavailable to her. Maybe it was the fact that she hadn't slept more than three hours at a time for almost a week. Or that every morning she pumped herself full of way too many espresso shots at the Morning Grind and couldn't concentrate in her classes. She carried far too much information in her brain to take everyone's advice. Just let it go. Let it come to you. *Fuck that.*

She woke up with a start, thinking about Professor Grady. The missing piece. She knew that was his freaking car. She knew he taught his last class at eleven, had office hours afterward, and then went home. She'd thought he took the train because of the two passes that clicked around his neck, but maybe she was wrong. Maybe some days, he drove that Audi to school and just didn't bother to unclip the train pass from his lanyard.

So when she went to the faculty lot after lunch and saw two gray Audis, one with a decal and one without, she was not at all surprised. And when she snuck by the parking attendant and the back door opened at her touch, she was not surprised either. Michael was right about parking lots — they didn't always lock the doors unless they left the lot, or maybe unless the owners tipped them mightily. And Bill Grady, she had a feeling, was cheap.

She saw the Semper blanket in his back seat and didn't think twice about what he used it for. She curled up underneath it on the floor. She was counting on him never even looking there, and she was right. He came out after his office hours and climbed in front without a single glance to the rear. After a few minutes, she risked a quick peek

386

out the window and saw he was heading down the same route he'd taken when he'd followed Mr. Maserati. The back way, along the river, avoiding the highway.

It was a long drive to Wayne, longer than she'd realized. He had a jazz station playing, and though she hated jazz, she was grateful for the background noise, since her stomach growled loudly.

Finally, he pulled into his driveway, got out. She lifted the blanket an inch, dared a glance out the window. Yes. It was the house she'd seen on Google Earth. Even smaller than she'd imagined from the front, but then she knew what secrets were held in the back, the spectacular landscaping, the second level. It was a beautiful day, sunny and probably warm enough to sit outside and enjoy the panorama of maples, oaks, evergreens. The kind of fall day that made you think winter was never coming.

The reds and golds against the blues of the pool. If it was heated, she was sure it was warm enough to consider a swim. She had a feeling he was heading for his pool house, his man cave. She got out and followed just far enough to see him heading down the path in his backyard. Yes, there he went. She watched as his shape grew smaller and smaller, till he was almost nothing. His eyes fixed on the slope ahead, not the flat, cool grass behind.

Good, she thought. That would leave her plenty of time to wait for his wife.

THIRTY-NINE

MAGGIE

The house was pretty, well cared for. A Cape Cod with brown wood shutters softened to gray and a bright-yellow front door. His wife's idea, stolen from a magazine? Or a nod to the school colors? Either was possible. The property it sat on wasn't particularly large, and it sloped downward precariously, backing up on a public walking trail. The neighbors' houses were fairly close by. People walked dogs up and down the sidewalks, heading to or from that trail, swinging small blue bags that were either empty or full of shit. It wasn't, Maggie decided, a good neighborhood to house sex slaves. No. The houses were far too close together for trafficking underage girls, and there were too many stay-at-home moms to not notice something was amiss. If her daughter was being held somewhere, her appearance changed, Maggie certainly didn't think it was here, but she hoped it would lead somewhere. Let Kaplan handle his angle; she would handle hers.

No Audi in the driveway, just a Subaru wagon. Green. A little muddy on the wheels, like it had just been driven up a dirt road. She glanced inside. No rope. No duct tape. No ball-peen hammer. She let out the breath she'd been holding, and it felt ancient, stale as a tomb. How long had she been holding that breath? How long since she'd brushed her teeth, combed her hair, slept?

She rang the doorbell, listened to it echo. Tile floors, she thought. Marble kitchen. Beautiful-looking but tinny and cold, the acoustics all wrong, and you didn't realize it until after installation when you had people over and they started talking all at once, and your ears rang. Maggie had been in so many kitchens like that. She'd go back to her small, snug kitchen, with its butcher-block counters and rugs and cheerful lined curtains on the windows and be glad for all the softer, kinder surfaces. When people came to Maggie, she could hear them.

The woman who answered the door was pretty but ordinary. No makeup, blue eyes. Slight, small as a bird. Her smile was automatic but also miniature.

"Mrs. Grady?"

"Yes?"

The woman glanced at the folder Maggie had in her purse, as if it held a clue.

"I'm Maggie O'Farrell. My daughter is in your husband's class."

"Oh," she said. "I never get involved in university business. If you have a problem with the grading curve or an issue, you have to call his secretary."

"No, that's not why I'm here."

"Okay," she said evenly.

"My daughter is missing."

"Oh, I'm so very sorry. How worried you must be."

"Your husband didn't tell you one of his students was missing?"

She blinked twice. "No, I wasn't aware."

"You don't think that's unusual? That he wouldn't mention all the flyers up outside his classroom? And that the police have interviewed him and searched for his car? The car that's registered in your name?"

"I'm sorry, I'm due somewhere in fifteen minutes. You'll have to excuse me —"

Maggie put a hand against the door. She knew she was strong, stronger than this small woman. If her head was in Maggie's shampoo bowl, she could snap her skinny neck.

"No," she said, "I will not excuse you."

Mrs. Grady flinched, took a small step back. She glanced over her shoulder as if wondering where her phone was, a weapon, something. When she looked back, her polite smile was gone, her face set firmly, her jaw tight.

"You are going to have to leave right now!"

"Look, my daughter was investigating your husband, and he was threatening her, and now she's missing! Do you really think that's a coincidence? Do you even know the man who lives here?"

"Look, Mrs. —"

"O'Farrell. Maggie O'Farrell. Mother of Emma, who is in your husband's Psychology 101 class, a straight-A scholarship student, daughter of a decorated cop who was gunned down in the line of duty, who sat in the first row and risked her life to write for the school paper."

The woman's face was a mask, yes, but her eyes were frightened. Maggie felt her power and also felt the risk she'd taken. She didn't know this woman. The car was registered to her, not him. If Mrs. Grady was lying and had found out her husband was involved . . . if she had misread Emma's intentions, was she strong enough to hurt her? Would she go that far to protect her husband? Maggie didn't think so. She saw a softness in her, around the eyes. Not much, but a little.

"I am begging you, woman to woman, to tell me what you know about your husband and his students. I just want my daughter back, okay? That's all."

Mrs. Grady swallowed hard. "There was a girl who came here a few nights ago, making accusations, paranoid, high —"

"It must have been another student. My daughter would not be high —"

"With all due respect, once you drop them off at school, you have no idea what they become. Okay? My husband and I have seen it all. This girl was crazy, off her meds or something —"

"Well, that's not possible. Was there someone else with her maybe? Waiting in the car?"

"She was alone, ranting and raving about my husband, so I called an ambulance."

"An ambulance?"

"Yes. Her pupils were dilated, her clothes disheveled. She needed medical care."

"Well, maybe she'd been held prisoner or harmed. You ever think about that?"

The woman blinked. Didn't have an answer, but Maggie had hers. No, no, she had not.

"You don't have kids, do you?"

"I have two sons."

"Sons," Maggie said. "Of course."

"What is that supposed to mean?"

"It means you walk through the world never knowing what it's like to worry every time your child goes out for a run or to the gas station at night or to a party filled with drunk boys who outweigh her. You don't know, and you'll never know."

The woman reached out her hand for the flyer. "Is that her picture?"

"Yes, this is my daughter."

She looked at it briefly and shook her head. "No, that's not her. The girl who was here had short, ragged hair. Like a little boy."

FORTY

EMMA

Emma didn't know day from night anymore. The light flickered, burned out. No one to replace it. She waited hours for the terrible food to come. She didn't know who slid it in, who made it, or how long she'd been there anymore.

She was being punished, and it was her own fault, she knew. When she let her thoughts travel in reverse — because from what she could see, in the murky, hazy present, there was no forward, only back — she saw where she had gone wrong. She could make lists of her own stupidity. No one needed to come in and torture her with idiotic questions. She could beat herself up just fine. Was that the point? Was that what all solitary confinement was for? To point you toward regret?

Finally, the tiny door opened. Light bled in from outside, brighter than sunlight, and once again, she could see the red marks on her ankles and wrists, from when she fought the shackles. From before she'd given up. *Here are your latest mistakes,* they seemed to say.

Squinting into the brightness, she could see there were two people this time, a man and a woman. One wearing white, one wearing black. If she was writing a story, a story that came to her, that detail would be significant. That's the kind of thing she needed to notice. Concrete, but a metaphor.

"Emma?" a voice said, floating toward her. No one else had used her first name. So formal with their inmates. So proper as they manipulated your body and asked so much, too much, of your mind.

"Yes," she said, in case a rescue was imminent, in case this person was a helicopter sent to ferry her out. In case this voice wasn't her roommates, her teachers, that asshole RA. She'd stopped saying their names, trying to tell her story, fearing they'd go get them. That speaking them was a summons, a prayer. She'd stopped telling them anything.

"It's Mom," the voice said.

"Oh no, they got you too," she said.

Maggie crouched down and held Emma's face in her hands. She smoothed her skin, fingered her short hair.

"It's okay, honey," she said.

"I had to cut it," Emma said.

"That's all right. We can fix it."

"It'll grow back."

"Yes, but I kind of like it this way. I can see your eyes."

"They took everything," Emma said. "They took all my stuff."

"It's all right, sweetheart," Maggie said. "We'll get you new stuff, I promise."

"How did this happen?" her mother said to the other one, the one in white. "How could she have been here for days without the police knowing?"

"She signed herself in," he replied. "Voluntary. We had no idea there was a missing girl in the area."

"I needed to sleep," Emma said. "They said I could sleep."

"You can sleep," Maggie said. "There's plenty of time for everything else."

"I'm glad you're here," Emma whispered.

"Me, too, Em. Night. I love you."

"Night. I love you," she parroted back softly before closing her eyes.

FORTY-ONE

MAGGIE

Maggie didn't have much fury left, but she summoned just a drop of it as she spoke to the head psychiatrist at West Pennsylvania Hospital.

"You blew it, you realize that, don't you? And the only reason I'm not suing you is because at least she was semisafe here. Although judging from the scrapes on her wrists, maybe not as safe as she could have been."

Dr. Rivelli's voice was calm, but beyond that, his whole body seemed to be contained, free of gesture or movement. As if he wanted to slip inside every situation and not create any waves in the atmosphere. In contrast, Maggie was on the verge of screaming. She spoke with her hands, her eyes, her shoulders, her whole self.

"Your daughter presented with classic symptoms, Mrs. O'Farrell. She was paranoid, unclean, kicking and screaming and completely out of control. The woman who called the ambulance was absolutely right to do so."

His measuredness, his self-possession, only amped her up more. She wanted to shout at him to *be real, to be a fucking human being.*

"And it never occurred to you to call the police? No, you let a stranger, a layperson, diagnose my daughter! My child!"

"Your daughter is an adult, at an age when many illnesses present in otherwise healthy people. Emma appeared to be in the midst of a manic or paranoid schizophrenic episode —"

"It's not paranoia when someone is actually following you!"

"Mrs. O'Farrell, this conversation is not productive in terms of helping your daughter."

"She needs to detox from all the drugs you pumped in to her. That would be productive."

"If you had seen her the night she came in, I think you would agree that she needed intervention."

"She needed the police. No, scratch that, she needed her mother. She needed someone to listen to her story and believe her.

And all she really needed was sleep!"

"Mrs. O'Farrell, an inability to sleep can be a symptom of several psychiatric conditions. Your daughter's theories and stories presented as obsession and possibly in line with someone experiencing a manic episode. Remember, we were there, and you were not."

But oh, what Maggie would have given to be there. If anyone had made the right phone call to the right person, she would have been. She felt tears pool in the corners of her eyes, and she held up her head, sniffing and blinking, to keep them from falling. She would not give him the satisfaction of seeing her weak.

"So you drugged her," she said. "That was your solution."

"She needed to be calmed down, and after a period of time, we opted to do that chemically. Also, she revealed there was a history of mental illness in your family."

"There is not!"

She felt his eyes hover on her. Maggie's hair was matted in the back, and her eyes were red and drawn and on the verge of tears. What was the difference between a person who was out of her mind with grief and exhaustion and a person who was out of her mind? How thin, how impossibly thin, was that line?

"Your mother?" he said gently, more gently, she supposed, than she deserved.

"It was menopause. She was under a great deal of stress."

"Okay, well."

"My daughter didn't know the full situation."

He nodded. "And what about your husband?"

"My husband?"

"The circumstances around his death were confusing, were they not?"

"My husband," she said evenly, "was killed by a drug dealer in a gang retaliation."

"Ah. Well."

"Did Emma tell you differently?"

Maggie thought of her daughter's connection, now, to Salt. Did they know something she didn't? Her mind lurched, and her head actually hurt, actually pounded with possibility. Frank, a suicide? A suicide they'd covered up so he could be buried with honor? And so she could get his life insurance, his pension, and her daughter's scholarship? No. She shook her head as if to wipe those thoughts away.

"She said he was deeply unhappy."

"Deeply unhappy? Good God, Doctor, I'm deeply unhappy, too! Show me one stressed-out, overwhelmed, working mother married to a man who's never home who isn't deeply unhappy! Deeply unhappy is not the same as depressed, and you of all people should know that."

He took in a deep breath, as if he was breathing in her monologue. Was that calculated? To make her think she was being listened to, when in reality she had sucked all the air out of the room, and he just needed oxygen? One of his hands moved, at last, up off the desk to smooth a lock of his hair that had fallen near his right eye. Unruly hair, but nice hair. A nice face. If she was going to be fair about it, she had to at least give him that. Finally, he spoke.

"That's true, and yet I also know that families, and children in particular, create many narratives and euphemisms around the reality of depression."

"Well, some people do, but I don't."

"Many young people feel tremendous pressure at college."

"You don't know Emma."

"No. But I've been doing this a long time. So I know a few things."

"Yeah, sure, doctor knows best," she said sarcastically.

"And I certainly know a closed mind when I see one."

Maggie should have been insulted, and she opened her mouth to tell him off but stopped. Her teeth made a small click as she nestled them together. Dr. Rivelli's eyes stayed fixed even though hers had wandered away. Maybe he was right. Hadn't Frank always said, when their discussions snow-balled into argument, that she'd already made up her mind, so what was the point?

"As I told Emma this morning, I suggest we release her to the general population of the hospital and let her be monitored for a few days. If she's better after a few days of sleep and talk therapy, then —"

"No."

"No?"

"She signed herself in, so I'm pretty sure we can convince her to sign herself out."

"This should not be about winning, Mrs. O'Farrell. This is not about you being right and me being wrong. But since you seem to be a truth seeker, well, this is about discovery. This is about knowing what is actually going on with her, metabolically, chemically. And yes, a lack of sleep can be hugely disturbing to the body. As I sense you may know yourself."

Maggie felt a burning in her throat. Rage? Coffee? Or just anger that he continued to see through her? Well, what a surprise. Now he could see that sleeplessness, anger, disbelief, and jealousy ran in families, too.

But she nodded her agreement. Especially when he added that there would be a lounge chair brought in, where she could rest right next to her daughter and be with her the entire time.

She walked outside to get some air. The hospital had valet parking, and people kept pulling up to the circle, handing over their keys. She thought about Michael suddenly and knew that he was the one person she would call besides Sarah. The last two she trusted, the same ones her daughter trusted. She was grateful that after all this had happened, one of them was male. That Emma wouldn't be ruined forever by a lack of trust. She thought of what Emma had told Michael about walking in on her father. She thought of the photo in Salt's apartment. She felt sick, suddenly, with the possibility that it wasn't Maggie and Frank that Emma had walked in on.

She sat down. How was it possible to know your daughter, your only child, so well you thought you had her memorized — every stubborn cowlick along her part, her earlobes that she always called fat, every mole at the base of her wrist, her right thumb that was so much larger than her left

— and not know something essential about her?

There was much to talk about. And now there was time. There was a whole school year ahead to talk about this and where to transfer. What smaller school, filled with people more like her, could take her next year. A journalism school? They'd have to see. See if she'd been ruined or inspired.

A police car pulled in the circle, no lights flashing, no hurry.

Kaplan got out of the car, closed the door. Moved slowly toward her.

"I had a feeling you might be here," he said.

"That's funny, because I had no feeling whatsoever that you would be."

"Well, it took me a while to think of the wife."

"Of course it did."

"I'm not sexist, despite what you may think."

"Oh, I know. Blame your biology. Blame your caveman DNA."

"You know, Maggie, you could have been a helluva detective."

"There's an essential difference between detective and mother," she said. "And you know what it's comprised of?"

"What?"

"Giving a shit," she said.

"Detectives can't afford to do that. There are too many. It's too much."

"You're wrong," she said. "You're dead wrong."

"We have to agree to disagree."

"I hate that phrase."

"Well, it is what it is."

"Hate that one, too."

"Well, if you change your mind, maybe you could consider the FBI. Lots of excitement."

"And give up the thrill of shampooing hair?"

He laughed.

"Kaplan," she said suddenly, sniffing back tears, "aren't you going to ask me how she is?"

"What?"

"Emma."

He swallowed hard, rubbed his chin.

"Point taken, Maggie. But I already spoke to the doctor. So I know she's fine."

"She's probably not fine. She's exhausted, she's going to be a whole semester behind in school, she's lost most of her friends, and she'll have to testify about it all if it goes to trial."

"Well, but she's —"

She held up a hand. "If you're about to

tell me she's Frank O'Farrell's daughter, so you know she's tough, I will hit you. I will physically assault you."

"I was going to say that she's your daughter, Maggie," he said softly. "And that's how I know."

He ran his hand across his shaved head, as if feeling for growth, for progress. She thought his hair looked a little longer than it had when she met him; when she squinted, she swore she saw it reaching forward, starting to curl.

"Okay," she said. "Maybe there's hope for you yet."

FORTY-TWO

EMMA

Her mother was printing something in the small office at the back of the hair salon. Emma heard the familiar sound of the laser printer starting up, even over the buzz of the electric razor Chloe had turned on. She'd already lightened Emma's hair on the ends, added tips of gold, then buzzed the sides just a bit. Maggie had always told Emma she had nice ears and nape and collarbone, and now she could see in her new reflection that maybe her mom was right. She'd always thought, *Who gives a shit about ears and necks? Guys like boobs and asses, right?*

Chloe warmed lavender pomade in her hands and raked it through the top of Emma's hair to give it more shape. The lavender smelled fresh and hopeful. It reminded her of their garden when they used to live in Philly.

"I like it," Emma said, looking in the mirror. She was actually amazed by the difference and how much, well, like herself she looked. As if she'd been hiding under all that hair, the golden shine masking the rest of her. And there was more to her, so much more, than that hair.

"It really brings out your eyes," Chloe said. "You look like an actress now, instead of a —"

"Homeless person?"

"You said it, not me."

"Well, I was, technically, homeless. Couch surfing. Sleeping in libraries."

Her mother came in from the back, holding out the piece of paper to her like it was a gift certificate. Since Emma was down to three shirts and two pair of pants, this would certainly come in handy.

She took it and read it, her face curving into a small frown. No gift certificate. No Groupon. An email, from some random dude at *Main Line Magazine.*

"What?"

"He's an old friend of your dad's, and I know it's in the wrong department, but the internship pays minimum wage, and he said you'd have access to all the reporters, and you could learn a ton."

"That's great, Mom, but how can I do a

full-time internship at a suburban magazine and still go to school?"

Maggie blinked, and then it was her turn to frown. "Well, you'll take a few classes at community college this year, and you'll save money from the internship, and then you can transfer to Pitt or Penn State in the fall."

Emma frowned, struggling to take this in. Her mother had mapped out an entire alternate plan without asking her? She'd just assumed?

"Transfer?"

"Yes."

"And lose my scholarship?"

Chloe and her mother exchanged a glance that Emma did not understand.

"The scholarship doesn't matter now, Emma."

"But I can't just leave. God, Mom!"

"Of course you can. And you should."

"No, Mom, I can't give up. I can't let them win!"

"It's not winning. It's just being practical."

"Practical?"

"Honey, those girls aren't going away. Tim Trenton is still an RA, Jason is still editor of the paper, and even Grady is only on temporary administrative leave. It will take months for the police to sort out your allegations —"

"Allegations? Jesus, Mom, whose side are you on?"

Maggie took a deep breath. Emma watched her like she was watching a foreign species, an alien. How could this person even share her DNA? Who the hell was she?

"After everything that has happened, Emma, how can you even ask such a thing?"

"I'm sorry, but how can *you* even think that I would leave?"

"How can you stay on campus, with everyone knowing what's happened? Who would want you in their dorm? Who would —"

"Jesus, Mom, I'm not going to live on campus. I'm not insane!"

"So you would . . . commute? From here?"

"If you'll have me, yeah. And if we can afford a train pass. I grew kind of fond of the train when I was doing surveillance."

"Surveillance," Maggie repeated with alarm.

"Don't worry, Mom, I'm not switching my major to criminal justice or anything. Your fear of me turning into Dad is not gonna happen."

Emma hopped down from the chair and took off the creamy-white nylon cape. She brushed a few errant hairs from her nose and cheeks and smoothed the front of her jeans.

Her mother's eyes were sparkling at the sight of her newly shorn hair. She smiled and held Emma's gaze as if waiting to be thanked and told she was right all along, that Emma should have cut her hair long ago.

"Sooo," Emma said slowly.

"Yes?"

"Any chance we can go to Target and get some new clothes?"

"Sure," her mother replied. "Any chance you'll switch your major to business instead of journalism?"

"Mom," she said and sighed. "Don't push your luck."

FORTY-THREE

MAGGIE

Maggie waited for Emma at the diner. She had been instructed by her daughter to stay off campus, to avoid Hoden House, to not go near the journalism building, and if any students came into the diner that she had interacted with, to not speak to them, not thank anyone or harass anyone, and not, under any circumstances, to write to the dean or the head of school while she was waiting. She was told to drink coffee and sit, and if Emma wasn't back in an hour and a half, then, and only then, could she text Sarah Franco or come looking for her. Parameters, once again, and Maggie would have to learn to live with them. Harder now than it had been before.

Emma had divvied up tasks and responsibilities between the police and herself, and Maggie was to stay home and blow-dry hair, unless Emma needed a ride and a meal. She

413

might ask her advice, but Maggie had been benched.

It was like a personal, one-on-one restraining order. Maggie didn't think she'd done any real damage — and she *had* saved her from the hospital — but Emma didn't want her making things worse. But Maggie knew if Emma knew everything, knew the whole story — every gesture, every word — that she would be embarrassed. She would understand, but she would still be embarrassed.

So she nursed a cup of coffee at the counter, memorized the menu, stacked the creamers in a pyramid, and waited for Emma to get back from her meeting with Jason. Or, as she'd put it, her intervention with Jason, since he'd refused to answer her calls, emails, or texts, and she planned to ambush him at his weekly newspaper meeting.

After what seemed like a long time and was only about a half hour, the door jingled, and Emma walked in cautiously, looking around to see if she knew anyone before sliding onto the red vinyl stool next to Maggie.

"So how'd it go?"

"Oh, fine."

"Really?"

414

"Sure, if fine means he called security and told me if I tried to slander him again, he would sue me, then yes, it went fine."

"Slander?"

"That's the part where I called him a man whore, a liar, and a bad journalist who would never get a job at a real newspaper."

"Very nice."

"I may have thrown in that he had a few STDs."

"Well done, grasshopper."

"What?"

"Never mind."

"He was remarkably calm as I shouted this into his weekly meeting. Until the point where I called him a bad journalist for killing the story after Fiona got to him. That's when he threatened to call his daddy."

"Daddy?"

"Well, when a kid threatens to sue and his dad is a lawyer, I kind of put two and two together."

"Ah."

"I can't believe I fell for his line of shit."

"Well, he's still a boy," Maggie said. "He still thinks with his penis. Come to think of it, most men do, too. But then . . . you know that, too, right?"

The question hung in the air, heavier than it should have been, and Maggie felt guilty.

This was why she wasn't allowed on campus. She was too sharp, too pointed, too unable to control herself. Emma picked up the menu and looked at it a long time before she answered. Measured and calm, those qualities reminded Maggie, with a pang, exactly of Frank. Now that Emma's hair was short, she looked more and more like him, too — the cowlick at the nape of her neck, her small ears. Those were Frank's. But any hair stylist knew better than to tell a girl with newly short hair that she looked like her father.

"Mom, if you're asking if I knew about Dad having an affair, then —"

"No, I know you knew."

"You did?"

"I found out from Salt."

"I only saw her a few times, and I thought she was just his friend, you know? I was young."

"I know. I don't blame you."

"And then the day I figured it out, there was this little shed at a picnic park, and —" She shuddered, not finishing her thought. "I didn't know what to do with that information. I couldn't really process it."

Maggie nodded but didn't let on that she knew what had happened. What Michael had said about Emma walking in on her dad. Her being a virgin. She thought back to that message Emma had kept on her phone from Frank, the repeated mention of the word *we*. She'd added two and two and two together and gotten a thousand. But now she knew she'd been right. But what good is it to be right unless you found out the right way? Not cheating, not sneaking around, not begging, just doing the right things that led you to answers? That was all her daughter was doing. Methodical, following procedures, not giving up.

"It's okay, honey," she said, reaching up to smooth a golden piece of her daughter's upswept pixie. "On some level, I knew, too."

"You did?"

Emma didn't squirm away from Maggie's hand. She let her pet her exactly as Maggie had when she was a baby and the first soft, magical growth had come swirling in and seemed longer every morning than it had been at night. Maggie wondered if she put her baby pictures side by side with a picture of Emma now if they might look identical. The curious upturn of their mouths, the openness in their eyes.

"Yes," she said, dropping her hand back onto the counter. "I just didn't want to deal with the consequences of it."

"So the woman who snuck into parties

and accosted my college roommates was afraid of something? Interesting dichotomy, Mom," she said and smiled.

"Everyone's afraid of something, sweetheart."

"See, that's what I'm counting on," she said.

"How's that?"

"To tie up my story. You need to find out a source's weak spot and use it to your advantage."

"Threaten them? Emma, seriously, you cannot go on like this. A story is not worth your schooling, your life, your —"

"No, Mom. You don't get it."

"Illuminate me, then."

"It's like Mr. Maserati," Emma said. "He was afraid his dead wife would be ashamed of him, so he wanted to do the right thing."

"You told him that?"

"Of course not. I just knew it. And this new sugar baby I'm interviewing? She was afraid she wasn't smart and couldn't do anything in life except use her body, and by contributing to the story, she is proving otherwise."

"A new source?"

"Yes."

"From school?"

"Yes."

"And you found her when, exactly? While you were supposed to be resting in the psych ward?"

"No, this other girl introduced me to her. Her boyfriend was the janitor at our dorm and had seen this pretty girl out back crying all the time. They mentioned it to me, and I put two and two together."

"Really," Maggie said and smiled.

"Remember the girl who found my shirt in the dumpster and then gave it back? Same girl told me this."

Maggie remembered the story. When she'd asked her daughter if anything positive had happened during this craziness. At first, Emma had laughed and said "Oh my God, roses and thorns, Mom?" because of the game they'd played at family dinners. Then, she had reluctantly admitted that there had been "this kid named Michael who was super helpful" and the dumpster shirt girl. Maggie hadn't pressed her for more detail on either one. She knew if she even said she'd liked Michael, too, that would be the end of it. Let Emma find out on her own. She'd also mentioned that the head doctor at the hospital was handsome, around Maggie's age, and didn't wear a wedding ring. What did they call that, when a patient turned their doctor into a father figure? There was some word for it Maggie couldn't remember. Still, she had a good laugh at the idea of her and Dr. Rivelli, who clearly thought she was a numbskull, then stopped herself. Maybe her mind *was* a bit too closed.

"Well," she said, "she sounds like a girl of character. A girl who would make a good friend."

"Yeah, why don't you call her mom and set up a playdate?"

Maggie thought about answering back but smiled and bit her tongue. "But your professor," she said, "other than investing in the club or going to the club, which I guess are both legal, what exactly did he do wrong?" She thought of his clueless wife, his nice house. Had it been worth it?

"You mean other than follow me and harass me? He had his secretary take photos of all the kids in his classes, claiming he had trouble remembering their names. Then he sent photos of girls he thought were good prospects to Tim Trenton. He'd try to get the other girls to recruit them."

"And why did the secretary tell you this? What was she afraid of?"

"She was afraid her twelve-year-old daughter would find out and stop speaking to her."

"And what did Trenton get out of it?"

"A cut of the club's membership fees, we think."

Maggie nodded her head. Of course it was all about money. She supposed Tim Trenton was a business major.

"So," she said, sipping her coffee, "if you wanted me to be your source, what do you think I'd be afraid of?" She posed her shoulders and pouted like the kids did in their selfies, a coquettish exaggeration of wistful.

Emma laughed, and her whole body shook when she did. Maggie had almost forgotten what that looked like, her daughter laughing, happy, not tense. How was that possible?

"Mom, do you really want me to go there?"

"So, what, it's obvious? I'm an easy source?"

She thought of Dr. Rivelli, his lack of hesitation as his simple words cut through generations of family pain and drama. Was she that transparent, that one-dimensional, a clichéd mother who feared her child wouldn't live to chase her dreams?

"I'm not doing this with you," Emma said. "No way."

"Well, someday, when you need a quote

from me, I'm going to say 'no comment.' "

"Okay then."

"Seriously, you will have to beg me to go on the record, come knocking on my door at night, like Robert Redford."

"You know I hate it when you make obscure film references."

"Well, someone has to educate you."

"Ha-ha. Right. I forgot. Thank you, Professor."

"One more thing," Maggie said. "Why did you go to the health center?"

"What?"

"The appointment you made that you didn't keep? What was wrong?"

"I just wanted to see what the beds were like in there, in case I could sneak in and get some sleep."

"Are you . . . sure that's the real reason?"

"Yes, Mom," she said. "What, you thought I was pregnant or something, is that it?"

"Oh, no. I thought you pulled a muscle jogging."

"Yeah, right," she said and laughed.

The waitress circled back, and Maggie started to order pancakes for them both, but Emma stopped her and told the waitress she wanted a spinach and mushroom omelet. Maggie didn't say, "I thought you hated spinach." Because wasn't spinach or blueberries or anything good for you something you could actually develop a taste for? Couldn't a person change, improve, grow, at any age?

Progress. They were both making progress. They were both becoming different people. Emma becoming bolder. Maggie growing softer. Maggie had been certain her daughter was not an escort, not suicidal. But there were more things to discover, more mysteries that would unfold. There would always be things she didn't know, and that would have to be okay.

Emma checked her messages on her phone, and Maggie sat still, not asking her who she was texting or what she was doing. Maggie was holding back, and Emma was forging ahead. All those times when Emma was a baby, when she'd wanted to speed her daughter up — *please start sleeping through the night, please start eating vegetables, please stop falling off your training wheels.* And now, all she wanted to do was slow her down. Suspend her in time so she could parent her, hold her, a little longer. As she watched her daughter doing something she did a thousand times a day, she was simply waiting. Waiting for the day when they would finally meet in the middle. In that warm, comfortable space between girlhood and adulthood, between parenthood and friendship.

"What's wrong?" Emma said. "You're making, like, a weird face."

"Nothing's wrong," Maggie said and smiled even broader, so wide it almost hurt.

"It's that face you make before you cry."

Maggie's breath caught in her throat. Maybe her daughter had been watching her all along. Maybe Emma knew Maggie's gestures and expressions, her precious tells, as well as Maggie knew her child's.

She swallowed and blinked back a tear. "I'm not crying. You're crying," she said, and they laughed, together, their lilting tones not the same but blended in harmony, filling the diner like a cathedral built for two.

READING GROUP GUIDE

1. In what ways do Maggie's pursuit of her daughter and Emma's pursuit of her story run parallel, and in what ways do they differ? Did you find their motivations and methods relatable?

2. Maggie's parental intuition is portrayed in stark relief to the more left-brained methods of the police. Have you ever acted on a hunch or intuition? What drove you to this choice . . . and were you right?

3. Colleges are frequently under fire for their tepid responses to crimes committed on campus. What might have happened differently in the novel had different policies or attitudes been in place?

4. The themes of women helping women and women hurting women are woven throughout the book. Did the betrayals

surprise you? Have you ever been on the receiving end of "mean girl" behavior?

5. Emma is accused of being judgmental toward sex work. Do you believe she was, and why? In your observation, even in this enlightened era, do you think most women are?

6. How did Maggie's experiences as a policeman's wife and widow color her responses? Was she fair, or did she overreact?

7. The "good old boys" network among fraternity brothers and alumni form a spine of suspicion in the novel. Do you find evidence of this in your own work, life, community?

A CONVERSATION WITH THE AUTHOR

All three of your daughters made it to three different colleges (congratulations!). Did any of your family's experiences on campus color the plot of this novel?

I don't think I realized, until I came up with the idea and started writing it, how extremely well prepared I already was! In some ways I had been collecting small anecdotes and details and stories for years, with nowhere to put them. Luckily, my two youngest were still in school, living in dorms, during the writing of it, so I could be more detailed in my research visits and ask them to help with certain topics, aiming for authenticity.

What factors went into choosing Philadelphia as the setting?

Given the different goals and majors of my kids, my husband and I sometimes feel like we've visited every college campus, from Ivies to state schools, in the Northeast, South, and California. So I felt pretty qualified to set a college novel in a lot of different locales! I knew I needed a city address, a state school, a rough neighborhood, and a traditional, male-focused alumni network. I considered setting it in Chicago for a while, but the clubby traditions of Philadelphia felt more right to me.

In the last few years, there have been a number of prominent real crimes at colleges in which parents are pitted against the administration. What changes in campus security or policy would you like to see happen?

Well, for starters, I am in favor of mandatory police involvement when a potential crime is reported. The whole tradition of campuses handling things themselves is ridiculous and self-serving. Many schools are developing new protocols and mandatory actions — like immediate, temporary suspensions — and my response is "Wait, you mean that's new? That's not how you did it before?"

There are mentions in the book about parenting girls versus parenting boys.

As a parent of all girls, do you believe there are differences?

There have been many lively discussions in my friend group about the different attitudes among parents of female teenagers and male teenagers. I've noticed differences, intentional or not. It takes a lot of empathy to raise kids to adulthood — you can't demonize other kids. You have to remember that these are children.

This is your fifth novel, and while all your books are propulsive in different ways, all of them hinge on a relationship with a child. Was this a conscious decision?

Gosh, I never saw that before! Wow. Well, no, it wasn't conscious, but I do think the secrets and wounds of childhood are at the core of most human suffering. So you can't really write an empathetic novel without considering someone's childhood, even if a child isn't a prominent character.

What are you working on next?

Well, my subconscious continues working overtime, because it's a book about two sisters and their . . . drumroll . . . kids(!), one of whom is accused of a horrific crime.

ACKNOWLEDGMENTS

Thanks to my family and friends, who always help and always ask and always seem so proud.

Thanks to my agent, Anne, and my editor, Anna, who are both so smart and helpful, even when I'm freaking out.

Thanks to the whole team at Sourcebooks, who work so hard on behalf of their authors.

And thanks to my huge community of writer buds: The Tall Poppy Writers and Bloom, The Liars Club & Writers Coffeehouse, and the Women Fiction Writers Association. You make a lonely job less lonely.

And thanks to the reader groups and book bloggers and Bookstagrammers who love reading as much as we do.

ABOUT THE AUTHOR

Kelly Simmons is a former journalist and advertising creative director. She's a member of WFWA, the Tall Poppy Writers, and The Liars Club, a nonprofit organization dedicated to mentoring fledgling novelists. She also co-hosts *The Liars Club Oddcast,* a weekly podcast interviewing top authors and discussing the craft and business of writing. Learn more at kellysimmonsbooks .com.